AF595829

PROMISE

FOR NOAH AND CAMERON

Omnibus Books
an imprint of Scholastic Australia Pty Ltd (ABN 11 000 614 577)
PO Box 579, Gosford NSW 2250. www.scholastic.com.au

Part of the Scholastic Group
Sydney • Auckland • New York • Toronto • London • Mexico City • New Delhi • Hong Kong • Buenos Aires • Puerto Rico

First published in 2019.

A catalogue record for this book is available from the National Library of Australia

ISBN 978 1 74299 198 6

Printed in Australia by Griffin Press.

Scholastic Australia's policy, in association with Griffin Press Group, is to use papers that are renewable and made efficiently from wood grown in responsibly managed forests, so as to minimise its environmental footprint.

10 9 8 7 6 5 4 3 2 1 19 20 21 22 23 / 1

ALEXANDRA ALT

An Omnibus book from Scholastic Australia

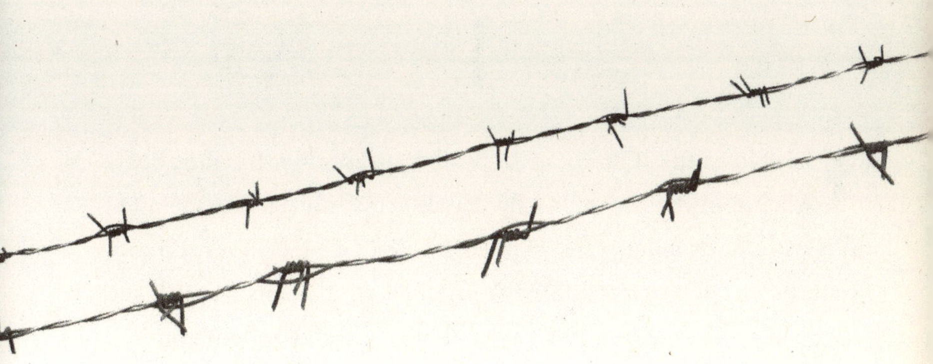

PART ONE

1942-1943

CHAPTER I

The cold of the concrete cellar wall seeps through the threadbare wool of my cardigan. It icily crawls across my back as the night fills with the droning of the enemy bombers. I close my eyes and concentrate on the touch of Ludwig's shoulder on mine, its warmth and shape like a fingerprint. For a second or two reality softens and I almost forget where I am, forget that I could be dead before I can take my next breath. Or kiss Ludwig.

I could easily sit like this forever, blind, shutting out that world I don't want to live in.

But I don't want to die with my eyes shut.

Ludwig sits straight-backed, tense, hands resting on his knees, listening for the approaching bombers in the sky above like the rest of us. We, in Berlin, are not used to this. No one talks. Even the babies are hushed and wide-eyed on their mothers' laps, their little toes twitching in knitted boots.

Our Flak is firing nonstop. The enemy planes are almost overhead now, the vibration of their propellers penetrating my bones. I hold my breath and my heartbeat slows, as though preparing my body for death.

I want to dive headfirst into the green depth of a lake, stay in a mermaid world and only resurface when everything that's happening above is over. I can almost feel the soft touch of slightly murky water on my skin, see the fable creatures gliding past, their mysterious smiles and their silvery tails. Everything is soft and muted and gentle and beautiful.

But re-emerge I must, to the cold grey, the harsh white, to the abyss of black and fervent red.

My bones vibrate and rattle inside my body. In an instant they could be scattered everywhere, mashed up with bricks and dust and mortar.

It's not us tonight. The bombers pass overhead and the droning fades.

Ludwig springs up from the bench and darts to the cellar door.

'Ludwig, it might not be over yet. Wait for *Entwarnung*,' his mother reprimands him.

Ludwig hesitates, turns around. Our eyes meet and I blush, my shoulder, my whole body still feeling that fingerprint of his touch.

'They are gone,' Ludwig says. His voice is guttural, as though he too has died in his head and now returned to the world. His eyes still hold mine and they tell me that he also still feels that touch.

And then he's gone. The steel door closes with a dull thud behind him. I long for the wailing sound of the air-raid siren but the all clear still doesn't come. Without Ludwig the small space feels more real, more crowded, but too empty all at once.

I avoid looking in the mirror as I twist my *Bund Deutscher Mädel* neckerchief through the leather woggle. I keep pulling and adjusting the fabric, but no matter what I do the neckerchief feels as tight as a claw around my neck. My mother fusses with my new skirt like I'm five and not fifteen.

'Mutti, please,' I protest, pulling away. 'Really, it's fine. You don't have to fuss like I'm one of your customers in the millinery shop.'

My mother ignores me. 'It's hardly noticeable that this is not the issue uniform skirt from the department store,' she says and plucks some imaginary fluff from the skirt's hem.

'I guess not.' I shrug, feeling indifferent.

My mother frowns at me. I know how difficult it was to find the cheap blue material that was a close enough match. And I know I should say something complimentary about the new skirt, about how well it has turned out, since sewing is not one of my mother's great talents.

'You haven't even looked in the mirror once,' my mother says, sounding hurt. She indicates our hallway mirror with the faded gilt frame next to the front door. The mirror is old, the silvering worn away in places and there are cloudy areas and black spots on the glass. I force myself to look at my smudged reflection. An average girl of average height. Braided brownish-blonde hair, lead-grey eyes, narrow shoulders. A nose that my mother always calls perfection but which is just a nose to me.

I detest the league meetings, the uniform on which we have to spend money we don't have, and I really don't care whether it's the regulation uniform skirt from the department store, like the previous one which I have outgrown, or not.

'I've got a sore throat,' I lie and cough. Getting a sick note from your parents is pretty much the only way to get out of the dreadful meetings.

My mother stops fussing with my clothes and tucks her wispy brown hair back behind her ears. 'Lene, not that again! I can't excuse you from another meeting. BDM is compulsory – it's the law!' There's a trace of alarm in my mother's voice. She knows the sore throat is a lie, just like the other maladies that I have fabricated in the past.

'Everything is compulsory. Everything!'

'Enough! That's selfishness talking. It's not up to me, it's the way it is.'

'BDM wasn't always compulsory,' I can't help but retort. Somehow, arguing makes me feel better even though I know I sound like a triumphant child who has uncovered an adult's secret.

'That's true, it wasn't.' My mother pauses as though thinking back to that other time, to that Germany I can hardly even remember, that Germany that died a decade ago. 'But that was then. Things are different now. They have been for a long time. If you don't go to the meetings and partake in the BDM duties you are going to get us all in trouble. We might already be on their radar because—'

My mother stops and nervously rubs the side of her face with her fingertips. I can tell she regrets her half-finished sentence, but she sighs and decides to finish it anyhow.

'—because you've missed at least half-a-dozen meetings this year. These things don't go unnoticed.' She pauses. 'And father's last letter was censored. That doesn't go unnoticed either.'

I nod. Causing my parents trouble is not what I want. 'I'm sorry, Mutti. But—'

'There is no but,' my mother interrupts me. Her voice is sharp but quiet, her mouth now in a thin line. A sure sign that I have exhausted her patience.

'We all have our duties. Just don't draw any attention to yourself, Lene, that's all I'm asking. All right?'

Of course, duties, nothing but duties! They are taking over my life. The meetings, the Winter Relief, packing parcels for the front, mending uniforms. There's never enough time for what I want to do, like studying or reading. Recently, some of the older BDM girls have even volunteered for the Flak. They spend the nights up on the Flak towers risking their lives operating the searchlights. I don't understand why you'd volunteer for that.

So I won't get that sick note, but I guess I knew that all along. 'I'd better be off then,' I say, casting one last glance at my imperfect reflection.

'Make a good impression on the new squad leader. A fresh start.

No more excuses and missing meetings.' My mother's eyes tell a different story. She's not a good liar.

'You still don't really want me to go, do you?' I say.

'It doesn't matter what I want, Lene.' She shoves me out the door.

Right. It doesn't matter what she wants. It doesn't matter what I want. Contributing to the war effort and final victory is all that matters!

I dawdle down the long stretch of our cobblestone street towards the intersection, glad for the cover of the soot-blackened balconies that hang above me, concealing my mother's view from our second-floor flat. Keeping my eyes lowered for the first few hundred metres, I navigate around a gang of preschoolers trading shell splinters, and a dog sniffing at one of the few neglected-looking trees while its owner is gossiping right in the middle of the footpath.

At the busy Prenzlauer Berg intersection, the sky opens up above me. The boulevard is wide and busy with pedestrians and traffic, the buildings tall and grand. Overhead, the familiar rumbling of the S-Bahn, and tatty-looking swastika flags flap like they've been doing for years and years.

I wait for a tram to pass, staring at a poster on a *Litfaß* column warning us about spies lurking in our midst, then cross the road, but instead of heading straight to the school hall for the meeting, I turn left. There's no way I can skip the meeting without my mother finding out but I definitely don't have to get there *early*. I take a detour past our local cinema, the Sternschnuppe, where a film starring Zarah Leander is showing. I slow and peek into the atrium. It's deserted. Potted ferns reach their leaves towards the glass dome for light. I slip inside, inching my way across the slightly worn marble floor to the closed theatre doors. I've done this before, sneaking into the theatre unnoticed, watching a film or newsreel without paying.

'Excuse me!'

I jump at the unexpected voice and stare at the woman whose shiny platinum-blonde head has popped up in the box office. She looks utterly preened. Her face is powdered too heavily, her lips are too red and her dress is a little too fancy for the afternoon. And I've never seen her here before. Normally there's a bespectacled man nearing middle age in her spot. And he never seemed to notice me sneaking in.

She looks me up and down, obviously enjoying my confusion.

'Are you on your way to the BDM meeting?'

Her face eerily reminds me of those Victorian post-mortem photographs I once saw in a museum. At first glance the person in the photograph looks quite pretty and like they really made an effort with their hair and clothes, almost doll- or mannequin-like. But when you look closer you realise that something isn't quite right, and it's then you grasp that the person is dead. Except those dead people don't wear Nazi party pins on the lapels of their dresses.

'Are you deaf? Why are you sneaking around like this?' she repeats, plastic blue eyes in a death stare. She is outright creepy.

I feel caught out even though I haven't actually done anything wrong. Not yet anyway. 'I'm not sneaking,' I finally say.

'Sure looks like it. Are you going to the meeting or not?' She scrutinises me, taking in my non-issue uniform skirt, the slightly too big, hand-me-down BDM climbing jacket.

'Yes, sure,' I say. 'It's Wednesday, meeting day.' Though I don't see why it's her business where I'm going.

'Aren't you running late?' she keeps quizzing me.

I feel like I have no free will of my own any longer. 'No, I'm not running late,' I say. Which is not true because if I don't get on my way now I will be late for sure.

'Ah, I remember we always had such a good time in the BDM,' she ruminates. 'Pity I'm not allowed to go any longer, now that I'm married. But rules are rules and you have to obey by them.' Her eyes blast freeze me to the marble floor.

Lying was a mistake. Despite the powder and lipstick, I realise she isn't actually that much older than me and knows exactly what time the meetings start. My eyes catch on her party badge again. It looks like a hole in her heart. I have to stick with my story now, though. I have to be careful. 'Yes, pity about that,' I casually say, then ask: 'Has the movie started yet?'

She blinks, surprised perhaps at my brazenness. 'No, I don't think so. The newsreel is still on.'

'Do you mind if I quickly duck in and watch the rest of it?' I'm throwing caution to the wind. This is risky. I don't think she's someone I'd want to know that I don't absolutely adore the League of German Girls. But here is my chance to see the latest newsreel. And tell Ludwig about it. And surely she would approve of my interest in the newsreel! 'And then I'll be off to the meeting.' I scrunch up my face as though I'm torn in a moral dilemma. I know I'm playing with fire.

But she doesn't fall for it anyway. 'I can't let you in for free.'

'I'll only stay for a few minutes,' I assure her. 'Really, I just want to see the newsreel, not the movie.' Which is another lie. I'd love to see the movie and I haven't been to the cinema in ages. Money is tight and we rarely go. And neither does Ludwig.

Meanwhile, minutes are ticking away. But then, to my surprise, she waves me through.

'Just this once,' she says. Her smile is sinister in its benevolence.

'Thanks,' I mutter.

I shiver, still feeling that cold blue freeze of her eyes. There's a funny feeling in my stomach, like when I ate a slice of my cake the night before my eleventh birthday, knowing full well that I'd be found out. Only the feeling is amplified a thousand times. I know I'll have to bear the consequences of my actions sooner rather than later.

But the minute I sit down in the very last row, I forget all about consequences. A report on the battle near Leningrad is on. Snow and ice everywhere, white on white. One of our infantry units barrages a Russian village. Houses take a hit and smoke streams from them into the sky, turning white into smudges of brownish grey. There is a cut to a snowed-in airfield. The commentary starts and I lean forward, drawn in by the high-pitched, over-dramatic voice of the commentator as Luftwaffe planes attack from the sky.

'Captured Bolsheviks are put to work!' the commentator shouts as the prisoners plough snow off the runway and cargo planes land. *'Our divisions have pushed far ahead and our outstanding transporter, the JU52, delivers fresh supplies for our soldiers.'*

The JU52 plane looks flimsy, like it's been built in someone's backyard from a few sheets of scrap metal. *'The JU52 also flies our troops to the front,'* the commentator elucidates.

Soldiers board the plane through a hatch-like door. A shot out of the plane's window follows and it's as though I'm there myself. Far below there's a snow-covered farm in the middle of eastern nowhere, a tall evergreen forest casting long shadows across white untouched steppe. I'm struck by how beautiful it looks. But then the camera shows a soldier's face, his breath steaming in the cold as he stares out of one of the plane's tiny windows. His face has that detached, faraway expression that soldiers have. But then he looks straight into the camera and I see it clearly – that fear and dread in his eyes. He wants this war as little as I do!

Suddenly a wave of shame hits me, shame about complaining over doing my bit for the war effort. But then I wonder if the war will really be over sooner the more everyone contributes. For a moment this new and sharp thought stumps me with its clarity.

An abrupt cut ends the scene.

'Mail arrives!' the commentator shouts. Mailbags drop out of the belly of the low-flying planes and are collected by soldiers.

Watching the mailbags being taken away, a painful knot forms in my chest.

My last two letters to my father remain unanswered and I am desperate for news. Mail from the front can take longer these days but it feels as though it has been way too long this time. The uncertainty is like a nagging pain that never goes away. Worst of all, we don't even know where my father is right now. There were hints in his last letter, the one that was censored, that he will leave France and that his Motorised Infantry division will be deployed elsewhere. We don't know where and we don't know how he feels about it, although his thoughts I am so desperate for are there, underneath those thick black bars staining the pages.

I've lost track of time, have no idea how long I've been sitting here. Ten minutes, fifteen, perhaps even longer. It's dark and cozy in here. The league meeting and the world outside seem far away. I feel closer to my father, sitting here in the dark, watching the newsreel pictures of the war raging on those countless far-away fronts. Another report starts. But I have to go. Now.

CHAPTER 2

I stumble out of the darkness and into the bright foyer, blinking my eyes. The young woman is still there, reapplying lipstick, flame red like the party pin on her dress. Ha, it looks like she has forgotten what she learnt in the BDM. Isn't the use of make-up forbidden and despised?

'Are you still here?' she asks.

I scuttle past. 'Thanks for letting me in,' I mutter.

'You are *really* late for your league meeting. You are going to get a fine!' Her sneer is full of *Schadenfreude* and disapproval.

I don't answer. I know I'm late. Very late.

I'm not the most proficient runner and my feet never seem to find the right rhythm, but now I'm sprinting back to the intersection, down the busy street as fast as I can without colliding into anyone, all the while searching for a plausible excuse for my tardiness. Avoiding a stack of boxes being unloaded from a delivery van, I nearly crash into a lantern post. I turn left, run past the mannequins in the shopwindow of *Modehaus*, the photo studio, and the pharmacy with a red, blue and yellow Pervitin advert in the window. I cross the road again, catching my breath and perilously navigating another tram, a couple of cars and several bicycles. Near Café Kramer I run out of steam and slow down. I desperately hope that the new leader is much like the last one who hated wasting time on latecomers and just gave a short stern reprimand. By the time I turn into the quiet back street where my school is, I still haven't come up with anything. Perhaps I can sneak into the hall unnoticed.

Crossing the schoolyard to the hall, I can hear the girls are singing one of those horrible folk songs I can never remember the lyrics for. Probably because I don't want to remember them.

Slightly breathless, I prop open the heavy wooden door and slip inside. Banners move in the draft and Hitler stares down at me from the huge portrait on the front wall. Heads start turning my way from the back row, first one, then another, then a whole row in front, then another row. Like a ripple that eventually reaches the squad leader. With a flap of her hand she cuts the singing, then waves me over. Her movements are sharp and precise, like a machine's.

As I walk up I am struck by the flawlessness of the squad leader's uniform on her athletic body. The regulation dark blue BDM skirt and white blouse are ironed and starched; her uniform jacket is a perfect fit, making her shoulders look straight and broad. The shade of her hair reminds me of the yellow in the Pervitin advert. It is immaculate, braided and pinned up, not a strand sticking out. She lives and breathes the league.

She glares at me, contempt, hatred and something stronger, a relishing of power, burning in her eyes.

'Why are you late?' she asks, appraising me coldly.

'I …' What I want to say is a jumble of words in my head. I start again 'I am—' .

'Stop.' The leader's palm slices through the air, mere millimetres from my face, as though she wants to slap me. Or chop off my nose. I flinch, barely controlling the reflex to veer backwards.

'Whatever you are going to say, it's bound to be a lie,' she declares loudly.

My face is aflame in an instant.

She grabs me by the arm, squeezes hard. 'I know a liar when I see one. If you are late again I will report you to our district leader.' The words are like a snake's hiss, casual yet menacing, reaching the very last row of the silent hall. 'There are no second chances in my squad!'

'It won't happen again,' I whisper.

'Punctuality and honesty are virtues that should be etched into the character of every German girl!' Out of the blue she's shouting. A droplet of her spit lands on my cheek. It burns on my skin like acid.

I nod. 'Yes, squad leader.' This girl is an absolute maniac. A manic little worker bee that's hatched from one of Hitler's hives. The urge to wipe the saliva away is overwhelming. But I control it.

'Sit down! You have wasted enough of our time!' She lets go of my arm.

I turn and trot past the rows of girls to an empty chair at the back of the hall. I look straight ahead, the girls to my left and right a blur of sniggering faces.

The squad leader's voice whips me to a halt again. 'No! I want you in the front row. Where I can keep an eye on you. And from now on I expect *outstanding* efforts from you in the Winter Relief.'

The Winter Relief. We've been collecting money since the beginning of October. It's early November now, so another four months of this!

I return to the front of the hall and sit down next to Annalisa who looks at me with revulsion. 'You are a disgrace,' she snarls loudly. Again, there are bursts of giggles everywhere.

'A disgrace to the Führer and to Germany,' Annalisa adds, earning approving sniggers all round.

Her words hurt. Annalisa and I met on the first day of primary school and became friends instantly when she asked me to come and play at her house after school. But now I can't even remember the last time we did anything together that wasn't school or a BDM activity. I shrug it off. As long as I have Ludwig I don't need other friends. Certainly not friends who berate me in front of everyone!

But humiliation and anger pulse through me. I want to confront the leader, challenge her, tell her to go right ahead and report me to the district leader. I want to tell her that I don't care. That I hate the BDM, the war. I have no idea what punishment I'd receive for such disrespect and disobedience, but surely it would be severe. And my mother warned me about drawing negative attention to myself.

I take a few deep breaths, the words of the leader's lecture washing over me, and the thought that there might indeed be a point in such a confrontation solidifies. I'm just not exactly sure what that point would be.

'*Ein Volk, ein Reich, ein Führer!*' the leader shouts when we finally finish singing, and, as one, we all repeat it after her.

I shake myself. It's time to set out with our Winter Relief collection tins.

To my surprise, Annalisa walks next to me. 'You really have to make more of an effort, Lene,' she says haughtily.

'Sure,' I reply. 'I'll start right now.' I rattle my tin.

'We all have to contribute more to the war effort,' she continues lecturing me, 'so you really have to get your priorities straight. For girls, school and studies isn't one of them. Which is why I've decided to leave school.'

'Really?' I ask. 'You get the best grades, though. Don't you want to finish secondary school?'

'Lene, what for? A woman's place is at home, raising children, nursing, cooking, looking after the house. I don't need to stay at school for that. Basic education for eight years is all that's necessary.' She eagerly looks at me for confirmation

'That's so stupid,' I mutter.

Her gaze turns icy. 'Which part exactly is "stupid"?'

'All of it.'

'I don't understand you and I don't think I want to.' Annalisa shakes her head. 'I think you are spending too much time with Ludwig. Ever since you started being friends with him, you changed.'

When we stand near the tram stop, Annalisa stays a few steps apart from me as though making a point. We start rattling our collection tins, pestering people for donations, not letting anyone get away who doesn't already wear the latest Winter Relief pin on their coat lapel. Annalisa says nothing to me for the rest of the afternoon.

'How was it?' my mother calls from the kitchen the minute I get home. She sticks her head into the corridor, a half-peeled potato in her hand.

'Boring as hell,' I snap, although it was so much worse than that.

'Lene! Don't talk to me in that tone!'

My mother looks shocked, her eyes that match mine, wide, but I am beyond caring. For a moment we stare at each other and I wonder if she will slap me for the first time in my life, but she doesn't. I storm past the kitchen, down the corridor to my bedroom and slam the door behind me, shutting her out. I wish I could shut everything out, that whole twisted world out there.

I pull a cardboard box from underneath the last two spare blankets in my wardrobe and sit down on my bed. The box feels light on my knees. I flick off the lid and run my fingers over my father's letters from the front. I know every single one of them by heart, know when they were written. The first one dates back to late August 1939, just before the outbreak of war, the last one to late September this year. In between I have seen my father half-a-dozen times, a week here and there, his short stays hazed over by those endless months of absence.

The day when he first left, more than three years ago, I can remember more vividly than any of his short leaves from the front afterwards. That day we walked together to the bakery next door to Café Kramer, just him and I, and bought a sweet treat, a rare indulgence – a plump *Pfannkuchen* thickly crusted with sugar. Pink raspberry jam oozed out all over our hands when we tore it in half to share.

My father wore his uniform and I wore my favorite summer dress. The colours of that day are carved into my memory. The faded yellow of my dress, the field grey of my father's uniform, the faint hues of orange and red in the trees, announcing that summer was almost over.

I remember the overwhelming feeling of something ending, not just summer, but my life as it was, everything changing. And I remember the feeling of my father's big hand squeezing mine, furtively, as though he knew exactly what I was thinking. I was perhaps a little too old to hold my father's hand, but all I wished was to never let go.

A few months later he came home on leave. There was a solemnity to his face that didn't gel with the newspaper headlines, the reports and constant speeches and news broadcasts on the radio of glory and lightning-fast victory or the proud face and gleaming eyes of our teacher as he moved the little red, white and black flags on the big map in our classroom further and further into Poland as their defense was crushed by the sheer speed of our surprise attacks.

'It'll all be over soon,' my father said. 'Let's hope it'll be over soon, let's hope it stops here.'

I knew then he didn't believe it himself.

And now, more than three years on, there's still war. We are fighting everyone, everywhere.

I randomly pull out a letter, feel the thin envelope with the *Feldpost* stamps between my fingers. The letter connects with the newsreel pictures, those mailbags dropping out of the plane's belly, the pale, scared face of the young soldier on the JU52. What if that's all that will be left in the end? Black-and-white newsreel pictures that make everything look less real, and thin sheets of paper.

'Lene?' The door opens a crack and my mother sticks her head in. 'What in God's name is the matter?'

'Nothing.'

'Are those Vati's letters to you?' She sits down on the bed next to me.

I nod.

'I'm sure we'll get another one soon.' There is a wobble in her voice. 'It's not been that long,' she adds, adjusting her tone.

'What if there isn't another letter?' I blurt out. 'What if he is …' The words stick like glue to the back of my throat.

My mother stops me. 'Don't think about the "what if". Vati is a professional soldier. He's been in the forces long before this war even started. He is doing his duty for Germany and he will do everything he can to come home to us. He's probably still in France and things are fairly safe there.'

I notice that my mother says that my father is doing his duty for Germany. She doesn't say the Führer. She never does. Like she wants to shut out the real world too.

'I'm so sorry,' I say to her for the second time today.

'All this rebellion,' my mother says and shakes her head. 'I guess you're at that age.'

It's news to me that there is an 'age' for rebellion. I wonder if that means that it is permissible to break the rules and laws, to disagree, to question things when those doubts about the way things are grow bigger and bigger.

'I'm sorry,' I say yet again. And I really am.

CHAPTER 3

I walk home alone without Ludwig in the cold misty rain after school the next day. It's Thursday which means our timetables don't match as he starts and finishes at his school early. It's one of my least favourite days of the week. Normally Ludwig and I take our time walking home. We talk and debate quietly and in riddles that only we understand. When we see the latest headlines plastered on the newsstands or pictures of the fat Goering in his ridiculous outfits – how did he ever fit into the tiny pilot's seat of a plane? – or the malicious-looking Goebbels, we raise our eyebrows. Sometimes Ludwig lets out a sneer on reading a headline. Or mutters something like: 'Whoever believes that is a fool'. Those sneers and comments have become more frequent of late.

I rush up the stairs to the Schluck's flat on the third floor when I arrive home. I want to tell Ludwig about the newsreel, but mainly I just want to see him. It's like he is the only person in the world I can really talk to, especially with Vati away. There's a sudden flutter of nerves in my stomach. I remember the air raid last week, his shoulder on mine, our eyes locked together for that short moment before he left the cellar.

'I thought it was you,' Ludwig says, letting me in. He's distracted, barely looks at me. I wonder if it's because I look like a wet rodent. But when he furtively checks the stairwell I know why. He quietly shuts the door behind me.

I follow him down the hallway to the kitchen, wiping my dripping face on the wet sleeve of my jacket. I glance into the small living room. The Schluck's radio, which is a slightly better apparatus than the standard *Volksempfänger*, is on but turned right down. Ludwig's mum doesn't seem to be home.

I stand by the oven in the kitchen, trying to get warm while Ludwig pours a small glass of milk for each of us with an unsteady hand.

'Have you been listening to … ?' My voice is an almost inaudible whisper.

He nods, pushing my glass of milk across the kitchen table. On his forehead, above his left eyebrow, a familiar small line appears.

There are chills of fear running up and down my drenched back. It's forbidden by law to listen to enemy stations and everyone knows what happens to people who get denounced or caught. Even right there on the radio is that sticker warning us!

Denke daran

Das Abhören ausländischer Sender ist ein Verbrechen gegen die nationale Sicherheit unseres Volkes. Es wird auf Befehl des Führers mit schweren Zuchthausstrafen geahndet.

I try not to think about it. We are only kids after all.

'What are they saying then?' I ask.

He shakes his head. 'Nothing much.'

'That's ridiculous! Don't you start keeping things from me, Ludwig. Please!' I find it hard to whisper when I'm annoyed.

'Stop it, Lene.'

Ludwig is keeping something from me. I know it. 'You have to tell me!' I say much louder than I should.

Ludwig puts a finger to his lips, silencing me. There are footsteps on the stairs outside the door, descending at a snail's pace from the attic.

'Sorry,' I mouth. I'm embarrassed about my outburst. And I seem to be doing a lot of apologising lately.

We wait for the footsteps to go away. They halt on the ground floor where an apartment door opens and closes quietly.

Despite the drizzling rain a brief flicker of weak sunlight angles into the kitchen. Ludwig takes a sip from his milk then carefully sets the glass down on the table again. 'It's fine, I understand,' he says and leans over, touching my hand. His eyes, the colour somewhere between hazel and burnt caramel, are intelligent and kind. Strands of his brown hair flop messily across his forehead. The little glimpse of sunlight reminds me of the summer just gone and how the late afternoon sun would bring out a copper hue in Ludwig's hair. The memory is like an ache, bringing with it a longing for something that is inevitably lost, something that perhaps had to be lost.

I remember how we stole into one of the tenement buildings on the south side of our block, climbing up a rickety ladder and out through an attic window. There was a stretch of flat roof there and weeds grew thickly everywhere. We lay in the sun, sharing a beer that Ludwig had pinched from his father's stash in the cellar, feeling nothing but the warmth on our skin, each other's presence and the thrill of doing something frivolous and forbidden. I was stretched out on my stomach looking up at Ludwig, who sat next to me, looking across the rooftops. It was the late afternoon and the sun, us under the blue sky above the city, the slight drowsiness from the beer, made the war not only seem far away but almost as though it didn't exist at all.

When we went up the next time, Ludwig said: 'I came up here by myself earlier this year. Very early in the morning.' His angular face tensed and darkened.

I was lazy and slightly sleepy from the beer but I sat up. Ludwig had spoken as though talking to no one in particular, but with urgency nonetheless. I moved closer.

'See that building over there.' He pointed across the rooftops to an expansive, nondescript rectangular building. From up here we could see a corner of its fully enclosed courtyard.

'Sure, the sanatorium, what about it?'

'It's not just a sanatorium any longer. Hasn't been for years, I think. That day, the courtyard was packed with people. And their luggage. I could tell that everyone was very upset. After a while, trucks came in, one by one, and took them all away, one truckload of people at a time. There were children too, and even from afar I could see that their parents didn't always manage to get on the same truck with them. Every time a truck drove away, the people who were left behind got more upset.'

'They weren't patients?' I asked, although I knew the answer as it is not a children's sanatorium.

Ludwig shook his head. 'Patients don't need SS guards with guns.'

I stared at the building, the now deserted courtyard.

'When they had all been taken away nothing happened for a while. Only all that luggage was still there. Then a different truck arrived and took the luggage away. It was from an auction house, it said so on the side of the truck.' He paused and we looked at each other. 'Why do you think those people didn't need their belongings any longer?' he asked.

The beer tasted stale and awful after that. We didn't even finish the bottle. And we never went up on the roof again.

After that Ludwig started listening to enemy stations.

I suddenly feel as though we are past a turning point and that we are slowly gliding into the blackness of an abyss from which there's no coming back. The feeling is so strong it's like a ton of rocks slowly being emptied on my chest, gradually crushing me.

'We tell each other everything,' I say to Ludwig. 'Please, tell me what you heard on the radio. I know it's something important.'

'You know that it's high treason,' Ludwig replies, his voice barely audible. 'For me to tell you what they said on the BBC or another enemy station.'

I nod. Of course I know and I don't need a lecture. 'I'm not going to tell anyone.'

'There are always ways to make people talk.'

I realise that he is scared. 'Who's going to know what we talk about?' I whisper. But I feel as though the concrete walls are leaning in to listen. It chills me.

'I know, you are right.' Then he gives in. 'Germany is losing battles on the Eastern Front. We are retreating. It sounds like the Soviets are gaining the upper hand and our losses are enormous.'

I'm stunned. 'But I saw the newsreel yesterday. There wasn't a word about retreat.'

Ludwig just looks at me. 'Well, they wouldn't want us to know, would they? They don't want us to know about a lot of things.'

I shake my head. 'They don't want us to know what's really going on. They're lying. That's why the reports said the opposite.' Then I also remember the soldier on the plane heading to the Eastern Front, the dread and fear in his face. 'What they say on the foreign stations might not be the truth though,' I ruminate. 'How do we know that it is?' I don't know what to believe any longer.

'Well, we can't know for sure,' says Ludwig. 'But there are clear indications that it is objective reporting. What's being reported in our newsreels, on our stations, isn't the truth. There is no independent reporting here. So we have no way of knowing what *exactly* the truth is and what isn't. But only an idiot wouldn't be able to put two and two together.'

CHAPTER 4

On Sunday my mother and I visit my Aunt Ilsa and my cousins Ophelia, Gertie and little Theo in Charlottenburg.

'I really don't know why my sister can't visit us for once,' my mother complains when we get on the tram heading to Alexanderplatz. She sighs, resigned. 'But I guess it's hard for her with the baby and all. Even though Theo is already two years old!'

I don't mind the once a month journey from the edge of Prenzlauer Berg across Berlin to Charlottenburg. It's a change from the humdrum of everyday life. However, the U-Bahn leg of this whole excursion is less than pleasant. I've taken the U-Bahn thousands of times, but recently a cold hand of claustrophobia clamps around me every time I descend underground. The stale smell is like an assault on my nose. I hold my breath as visions of being trapped in the dark ambush me. I see the narrow tunnels being hit by a bomb and flooding or fire spreading rapidly into the underbelly darkness of the city.

As we wait with the rest of the crowd on the platform my mother glances at me, an eyebrow raised. I grasp her arm for almost the entire train ride and I try to hide my relief when we resurface in Charlottenburg. I breathe more freely when we get on the bus and during the short walk along the elegant streets to the apartment.

My aunt is a typical upper middle-class housewife. She married my uncle, who comes from a Prussian well-to-do family, travelled all over Europe before my cousins were born, then settled into motherhood. They live in a rather grand turn-of-the-century apartment. The entrance hall has a black-and-white chequerboard marble floor, bas-reliefs and gleaming floor-to-ceiling ornate gilt mirrors. The mahogany stairs are dressed in a ruby carpet and there are kaleidoscope-like stained-glass windows on every landing. There's even a lift! It's quite the contrast to our dim, slightly dank stairwell with the worn stairs, flaking paint on the window frames, and draughty vestibule at home.

We don't wait for the lift and instead climb the sweeping stairs to the second floor and ring the doorbell. Nothing happens for a long time. Inside it's unusually quiet.

'That's odd. Ilsa is expecting us,' my mother says and rings the bell again. 'Ilsa,' she calls and stands on tiptoes, pressing her face against the door's frosted glass window, trying to look inside.

At last there are footsteps. They are slow, heavy. They don't sound like my cousins' or Aunty Ilsa's who, although big-boned and curvaceous, usually walks as lightly as a ballerina.

The door opens and Aunty Ilsa's distorted face peers out at us.

'Ilsa, what's wrong?' My mother closes the door behind us and switches on the light. 'It's all dark in here. Why haven't you opened the blackout blinds yet? It's midday.'

Aunty Ilsa is motionless and slack, lifeless, like a shop mannequin. The only movement comes from her tears dripping from her chin onto the collar of her silk blouse. I watch a single teardrop land on her double-strand necklace and slither down the smooth white surface of a pearl.

'Where are the children?' my mother asks.

'Oh God,' she cries as some life returns. She unclasps her hands and places them over her face, her fingernails digging into her cheeks so hard it looks painful. A scrunched-up piece of paper sails to the floor. My mother picks it up, then wraps her arm around Aunt Ilsa's shoulders and slowly walks her to the kitchen.

'Well, at least the blinds are up here,' my mother mutters.

I follow them to the kitchen where my younger cousin Gertie is hunched over a pot on the stove, mashing potatoes with abrupt, jerky jabs that make her whole body shake as though it were clenched by sobs. Her blonde angelic curls hang down in a mess. She looks up briefly; her eyes are red rimmed too. Her older sister Ophelia, with two-year-old Theo hoisted on her hip, stands by the kitchen window dressed in her BDM uniform, almost as tall and big-boned as my aunt. Her heart-shaped face, framed by long wispy brown hair, is like a mask, and the anaemic autumn light filtering in makes it appear even more lifeless. Her eyes aren't red; they are as hard as river pebbles.

Aunt Ilsa collapses on a kitchen chair and my mother puts the sheet of paper on the table and smooths it out. It looks official, with a letterhead I have never seen before.

Before I've even read it I realise what it is.

A notification.

My uncle, a Major General in the *Wehrmacht*, is dead. Fallen for the Führer, the German people and the Fatherland, the notification says. *Gefallen für Führer, Volk und Vaterland.*

Would the German people really have wanted him to die for them? I didn't want him to die for me. I feel helpless with a heavy sadness that hits me as I process the news. I glance from Ophelia to Gertie to my aunt, all of them in their orbs of grief; everything has changed suddenly, everything is so overwhelmingy different than the last time we were here. I don't know what to do; I can't console Gertie as I would have done if she'd scraped her knee, or Ophelia if she hadn't done well in an exam. But I walk over to the window and stand next to Ophelia.

At last Aunt Ilsa speaks, her voice monotonous. 'Last time I saw Manfred, he told me that if he had a choice he would abandon the Eastern Front. If it were up to him, he would pull out of Russia. He was considering putting in a request for transfer for his men so they could get moved further back temporarily. He even asked for leave for some of them. They were all battle weary, sick and weak. They sometimes didn't sleep for up to three or four days. He said they didn't stand a chance in the shape they were in and they hadn't had any leave in over a year.'

Thump, thump, thump goes the potato masher. As monotonous as my aunt's voice.

My mother's eyes dash to us children. She puts her hand on my aunt's. 'Ilsa, please, you have to calm down,' she says, even though my aunt doesn't seem hysterical or agitated at all. Though her words are of course scandalous.

Gertie drops the masher and storms out of the kitchen, sobbing. I'm about to follow her but Ophelia stops me. 'Here, look after Theo.' She puts Theo into my arms and finishes mashing the potatoes.

Thump, thump, thump.

I sit down at the kitchen table. Theo reaches for my nose and traces his little fingers along its bridge. 'Vati gone?' he asks.

'Yes, Theo, Vati is gone,' I reply, trying to steady my voice. I know Theo doesn't understand that his father is dead, just that he's not here like he hasn't been for most of Theo's life.

My aunt suppresses another sob.

'I'm so very sorry, Ilsa,' my mother says, awkwardly touching her sister's arm. 'He was a good soldier, a good man.'

My aunt shakes her head, refusing to listen. 'He said it was hell out there on the Eastern Front. The cold at night was unimaginable and they were waiting for warmer uniforms that just didn't arrive. They were running out of fuel and food and the relief units had been cut off.'

'Ilsa, stop it right away,' my mother says, sounding breathless with shock at my aunt's words, her frankness and criticism of the war. 'You are talking nonsense. It can only be a matter of weeks before Stalingrad falls. They just have to persevere.'

'Yes, that's what I thought. But Manfred didn't, and he would have known, wouldn't he? And now he is dead.'

I've never heard adults talk like this before. People just don't say these kinds of things out loud. I didn't even know anyone *thought* those things. Pulling out of Russia, doubting the superhuman strength and spirit of our soldiers. But wasn't that exactly what Ludwig had heard on the foreign stations? What they said had to be true then. I feel stupid now for doubting it. Putting two and two together, Ludwig had said, only an idiot wouldn't be able to. Oh, how I wish he were here right now and I could talk to him.

Ophelia slams the oven door. 'The *roast* is done.' Her voice is brittle and hostile. Why is she behaving like this?

Aunt Ilsa shoots her a forlorn look. Ophelia fiercely returns it. When she finally lowers her eyes her bottom lip is trembling.

'Do you want the table set in the dining room?' my mother asks Aunt Ilsa. Her voice sounds helpless.

'That was Gertie's job, but I guess I'd better check that she's done it.' Ophelia wipes the back of her hand across her eyes and clears her throat. 'Roast on *Eintopf Sonntag*, it's a disgrace. It's undermining the spirit and resolve of the people's community. I'm sure everyone in the building can smell it too,' she then mutters, stalking out.

We are meant to forego the roast on *Eintopf Sonntag* and donate the money we would have spent on it to the war effort and the Winter Relief. We are supposed to eat a vegetable stew instead. The whole of Germany is. But that Ophelia would be bothered about it on a day like today makes no sense.

'What do I do now? Three children and there's not even a grave to go to,' Aunt Ilsa whispers to my mother.

A shiver spirals up my spine. I bury my face in Theo's hair and smell his baby smell. He leans back into my chest and clamps his pudgy little hands around my forearm.

Next time it could be us getting a notification in the mail.

I glance at my mother. She has blanched to the palest shade of white.

We hadn't planned on staying. But my mother doesn't want to leave my aunt and we end up spending the night at the apartment. At bedtime, I put on one of Ophelia's slightly too large nightgowns and climb into bed in the girls' bedroom. I watch as Ophelia methodically takes off her BDM uniform, puts the jacket and skirt on a coat hanger. She tosses the white uniform blouse in the dirty laundry basket and whisks a fresh one out of the wardrobe. Inside, I see three blouses neatly lined up.

Three, plus the one she's just worn! I only own one and it's not even the regulation uniform blouse. Not that I care about the uniform, but seeing the blouses all crisp, pressed and brand new like that, reminds me of how privileged my cousins are. Although now even Gertie has to wear Ophelia's cast-offs.

After replacing the dirty blouse with the fresh one, Ophelia hangs the complete uniform on the outside of the wardrobe door, ready for the next day. She meticulously adjusts the jacket, then steps back, tilts her head and admires her uniform.

'Do you think I should have the sleeves taken up on the jacket?' she asks me. 'I think they are a tad too long.' She immediately answers the question herself before I have a chance to say anything. 'Yes, that's what I will do. I'll take it to the dressmaker tomorrow so it'll be done in time for Wednesday's meeting.'

Her father has just died on the Eastern Front and all she's concerned about is the fit of her BDM uniform! But Ophelia has always loved the BDM and I know she wants to become a squad leader.

Ophelia hops into bed next to her sister, who is staring at the ceiling, her face scrunched up as though it required all her concentration to not start crying again. 'Move over, Gertie. Goodness, you are taking up so much space.'

'I can share with Gertie if you want,' I offer. I'm only four months younger than Ophelia but I'm closer in height to Gertie, even though she is two years younger than Ophelia and me. 'Gertie?' I reach across the space between the beds.

Gertie shrugs and continues to stare at the ceiling.

Ophelia shakes her head. 'No, it's fine.' She grabs the latest copy of *Das Deutsche Mädel* magazine from the bedside table and starts reading, frowning a little as Gertie cuddles up to her. 'Do you want to read one?' Ophelia asks me, indicating the stack of magazines on the bedside table.

'No, I'm too tired.' Which is not true; I'd love to read one of my science books. There's one about subtropical insects that I'm reading at the moment. It gives me a little thrill every time I open it as I escape to a world far away. But I'd rather not read that awful magazine. 'I'll turn the light off in a minute,' Ophelia says, her eyes glued to a story.

'I'm really sorry about your father,' I say after a while.

'He died a hero's death,' Ophelia replies shortly. Her eyes don't divert from the page, though I can tell she's stopped reading. 'For the Führer and the greater good of the German people. It says so on the notification. It's an honour to give your life for the Führer.' Her voice sounds a little funny and she quickly clears her throat.

Gertie starts sobbing. Sitting up, Ophelia yanks her shoulder out from underneath Gertie's head. 'Will you stop it, Gertie! I really can't stand the weeping any longer. You should be ashamed.'

'No, you should be ashamed,' sobs Gertie. 'You haven't shed a single tear. It's like you're not even sad.'

'Maybe I'm not,' says Ophelia.

'How can you not be sad?' Gertie cries.

'I'll tell you why! Because his death saved him from being branded a coward. Now he's a hero!'

'Your father wasn't a coward,' I cut in. 'How can you even say that? He was looking after his men as well. All he wanted was for them to get a break from the frontline.'

'Only a coward would consider begging for a transfer from the front,' Ophelia replies.

'He didn't beg,' Gertie cries. 'He didn't even request it.'

'It still makes him a coward. Even thinking of such a request is a disgrace – thinking that we are losing the war against those Bolshevik sub-humans! How dare he!' There's chilling rage in Ophelia's voice and the bone-deep conviction of her words stifle my reply. Despite the warm quilt and the flannel nightgown, another shiver spirals up my back.

'You are a monster,' Gertie says, choking. She turns away from Ophelia and moves to the very edge of the bed.

Ophelia flings the magazine back on the bedside table and switches off the light. Her words hover in the dark room like malevolent ghosts long after her regular breathing tells me she's fallen asleep.

Theo's crying wakes me in the middle of the night. Disoriented, I lie in the strange bed for a moment before realising where I am. The door is ajar and a thin sliver of light cuts through the darkness. I hear my cousins shifting restlessly in their sleep in the other bed. As I get up and go to the nursery next to the girls' room, I see that the light is on in the kitchen. My mother and Aunt Ilsa are still up, talking.

'What's the matter, Theo?' He's standing in his cot, his fine reddish hair plastered to his sweaty forehead. I pick him up, and sway him on my hips. 'There, there,' I say, soothing him, and he settles until he falls asleep, his head resting on my shoulder. After a few minutes, I gently put him down again and slip out into the hallway, tiptoeing across the chilly parquetry floor towards the voices in the kitchen.

'You have to be strong, Ilsa,' I hear my mother say. 'The children need you now more than ever. Especially the girls. They are at a difficult age.'

'I know they need me. At least Gertie does. All Ophelia thinks about is the BDM and the war effort. Sometimes I catch her looking at me with such derision. Like this afternoon when she lectured me about cooking a roast. *Eintopf Sonntag*! What difference is it going to make?' She pauses. A pipe is clanking in a bathroom somewhere above us. Outside, a cat hisses loudly on the roof.

'I'm scared. Do you know what else Manfred said the last time I saw him?' There's another pause. 'My god, it was only three weeks ago that he sat in this very spot.' Her voice trembles and she's lowered it in the way people do when they are about to say something they think they shouldn't.

I move one step closer, breathing shallowly.

'He said that we weren't going to win the war in Russia, that German losses were high and the Russians had vast reserves of men, and Hitler was insane – *insane*, that's the word he used – if he thought we could still win. That invading Russia was the biggest strategic mistake he's ever made, the decision of a lunatic.' She pauses again and lowers her voice even more. It's no more than a whisper.

I take another step closer, not wanting to miss a word.

'He said the invasion of Russia was the beginning of Germany's defeat and downfall.'

'It can't be true,' my mother says. 'Defeat? We can't lose. It's unfathomable. Not after all the sacrifices we have already made. Anton has been away for so long.' She sounds breathless.

'That's what I thought too. I thought that perhaps Manfred was the one who was insane. But then he said there were many others who shared his view. That it was not too late to turn things around, to prevent things from getting much worse. For us and for others.'

'Getting worse?'

'He said we've already done enough harm in the east with what has been done to the civilians. There's been total annihilation.'

There's silence. The word 'annihilation' floats down the hallway to me and hovers, like those other words, the ones Ophelia said, haunting me and inciting me to think, to form images in my head.

'How can we go on if we allow ourselves to get carried away with thoughts of losing, of doubting? We Germans are not like this,' my mother finally replies.

She's trying to convince herself. I recognise that slightly off-pitch tone of her voice. No, my mother is definitely not a good liar.

'Just think of your children, of baby Theo,' my mother adds.

'Theo won't even remember his father.' Aunt Ilsa blows her nose. 'But I wanted another child so badly. Just in case.'

My mother sighs. It's a strange sigh, full of longing.

'The revenge of the enemy—' my aunt starts, but her words are drowned by the wailing of the air-raid siren. For a second or two I freeze, trying to figure out the rest of my aunt's sentence. Then I turn on my heels and hurry back down the hallway. My toes catch on the hem of the too-long nightgown and I stumble and nearly fall. I pluck Theo from his cot again and hastily wrap him up in a blanket. He stays blissfully asleep. With Theo in my arms, I scramble back to the girls' bedroom.

'Gertie, Ophelia! Air raid, get up!'

Half-asleep, my cousins tumble out of bed, searching for their dressing-gowns in the semi-dark. My mother and Aunt Ilsa rush into the room.

'Quickly everyone,' my mother calls. 'Away from the windows.'

The Flak starts firing. And there is another sound, one that I have never heard before: a faint whistling followed by a powerful boom. An explosion! The house shivers and fear arrows through me.

My mother takes Theo off me and we race to the apartment door. I'm pushing my aunt, who seems slow and disoriented, up the hallway and we scurry downstairs with the rest of the dressing-gown-clad residents. By the time we reach the ground floor and race to the cellar door leading down to the air-raid room, there's another explosion. It sounds terrifyingly close. Gertie lets out a shriek.

I've never experienced an air raid like this before. Berlin, unlike other German cities, has been largely spared so far. Where we live, only one building a few streets over was bombed in 1940. But here, we are not too far from Tempelhof Airport and there's also the industrial area of Siemensstadt – ideal targets. 'My God, hurry up.' My aunt's voice is breathless with fear.

But even if we tried, we couldn't go any faster without falling. As I scramble down the last steps, there's only one primal thought in my mind – *don't let it be us*.

The moment I launch myself through the steel door there is a deafening boom. The floor shudders beneath us and the building shakes on its foundation. I throw myself on the concrete floor, wedge my head between my knees and fold my arms over it.

Silence follows. Or what I perceive as silence after the noise of the explosion. The Flak is still going but the bombs have stopped. I stay in the same position for a long time, wrapped in a parcel on the ground. Finally I open my eyes and tentatively unfold myself, checking for broken bones, for blood. But I seem to be all right. The cellar ceiling is in one piece and so are the walls and everyone around me. Ophelia and Gertie still cower on the ground like me. My mother and Aunty Ilsa, who is clutching Theo to her chest, huddle on the benches, shaking. A building very close must have taken the direct hit.

I get up, brush the dirt off my nightgown and sit down on the bench next to my mother. I look at the concrete floor, my bare feet, but I don't feel the cold.

No one says much more than a few whispered words until the all clear comes. We climb up the cellar steps and some of the other residents go outside. Through the open front door, I can see a wall of flames licking at the night sky where down the road an apartment building stood this afternoon. The fire feels hot on my face, like a furiously hungry and revengeful beast.

CHAPTER 5

The next morning before we leave, my cousins and I take a closer look at the bombed building. A fire crew is still dousing a section of the ruin close to the neighbouring apartment block that seems to have reignited, but everywhere else the fire has stopped burning. Heat is radiating from the blackened ruins. It smells of smoke, cement, pulverised bricks. Above, the sky is a mocking powder blue.

The destruction is sharp like a stencil cut-out in the glare of the morning light. All five floors of the front building as well as the rear building have collapsed onto the cellar. Sections of a back wall still stand erect, shaped like a chain of fragile, bizarre exclamation marks. It could all crumble without any warning.

I wonder how many people are buried down there, and I feel deep, guilt-drenched relief that it's not us in that horrible tomb of the cellar.

'The enemy will pay for this. Just wait until our bombs drop on their cities again,' Ophelia says. There it is again, the cold, vengeful tone.

'What's the point?' I say. 'They'll just come back and bomb us again.' Suddenly feeling uneasy, I look up into the sky. What if they come back now?

'They are enemy scum,' says Ophelia. 'And they hate us and the Führer.'

'You should hear yourself,' I say. 'When will it all end? When everyone is dead?'

'Shut your mouth, Lene! Everyone can *hear* you. You should remember that what we think doesn't matter – *we* don't matter. What the Führer wants matters because he knows best. We belong to him and we will die for him if necessary.' Her voice sounds trance-like suddenly but at the same time deeply resolved, convinced of that only truth.

But I feel mad, furious anger. 'That's right, we don't matter! The Führer would sacrifice all of us without blinking! Our soldiers, women, children, everyone, if that means he gets what he wants. Because that's the only thing that *really* matters to him.'

'What you say is bordering on treason, Lene,' Ophelia says coldly.

'It's the truth that I believe.'

'Those poor people,' Gertie whispers. 'We knew them.'

'For goodness sakes, don't feel pity,' says Ophelia. 'It weakens your spirit. A German girl has to be strong.'

I've had enough. 'It's not wrong to feel sorry for others. Those people died a horrible death!' I don't even lower my voice. I don't care who hears me.

'Feeling sorry won't bring them back, will it?' Ophelia retorts. 'Pull yourself together, Lene!'

'What if it's us next time?' asks Gertie.

'So be it. I wouldn't want anyone to feel pity for me. I would give my life for the Führer. I would sacrifice everything and everyone for him, just like Lene said.'

Has Ophelia gone insane? It's like Theo, Gertie and her mother mean nothing to her and only what her Führer wants matters. I wonder if the shock of her father's death has done something to her. It's as though someone's put a pair of ugly scull-embossed wings on her and she's happily floated into the abyss without even looking back. Only she doesn't see the ugliness of her wings and she thinks it's beautiful where she is going.

Gertie looks like she's close to tears again and I don't want to upset her more than she already is. I quickly pat her shoulder; it feels tense beneath my hand.

'I really can't stand watching this any longer.' Ophelia indicates a crew of prisoners of war who have arrived with a guard and now start digging in a particularly dangerous-looking section of the rubble. Ophelia's lip curls in disgust.

I watch the POWs and wonder what nationality they are. Their faces are thin, strange and foreign. They are dressed in dirty rag-like clothes.

'I hope it doesn't collapse on them.' I point at the crumbling back wall.

Ophelia looks at me with utter incomprehension. 'Who cares if it does, those are not Germans. They are disgusting. I don't even want to look at them.' She shakes her head as though I were someone slow and stupid. 'Let's go back inside,' she orders us. 'It smells of gas. There's a big leak somewhere.'

She's right. I sniff and now smell the gas from the busted mains as well.

Glass from the shattered windows and broken roof tiles crunch under our feet as we walk back down the street to my cousins' building. I don't want to go back upstairs, though, and I don't want to be around Ophelia any longer.

'I'll wait outside. We'll be heading home soon.' I suddenly can't wait to get back to our little flat, back to Ludwig, away from Ophelia, away from the ruin, away from the house that has become a tomb.

'Fine, suit yourself.' Ophelia marches off and disappears upstairs.

'Bye, Lene.' Gertie's voice is small and wobbly. 'I hope we see each other again soon.' She reminds me of the little cherub child she still was, a few years back, when Ophelia and I had suddenly shot up, our faces and bodies changing, and Gertie started looking up at us like we were adults.

'Adieu, Gertie, until next time.' My throat feels tight. 'Gertie …'

'Yes?'

'Nothing.' I can't bring myself to tell her I fear that I might never see her again, that next time we visit there might be a ruin in the place of her lovely apartment building, just like the one down the road, with them buried beneath it.

'Take care, Gertie,' I say. My voice is unsteady too, I can't control it, and I know that it's obvious to Gertie what I'm thinking.

'I'll try.' Gertie turns to go back inside but halfway up the portal steps she stops and spins around. She flings herself at me, wordlessly hugging me tight, before running back inside without another word, passing my mother who is on her way downstairs.

Right then there's commotion at the bombed building.

'Don't look!' my mother shouts.

But it's too late. I have turned around, have already seen it. A body is pulled from the rubble by one of the POWs. It's small and black. Stiff and charred, like a burned loaf of bread. I draw in a sharp breath, thinking that those people were still alive yesterday.

'I said, don't look!' my mother calls again. She grabs my arm and pulls me away. 'Look away and move along, Lene. For goodness sake, just do as you're told!' There is a new shrill edge to her voice.

I don't reply. I don't think my mother expects me to. Things don't stop happening only because one looks away. They happen, so one must look.

Once we've left my cousins' street behind everything seems normal again. And yet I know nothing is. The bus is late and we decide to walk to the U-Bahn. I'm feeling even more uneasy than usual when we descend underground. The crowd sweeps us along, down into the tunnel and onto the packed platform.

'Such a close call last night. I think we might be less at risk where we are. They are coming for Berlin now,' my mother mumbles.

I suddenly think that it is perhaps nothing more than an illusion believing that we are safer where we live.

'I should request getting you posted with the *Kinderlandverschickung* as a supervisor. At least you'd be out of harm's way in the country.'

'No!' I protest. 'I don't want to leave school.' *And I don't want to leave Ludwig.* But my mother doesn't need to know that.

'School!' my mother exclaims and shakes her head. 'When I was your age I was working, earning money. I left school when I was fourteen.'

'I know that, Mutti. But I always thought you and Vati wanted me to get a higher education, so I can go to university,' I whisper. 'Don't you want me to have the opportunities you weren't able to have?'

'We still do. Of course we do. We want you to have choices, and you are certainly bright enough.' My mother reassuringly pats my arm now. 'But if last night is a taste of things to come, school, or any sort of higher education let alone university, will be the least of our worries.'

Was she right? Was university nothing more than a pipedream, an ambition I shared with Ludwig? As a girl it's almost impossible to get the qualifications needed for university entry. I'm lucky my school still teaches subjects like Latin and chemistry to the girls who want to take those subjects. But for how much longer? Oh, how unfair, how angry it makes me that my life is being controlled like this. I refuse to accept it! I know with crystal clear certainty that I want to go to university. I want more knowledge, I want to know about the universe, about how the human mind and the human body work, about the animal world, flora and geology, and how it's all connected. I don't want bearing children, cooking and looking pretty to be my only purpose in life!

I look up at the low, vaulted ceiling of the underground station, one of the oldest in Berlin. Was my mother right, though, was my education perhaps really the least of our worries? What if there was an air raid right now? Would the ceiling even be strong enough to withstand the bombs? My guess is, it wouldn't.

I step forward and peer into the tunnel worming away into the darkness, checking if a light isn't already approaching. Meanwhile, more people spill from the streets above down into the tunnels and onto the platform. I'm getting pushed closer to the tracks. The tips of my shoes are almost at the platform's edge.

'Heavens, where's that train?' my mother says. She has grabbed hold of my arm again, drawing me back.

'Running late, busses too, because of the bombings last night,' says a woman wearing a prim little hat with a bow. 'Apparently, there's some damage to an underground shaft.' She shakes her head. 'A terror attack! Such cowardice!'

'It is very unfortunate,' my mother replies shortly.

At last I can hear the train approaching. A murmur of relief goes through the crowd. Carriages rattling past bring more gusts of stale underground air with them. The train is already packed to near capacity and very few people get off. But we manage to squeeze in, pushing and shoving our way into the carriage.

As the crowd adjusts, drawing even closer together, I'm jostled against the edge of the still open door. I feel my stockings catch on something just below my left knee. It's sharp and cold, and there's a pulling and tearing sensation. Then the pain hits. My shin starts throbbing and I feel something warm and wet trickling down my leg and ankle into my shoe. I bite my lip. My face is pressed into the overpowering mothball smell of a stranger's wool coat. I'm packed in too tightly to see what's happened. I suddenly feel queasy.

'How on earth did you manage to do this?' My mother shakes her head, dismayed. 'So clumsy.'

My stockings are torn and the moss-green wool has turned a ghastly brownish red all the way down from my left shin to my ankle where drying blood cakes the wool to my skin. From the deep thumb-long gash, blood still trickles.

'I'm sorry, Mutti,' I say. 'It was such a crush on the train and everyone was pushing. I couldn't help it.' Carefully I peel the torn wool off, the cold in the still chilly kitchen creeping up my bare legs.

My mother takes a closer look at my leg. 'Well, this is certainly more than just a scrape.' She then holds up the stockings, inspecting the shredded wool. 'These might be beyond repair. And they are brand new too.' She throws them over the back of the kitchen chair, then starts cleaning my wound. 'This is really deep. Let's hope it doesn't get infected. It's the last thing we need right now. We should have never gone and visited.'

'Let me do it,' I say. I take the cloth out of her hand and dab antiseptic on the cut. Tears shoot into my eyes from the sting. I'm embarrassed that this has happened, that my mother is fussing over me like I'm a little girl. I'm upset that I ripped my only pair of winter stockings. But most of all, I'm upset for being upset over a scratch, while on the other side of town in Charlottenburg, people are dead beneath the rubble.

I put my leg up on a chair to stop the bleeding while trying to hide my tears. But my mother has seen them anyway and starts bustling about. She takes the soiled stockings, fills a tub with water and soap in the kitchen sink to soak them, while mumbling to herself about running out of flour and oats and getting started on dinner.

I move my chair closer to the table, hobbling on one foot, when there's a knock on the door.

My mother frowns. 'Who could that be, right at dinnertime?'

I shrug and get up but she tells me off. 'No, you stay put. We don't want the bleeding to start again. I will get it. It's probably Frau Schluck.' She leaves the kitchen and her footsteps tap down the corridor.

I collapse back on the chair and start unwrapping the slice of leftover roast my aunt has given us. I wipe the grease off the butcher's paper with my finger and lick it. Furtively I pull a tiny piece of meat off and pop it in my mouth. God, it tastes so good.

I chew as slowly as possible, savouring it, while my mother is talking to someone. I can clearly hear a self-assured, clipped male voice.

'Frau Trauber? *Geheime Staatspolizei*.'

I freeze and stop chewing, an icy spike of fear piercing my spine.

The Gestapo!

'If you could spare a moment of your time we would like to talk to you,' says a second male voice. Polite but oh so reticent.

What are they doing here?

They don't wait for my mother's answer. I can hear them tramping into our corridor, fast and resolute. The apartment door snaps shut. I gulp down the small lump of meat in my mouth, toss some scrunched-up butcher's paper on the slice of roast, covering it as though the meat were evidence of a crime. Which it might well be in the eyes of the Gestapo.

Two men enter the kitchen. They are in civilian clothes and long black leather coats. They don't take off their hats.

My heart is racing. I see my presence registering with them. They see the half-unwrapped parcel on the table and a quick glance passes between them. I start sweating, my pulse racing faster still. I feel sweat pouring out of me, running cold on my skin in the chilly kitchen.

The acuity – knowing about the conversations between my mother and my aunt, about Ludwig listening to enemy broadcasts, my absence at the BDM meetings in the past, the run-in with my leader, my argument with Ophelia, my father's censored letters – all of it comes rushing at me in one big nauseating wave.

What if they know about all of it?

And then there's also the meat on the table. Hidden by the paper but somehow I'm sure that they can smell it, that they can smell that it's yesterday's illegal roast. That they can smell from afar if someone has broken one of the countless and ever-changing laws of our state.

'Please, take a seat Frau Trauber,' they say to my mother who is standing in the doorway behind them, not moving, hands on her hips, looking outraged.

'I'd rather stand,' my mother says coolly. 'Can I see some identification, please?' she then requests.

'Certainly.' They produce their badges and my mother inspects them carefully.

Her assertiveness is both unsettling and reassuring. Our eyes meet and there's an almost indiscernible movement of her head, telling me to leave the kitchen.

I get up. My legs, not just the one with the cut, feel wobbly.

'An injury?' one of the Gestapo men unsympathetically asks, raising an eyebrow.

I nod. 'It's nothing.' My voice sounds rasping, my throat is dry. I hobble out of the kitchen, not looking at anyone, expecting to be stopped, ordered to stay, to be questioned. But no one does. In the relative safety of my bedroom at the far end of the corridor, I position myself behind the open door, my leg throbbing, my heart pounding. In our small flat I can hear every word of the conversation in the kitchen.

'We won't keep you long, Frau Trauber,' says one of the Gestapo men.

'I appreciate that,' my mother says shortly. 'I have dinner to prepare and chores to do.' I can hear her opening a drawer and I think she's taking out her apron, putting it on.

'You are not a member of the National Socialist German Workers Party,' the other Gestapo officer says.

'No,' my mother replies. 'We have never been members.'

A pause. I hold my breath.

'Or of any of its affiliated organisations,' my mother then adds coolly.

'It sounds as though you are rather pleased about that,' says one of them, his voice almost casual, though at the very core of it I can hear deathly ire.

'That's your interpretation,' my mother replies, but her tone clearly implies that she is.

I know that my parents, like many others, were Social Democrat supporters before their party, along with all other parties, got banned by the Nazis in 1933, only months after they seized power. And I'm sure the Gestapo knows that too. Oh, they are so skilled in intimidation!

'As you know, there's a lot women can do on the home front and in the Women's League to contribute to final victory and to strengthen the people's community.' This is fired at my mother now, precise and steely like a butcher's cleaver hacking through meat, all pretend courtesy gone.

For a moment there's silence. Then I hear my mother move, one step, two. She must have been standing over by the kitchen sink, but now moves toward the table where I'm assuming the two Gestapo officers are standing.

'Now listen,' my mother says, her voice matching the cold steeliness of the interrogator. There's wrath in it too. I'm frozen with fear, scared for my mother. That tone she's using!

'This is quite an outrage,' my mother continues, 'calling in at such a late hour. Questioning me about my integrity, because that's what this is about, isn't it? Our integrity! While my husband, a professional soldier, is fighting at the front for Germany and has been serving the Fatherland since 1934 when he enlisted in the Cavalry so he could put food on the table!'

'You are mistaken in thinking—'

'I have not seen my husband in ten months. So why don't you come back and discuss our *participation* with him when he comes home on leave!'

So many unsaid words, but her meaning is clearly there, readable, obvious. *Why are you two not serving at the front, fighting the war that you wanted? Why does my husband have to fight a war he never wanted?*

However, the fact that the Gestapo is here, in our kitchen, is the only reality at this moment.

There's silence, then a shifting, crackling of leather, boots shuffling on the floorboards.

'Very well, Frau Trauber. It was certainly not our intention to disrespect the *sacrifice* you are making. We will call in again.'

Multiple footsteps walk down the corridor, only a few metres from my door. I hold my breath.

A unison '*Heil Hitler*' is shouted. Then the front door shuts and my mother exhales audibly. It's like a shudder, sounding wheezy and high-pitched, somewhere between a gasp and a sigh.

CHAPTER 6

The cold late autumn air bites my bare legs.

'What happened to you?' Ludwig asks, glancing at my leg.

Despite the cold, I'm wearing a pair of white summer ankle socks because the torn wool stockings are still drying in front of the oven and I haven't been able to mend them yet. Combined with my fur-rimmed leather ankle boots, a rare hand-me-down from Ophelia at the end of last winter because they were still much too big for Gertie, and bare legs, I simply look ridiculous. Plus my nasty injury is on show for Ludwig and everyone else to see.

'It's no big deal.' I try to hide the ugly, scab-covered gash behind my school satchel.

'It looks terrible,' Ludwig comments.

Does he mean the cut or the way I look in those socks and boots? I pull my socks up but it's useless; they are too short to cover anything.

'I just meant that it looks like it hurts,' says Ludwig. 'How did it happen?'

'Doesn't hurt any more.' I say it more brusquely than intended. And it's not quite true anyway as my shin still stings and throbs. 'It happened on the train coming home yesterday.'

'Aha. I wondered why you weren't at school,' Ludwig replies. Uneasy, he glances ahead.

'That air raid, it was scary. The apartment block across from my cousins' was hit. It was so close the whole building shook. A lot of the windows got blown out …' Irritated, I stop. 'Ludwig, are you even listening to me?'

'I am, I am. Sorry. Luckily there were no hits here. But we had to assemble straight after and put out a fire on the other side of the park.'

Ludwig is nervous, distracted. But what by?

I scan the street. It's early morning, just before eight o'clock, and the footpath in our street is busy with children rushing to school, people on their way to work, soldiers on leave and old ladies and men taking their dogs for their morning walks. Then my eyes catch on two older boys in Hitler Youth uniform. They roam along on the opposite footpath, saluting soldiers, staring at people openly and hungrily as though ready to pounce on anything out of the ordinary.

Ludwig's jaw clenches. 'Not them again,' he mutters under his breath, then pulls his cap down over his forehead and into his eyes, hiding as much as possible of his face beneath it. But it's a mistake. The movement catches their attention. Or perhaps they have already developed a heightened sense for detecting people who wish to avoid them. They exchange a glance, a few words, then quicken their steps and cross the road, heading straight for us.

'What's going on, Ludwig?' I ask quietly. I wonder if the Schlucks had a visit from the Gestapo too. I was going to ask Ludwig but now definitely isn't the right time.

'I didn't go to the drill last Saturday. And these two have got it in for me. Squad leaders, like a pair of bloodhounds, they are,' Ludwig says under his breath.

I feel a flutter of alarm spreading upwards from my belly. Hitler Youth for boys, especially for the older ones, is incredibly regimented and strict.

The two squad leaders look older than Ludwig, not really boys any longer, but almost men. One is stocky like a young bull and has a face like a squashed pancake with a sprinkling of pimples. The other one is towering over us, even over Ludwig. He's lean and angular with wide shoulders. His blond hair is long on top and clipped very short underneath, parted on the side and slicked back.

'Hey, Schluck,' the stocky one now shouts. He almost runs the last few metres, then comes to a halt in front of us, blocking our way. '*Heil Hitler*!' Like a reverse guillotine, his arm slices past our faces for the greeting.

'Morning, Horst,' Ludwig says.

The two leaders exchange a quick look. Ludwig has not returned the *Heil Hitler*.

'*Heil Hit-ler*,' the tall one reiterates, over pronouncing every syllable.

'Good *Mor-ning*,' Ludwig repeats, also over pronouncing every syllable. 'Excuse us, we're on our way to school.' He tries to move past them, but they slink in front of him, creating a solid blockade across the width of the footpath.

They cackle, though their jaws are clenched with rage. 'Still at school, you little genius? Planning to go to university, are you? Shouldn't you be doing something more useful, like volunteering for the front?' Horst, the stocky one, sneers.

Ludwig doesn't reply. He steps onto the road, trying to bypass them again, but they are quicker and obstruct his way. 'What do you want?' asks Ludwig, exasperated.

'You weren't at rifle shooting practice on Saturday,' Horst barks. 'The second time since September. I warned you about missing any more drills and meetings. And yet you didn't show.'

'I couldn't make it, I was busy.' Ludwig shrugs.

'What with?'

'Homework.'

'A bookworm,' the taller boy interjects now musingly, almost benevolently. He smiles briefly, showing a neat set of glossy white teeth. His eyes brush mine. They are sharp and piercing and I notice their colour: a washed-out blue with strange greenish flecks. Like the eyes of a sleek, sly predator. The smile disappears as he suddenly moves toward Ludwig.

'Don't worry, I got this, Kurt,' Horst says to the other leader, then grips Ludwig's arm. His face is hard and ugly, his eyes angry and narrow, like the slits in a dirty drain. 'Let me refresh your memory, Ludwig.' His boot comes down hard on Ludwig's foot. Ludwig flinches. 'Participation in the Hitler Youth is compulsory,' he hisses. 'And remember that oath you took on the Führer?'

I can tell from the expression on Horst's brutish face that he is about to unleash more violence. Ludwig tries to free himself. But Horst's grip is vice-like, his boot still crushing Ludwig's foot into the ground.

'I *am* in the Hitler Youth. And I sure remember taking that oath.' Ludwig doesn't manage to hide his contempt when he says the words 'Hitler' and 'oath'.

Horst's face turns a dark shade of red. His fist clenches. I can see the muscles in his short, chunky arm tensing under his uniform jacket.

'Let him go!' I call out sharply. My body floods with adrenalin. 'Let him go,' I repeat even louder, more commanding.

Slowly, his hand still gripping Ludwig, Horst turns his head and appraises me as though he has only just noticed me. A ghastly grin appears at the corners of his mouth.

'Who's she?' he asks Ludwig. 'Your girlfriend? Now, isn't she something else!'

'She's my friend.' Two red patches form on Ludwig's cheeks, but his eyes are locked into Horst's. 'You leave her alone,' he says and looks at me for a split second.

It's all there in that glance, all our adversaries need to know. They laugh. One vicious, the other measured.

'You know, soon you two can get married and have lots of babies for the Führer,' Horst sneers. 'Boys preferably.' He gives me another stare. 'And if he,' Horst yanks Ludwig's arm, 'isn't up for it, I'm more than happy to perform this pleasant duty for the Führer myself.' His leer morphs into a nasty grin.

Kurt looks me up and down with his sly eyes. A barely discernible smirk hangs in the corners of his mouth.

My neck and face explode with heat.

'You leave her alone,' Ludwig says again. His voice is quiet but resolute.

'She'd better pay attention in the League of German Girls so she learns how to raise good, healthy German children. Do you reckon she *is* even in the League?' Horst says to Kurt as though I'm not even there.

'What kind of a question is that?' I cross my arms and stare at him, wanting them to notice me. It works.

'Are you?' Horst accuses, turning to me.

'Am I what?' I ask.

'Lene, don't,' Ludwig says quietly.

'Are you in the League of German Girls; are you doing your duty for Germany and the Führer?' Horst repeats, his voice undulated with cold rage. 'Or is there something *wrong* with you?' He suspiciously looks me up and down, moving a few inches closer without letting go of Ludwig. 'You are not wearing your uniform. As far as I know most girls are collecting for the Winter Relief after school today.'

'I'm not accountable to you,' I reply. 'And membership in the League of German Girls is compulsory for all girls over fourteen years of age. Don't you know that, Horst?' It's obvious that I'm mocking him even to a nitwit like him.

He gawks at me for a short moment, speechless at my audacity. Or perhaps my stupidity.

'It's only compulsory for pure, healthy Aryan girls,' he hisses. 'What's your last name, Lene?' he then snarls.

'Enough! She's got nothing to do with this,' Ludwig interjects before I can say any more. 'I'll be there on Saturday, all right?' He's gone pale and small beads of sweat have formed at his hairline. His eyes warn me to back off.

'Don't miss it, or else,' Horst threatens, finally releasing Ludwig's arm from his grip. 'Shooting exercises for the whole district are planned again for that whole day.'

Ludwig quickly shifts away, creating a safer distance between himself and the two squad leaders. I quickly move to his side. 'I'll be there. Even if my father comes home on leave.' Now Ludwig drills his eyes into his adversary's. 'I hear *your* old man has been declared unfit for service, Horst. Something about his heart? Or was it his head?'

Horst takes the bait. 'His hearing,' he grunts through clenched teeth. 'He's deaf in one ear.'

'Ah, right. Such a shame really. It's so disappointing, isn't it, when one's own father can't fulfil his duty for the Fatherland and the Führer? But, you know, it sounds a bit like an excuse to me, the whole thing about his ears.'

Horst lunges at Ludwig, but he sees it coming and bounces out of the path of Horst's fist flying at him like a projectile.

'You little bastard,' Horst grunts. 'He does *more* than his fair share for the Fatherland. He has already denounced seventeen Jews who tried to pass themselves off as Aryans!'

'Seventeen, wow. Keeping a tally, is he?' Ludwig says. His voice has suddenly gone icy, without a hint of fear in it.

'Horst, let's get going now,' the tall squad leader, Kurt, who has said so little throughout the whole exchange, interjects. 'I think we've made our point,' again his eyes brush mine, 'and so have they,' he ominously adds. And then, he briefly stares at my bare legs. Embarrassment pulses through me once more.

Ludwig grabs my wrist and drags me away.

'You'd better be there on Saturday,' Horst shouts after us. 'And you, Lene, you should be training as a nurse or a nanny. You don't belong in school any longer! And put on your BDM uniform and lose those boots!'

Who the hell does he think he is telling me what to wear, and where I do or don't belong?

'That was close,' Ludwig mutters when we are out of earshot.

I shrug. 'I think it was right that you stood up to them.' Isn't that what my mother did with the Gestapo last night? 'And you haven't really done anything ... just missed a few meetings.' I say this to calm myself, remembering the wave of nauseating fear that came rushing at me last night when the Gestapo stood at our doorstep. What if they know what we really think and talk about, know that Ludwig has been listening to enemy stations? The flutter of alarm in my stomach persists. Of course I know they are dangerous. They could report us. I don't want the Gestapo back in our kitchen. What if we have gone too far? It sinks in that they don't need evidence of our true thoughts, or of a crime; all that's needed is the suspicion that we might be harbouring anti-Nazi feelings.

'Will you go to the shooting practice?' I ask, trying to drown out that flutter.

'I have to. It'll keep them off my back for now.' Ludwig shakes his head. 'All those drills, the exercises, the fighting – I detest it! "*Swift as greyhounds, tough as leather and hard as Krupp steel*". Ha! How I hate that stupid motto. Now even the younger boys can't wait to go off and fight. They all want to be in the SS and all they know is to follow orders,' Ludwig says glumly.

'I know what you mean,' I say.

'This Germany,' Ludwig makes a gesture with his arm indicating the soldiers on leave, Nazi flags framing a shopfront, the newspaper headlines at a kiosk denigrating the Soviet Bolshevist enemy, 'is all they have ever known, from the day they were born, and they will make perfect little soldiers.' Angrily Ludwig shakes his head.

I can relate to his outburst of anger. We are joining puzzle pieces, trying to figure things out, what we see, what we feel, what we think is true, what is expected of us. Though I get the feeling that Ludwig already sees things a lot clearer than I do. I feel so confused about everything that is going on, what we are told, what I really think, but I'm not allowed to say out loud.

We walk in silence for a while. 'Your father isn't coming home on leave, is he?' I ask when we turn into the street where our schools are.

'No. His division is headed further east. He's not coming home for a long time. Probably never.'

'Don't say that.'

'I'm not closing my eyes from the truth any longer.'

'My uncle has fallen on the Eastern Front. We found out on Sunday.'

'That's the worst news. I'm sorry, Lene.'

I nod, silent. I don't want Ludwig to think that his father isn't coming home.

Even though our whole conversation so far has been conducted in a whisper, I still look over my shoulder, making sure the squad leaders are gone. They are, but there are plenty of other people about, including a group of pupils from our schools ahead of us. There are ears everywhere.

'On his last leave, my uncle said that he thought we weren't going to win the war against Russia, that German casualties were high and Hitler was,' I lower my voice even more, barely mouthing the next word, 'insane if he thought we could still win.'

Ludwig nods. 'And there are those rumours about Paulus's Sixth Army. They are in danger of being encircled at Stalingrad if they don't retreat now. If they are encircled, hundreds of thousands of our soldiers will be left to starve and freeze to death by our beloved Führer. Because he will never let Paulus retreat!'

I shake my head, silent. It's not what the papers, the broadcasts or the newsreels are reporting, but it sounds similar to what my aunt said.

'Your uncle was an officer quite high up?' Ludwig asks.

I nod. 'He was.'

'I think he was right.' Ludwig pauses. And someone has to replace all the losses. And soon, those who will replace the losses will become younger and younger.'

My stomach suddenly churns as though it was hanging upside down. Ludwig is sixteen.

'The war can't go on for much longer,' I say. 'It just can't. Final victory can't be far off.' The words 'final victory' almost make me gag, like they shouldn't even be coming out of my mouth. But I don't know what else to say even though I know it sounds like a stupid lie.

'Final victory!' Ludwig, predictably, exclaims. He lets out a weird laugh. 'As if we will wipe out the entire Soviet army overnight! And Hitler will never sign a surrender agreement with the British and the Americans!'

The truth is I don't believe that we will do either of those things. But I'm not ready to accept this. Perhaps somehow, someway everything will be all right.

CHAPTER 7

A week later the long overdue letter from my father finally arrives. My mother fumbles with the envelope, drops the letter opener. Tears glitter in her eyes. There are two sheets in the envelope: a letter for my mother, and a separate one for me.

As I unfold my letter, relief washes over me. But then disappointment hits. The letter is short, no more than a note.

5th of November, 1942

Dear Lene,

I know you must be worried that I haven't written for a while. I am well, we have enough food and warm uniforms. I am thinking of you and Mutti every day. Please always be sensible, Lene. As much as you possibly can.

Your Vati

I show my mother the few lines. Short and odd. But she doesn't even glance at them. Her eyes are glued to the letter my father has written her.

'Not now, Lene,' she says. 'Go get started on your homework.' She disappears into her bedroom with her letter and shuts the door.

Get started on my homework? We just got long-awaited letters from my father and that was all my mother had to say? Usually, when a letter arrives, we sit together at the kitchen table or in the rarely used sitting room to read it. This is beyond peculiar. I stare at her closed bedroom door, wishing for X-ray eyes.

What news does my mother's letter bear that she feels the need to be alone? And my letter is so short and cryptic: *Be sensible, Lene. As much as you possibly can.*

Not a word about keeping up my good work at school. Before he went to war, we would talk about this, my father and I, about university, and weigh up the different options and choices. He'd laugh a little when I'd pretend to consider enrolling in a particularly obscure course I'd heard about such as geology or entomology, and then he'd say, 'Why not, Lene, why not?' And now all my father tells me is to be sensible! And hardly a word about how he is doing. Had my mother complained to him about my 'rebellious' behaviour?

I go over my letter a few more times, trying to read between the lines. Trying to read the things that can't be said. But I can't decipher white space and eventually I do get out my homework. But it's unsettling that the bedroom door stays shut for such a long time. I want my mother to emerge, for information to come forth. My homework blurs in front of my eyes and I stop writing mid-sentence. I accidently drop my pen and it rolls across my half-finished essay, splattering it with ink. What a disaster.

'Lene?'

'Yes?' I quickly hide the mess.

My mother is still holding her letter. 'Vati wants you to know that he's very sorry that his letter to you is only short this time. He's well and he sends you his love.'

I nod. I catch a glimpse of my mother's letter. It is littered with fat black bars. Again. Some concealing whole paragraphs of my father's angled, rushed handwriting. 'It has been censored again,' I say.

'They've become even more vigilant, I guess,' says my mother. She looks worried. 'There's more they don't want us at home to know.'

'Like the heavy losses on the Eastern Front.' It just slips out.

My mother blinks slowly, once, twice. Then she says: 'Lene, Vati has been ordered to the Eastern Front.'

'That's bad news,' I whisper. But deep down I knew this would happen. *Someone has to replace all those losses.* 'When? Will we see him before he goes?' I ask.

Slowly my mother shakes her head. 'No, Lene. He won't be able to get any leave.' There is a pause. 'But his division will have a one-and-a-half-day stay in Hanover on their way through to the Eastern Front.' I can tell she's choosing her words carefully, as though she were explaining something to a small child. Her tone is soft and gentle. 'I will travel to Hanover next week to see your father before he leaves.'

'But you can't go without me!' I jump up. I want to argue, debate this; I want to change it. How far away was Hanover, two hundred kilometres perhaps? Three or four hours on the train?

'Don't, Lene.' My mother shakes her head again. 'Don't argue. Not this time. I'll only be away for a couple of days.'

'Days? But you can't leave me here alone. Why can't I come?'

'I will not take you.'

There is a firmness in her voice, her face, and I know that asking questions will be pointless. They will not be answered.

'It's too risky with the bombings. The train could get hit.'

I stare at my mother. And she realises at once what she's said. If the train gets hit, she might die.

'Which won't happen, Lene, don't look at me like that.'

'If I can't come I might never see Vati again.' I know I shouldn't say this out loud but it's all I've got, all I can think of. The force of hot tears takes my breath away.

'That's enough!' My mother seems far away, removed from the argument. She gets up from the table and tucks her letter into her apron pocket. 'You can write to Vati but you will stay here, and that's the end of it. We couldn't afford two train tickets anyway.' She leaves the kitchen, gently patting the letter in her pocket.

The finality of her words, the stifling sobs in my throat, knowing that my mother too believes that my father will not come home from the war, is almost too much to bear. I'm clinging to the edge of the abyss by my fingernails.

As my letter is not getting posted and potentially checked I write more freely. But with that feeling of an enormous black chasm below me, refusing to subside, I take care not to write too openly and call things by their real name. The letter could still end up in the wrong hands.

Berlin, 19th of November, 1942
Dear Vati,

I'm able to find some consolation in writing this letter to you knowing Mutti will give it to you personally in Hanover. So many things feel overwhelmingly wrong, have felt wrong for many years. Though, at the same time, things make more sense as I am able to see them much more clearly.

Remember when you came home on your very first leave? How we all hoped it would be over soon. And now I find myself wondering how we got to where we are now, how it feels as though it is all sliding towards ... a horrible uncertainty. I am trying to be sensible, like you said I should, though it gets harder and harder every day, when in order to do that you have to hide your true thoughts and feelings and there are only very few people who one can really talk to. I fear, and yet I know I have much less to fear than others.

I find myself desperately trying to remember the time before you enlisted, when I was perhaps four or five years old. Before everything started changing. I know things weren't easy then, and I remember that you had a hard time finding work, and so did many people. Back then, you decided to join the Cavalry. Now there's so much work in Germany. Most of it to keep the war going. And all of us must help to keep it going. You are out there fighting on the front, soon the most terrible of all fronts, and I know we must all chip in and support the war effort and yet my feelings about it are conflicted. I am ashamed. And sometimes I wonder how supporting the war effort will help you to come home to us.

I'm so desperately hoping you can come home on leave very soon, or for good. But at least Mutti is able to see you and I am grateful for that. My dear Vati, please stay well and I hope and pray that I will get to see you too. I miss you and there are so many things I want to talk to you about!

Your loving daughter,

Lene

When I finish the letter I'm suddenly unsure. What if it upsets my father? Normally I don't write about anything that really worries me. I try to be upbeat, write about school and my visits to see my cousins. Not just because the letters could get checked but also because I don't want to make it any harder on my father. But this time I cast those rules aside. I feel that I have to and that he will understand.

The dreaded day of my mother's departure has arrived. To add insult to injury it is a Wednesday, which means BDM.

'I'll be back before you know it, you'll see, Lene.' My mother picks up her overnight case and presses a kiss on my cheek. 'I've told Ludwig's mother that I'm away. You can always go and see her if need be.'

I search her face for any indication that she is changing her mind at the last moment, taking me along after all. But there is nothing.

'Don't forget to give Vati my letter.'

'I've got it right here.' My mother pats her coat pocket. 'And, Lene, don't miss your BDM meeting again! Be sure to make an effort.' She pushes down the doorhandle, gives me one last nod and shuts the door firmly.

I shuffle back to the empty kitchen and sit down at the table. I pile my schoolbooks into a tower, then dismantle it again. The next two days stretch like an eternity in front of me. There's an essay and a chemistry assignment with illustrations to be done. And now, of course, the dreadful BDM meeting.

I get ready in front of the mirror, looking at myself properly for once, taking care with my appearance, my uniform, making sure the neckerchief is not askew, that my skirt is free of creases and lint. I attempt to copy my squad leader's complicated braided hairstyle. It looks good enough but not as perfect as hers. I keep thinking that if I do everything right from now on, my father will come home.

I leave with too much time to spare but I still take the direct way to the school hall, no detour past the Sternschnuppe this time. The sky is a grey lid, dull and low. It will be dark early.

As I approach Café Kramer, I notice a tall figure dressed in a Hitler Youth uniform. The recognition is instant. Kurt, the squad leader, who stopped Ludwig and me the other day. My heartbeat jumps into my throat. I duck, trying to take cover behind one of the other pedestrians. But there's no point. I'm close enough to see those eyes, the predatory glint in them. They are vivid; harsh bursts of colour in the dull afternoon light. And I know he's noticed me even before I saw him, watching me approach. He catches my eye and smiles, full of self-assured arrogance.

I pretend that I don't remember who he is. I keep walking but he smoothly peels away from the wall.

'I've been waiting for you, Lene,' he says.

I nod a short impersonal greeting, my heart racing. Why has he been waiting for me?

'Mind if I join you?' In an instant, he's striding next to me.

I shrug without looking at him and speed up. I want to shake him off.

He chuckles. 'BDM meeting?' he asks as though this was a perfectly normal situation, as though he's walked next to me a million times before. As though the other day, when he and Horst harassed and threatened us, had never happened.

I don't reply.

'How's the Winter Relief coming along? Getting plenty of donations?'

I walk even faster.

'The boys in my squad have been doing an outstanding job collecting scrap metal. Even the smallest piece counts and can be turned into a bullet.'

I say nothing.

'You look nice in your BDM uniform, your hair pinned up like this.'

I can feel his eyes on me, assessing me, like he did the other day when he stared at my legs. I don't want his compliments and I self-consciously touch my hair, regretting that I even made the effort. I'm now almost running.

'You don't have to be scared, Lene.'

'I'm not.' The firmness of my voice surprises me. I stop and look him straight in the eye. 'Why should I be scared?'

'I don't know. You tell me. You sure look scared.'

I start walking again. 'I'm not scared of you. I just don't like you. I'm allowed to not like you.'

'Of course.' He sounds amused. 'Seems pointless though.'

'It's not pointless to me. You had no right to harass us the way you did the other day.' It's important that he knows that I dislike him. And I don't know how I ended up getting into this exchange of words, into this conversation which feels too personal.

He laughs but there's no humour in his voice. 'You will find that we do have that right. And sometimes people have to be pulled back in line.' He looks at me narrow-eyed. 'A lovely girl like you shouldn't hang around certain boys. Boys whose attitudes are more than questionable.'

I shrug, desperately trying to pretend indifference.

'You know who I'm talking about, don't you?'

'I have to run,' I say, 'or I'll be late for the meeting.' Blood is roaring in my ears; all I can think of now is that I mustn't let Kurt see that I am scared. That I mustn't let him see how important Ludwig is to me.

Kurt glances at his expensive-looking wristwatch. He raises an eyebrow. He knows I'm early.

'I'm helping. With the set-up. We are getting more sewing machines today,' I add quickly.

But he's already a step ahead of me.

'It'll be getting dark by the time the meeting is over. Is anyone walking you home?'

'No!' I immediately realise my mistake. I should have said yes, but my nerves are ruining my thinking.

And then I break into a run, gaining speed as I sprint away from him, shortcutting down an alley, ducking behind a *Litfaß* column covered in notices, announcements and posters when I reach the road where my school is.

I lean against the column as I try to steady my breath and peer around. He hasn't followed me. But I'm humiliated. Running away like this. Especially when it's pointless as he knows where I'm going anyway.

Sure enough, after the meeting he's there, waiting in the vestibule outside the hall. I stay inside, watching my squad leader walk past me to the vestibule. Her face brightens. '*Heil Hitler*, Kurt.'

They know each other! For a moment I hope that this means that I can sneak out with the rest of the girls. I start moving towards the door.

But Kurt only curtly nods at my squad leader, looking uninterested. '*Heil Hitler*, Regina.' He immediately turns his attention to me. 'Are you ready to walk home, Lene?'

Regina's face kind of collapses, first into surprise, then repugnance; she can't veil it. She hates me even more now! Her lips curl into a thin, grim smile. I wish I could relish the moment because I dislike her so much, but I can't because I detest Kurt even more and I don't want his attention. I desperately wish he would chase her instead.

'Lene, wait a minute,' Regina says. She indicates for me to follow her back into the now empty hall.

'Don't be too long,' Kurt says. 'I'll be outside.'

Feeling uneasy, I stand in front of Regina. For a moment she completely ignores me, sorting through bundles of leaflets and magazines in the wall rack. I feel as though I'm caught in a trap; Kurt's waiting outside, Regina's got her fangs in me inside.

'Did you hear about Sigrid?' she finally asks. 'She's broken her wrist, the clumsy girl.'

Sigrid is one of the older girls in our group, who is now a Flak helper. 'Yes, I've heard. It's a complicated break they say.'

'Indeed.' Regina stops sorting. 'How old are you again, Lene? Sixteen?'

'Fifteen.' There's a funny feeling in my stomach. A soup of nausea and dread.

'Oh, that's right, only fifteen.' She sounds disappointed. 'Turning sixteen, when?'

'In May.' The soup in my stomach is threatening to boil over, slowly rising upwards into my oesophagus. I'm pretty sure one has to be at least seventeen to volunteer for the Flak and operate the searchlights. But perhaps that has been revised.

'I could still try to get you in. To serve the Führer and contribute more to the war effort and final victory.' The wink she gives me makes me shiver. 'A rule is not always a rule especially where girls like you are concerned.'

There's no doubt in my mind that Regina could easily make an exception for me.

'I don't think my parents would give their approval,' I say.

'It's not really always up to the parents, though, is it?' Regina smiles. 'Remember that at the end of the day you belong to the Führer! And if it is required to serve, you serve where and how you are told, no matter your age!' For the first time I notice that she has ugly teeth, thin and pointy like a yapping little lapdog's.

I shake my head, then nod. 'It's not up to the parents.'

'Oh, never mind,' Regina says. 'I'm sure a replacement for Sigrid will be found quickly. It is such an honour to serve the Führer after all.'

'Yes, a replacement will be easily found. Yes, yes.' My head nods like a puppet's.

Regina has gone back to collating her leaflets. 'I could use a hand here, Lene,' she says. She hands me a stack of BDM magazines and guides. 'Sort them chronologically by title and issue date. Someone's made a mess.'

'Sure,' I say. I wonder if Kurt's still there or if he's given up waiting. But I doubt he's deterred that easily. The other girls' chatter outside is thinning.

'This is one of my favourites.' Regina fans the magazines out on a table, messing them up even more, then she pulls one out, holds it up for me to see. 'Doesn't he look dashing?' She has lowered her voice.

'Sure, he looks handsome,' I say, glancing at the Hitler Youth squad leader on the cover.

'Handsome like Kurt?'

'Perhaps a little.' The soup in my stomach is bubbling and churning, rising like acid. I swallow half-a-dozen times but it doesn't go away.

Regina starts talking in a hasty whisper. 'Let's cut to the chase, Lene. I like Kurt and I thought the feeling was mutual. We are very like-minded, me and Kurt. And we perfectly fit the Führer's ideal of young Aryans. We could be on the cover of one of those magazines!' She straightens and pulls back her shoulders as though posing.

'And, honestly,' she goes on, 'I don't think *you* quite fit that ideal. I mean, look at you! You might have pure Aryan blood flowing through your veins, but you certainly don't look perfectly Aryan. I give you that much, you are sort of *dark* blonde and your eyes are kind of bluish-greyish, although they do have a really obvious mud-coloured tone to them.' She walks off and rummages in a cupboard. When she returns, she clutches one of those horrible eye colour charts and holds it up next to my face. 'I don't think your eye colour even matches any of these.' She snaps the little metal case shut and regards me, trying to find something else that she considers a flaw. 'And you are short for your age.'

'There's nothing between me and Kurt. I hardly know him. And I really like someone else,' I add.

Regina brings her face close to mine and smiles her skinny-teethed smile. 'Don't get in my way,' she hisses, and then she lets me go.

I step out into the shadows of dusk, feeling Regina's eyes drilling into my back. I can't see Kurt anywhere and I hurry out of the school grounds, starting to feel vaguely optimistic. Perhaps he's taken a liking to one of the other girls and decided to chase them. Surely he would have noticed how extraordinarily pretty some of them are!

I walk behind a middle-aged couple; the man carries a briefcase and the woman a canvas shopping bag. When they get to the *Litfaß* column they slow, looking at a poster that's plastered there. They exchange a quick glance of silent disdain and then keep walking. When I take a closer look, I see it's just a poster warning about the dangers of shell splinters during an air raid.

'I was starting to think Regina would never let you go!'

I jump. Kurt!

He lets out a gruff laugh. 'Can't help that *I'm* not keen on her.'

'I thought you'd gone!' I coldly say, though inside my chest my heart is pounding

He lights a cigarette and effortlessly aligns his step with mine.

I look down at the footpath, trying to ignore him, walking fast, just stopping short of running. His black boots are like polished gunmetal in the dark.

'Apparently donations for the Winter Relief are down slightly,' Kurt says.

'Usually everyone gives something,' I defensively reply.

'Sure. But the war will be over before spring anyway, trust me. Final victory is near and things will be glorious for all Germans then.'

Right, before spring.

'You don't believe it?' asks Kurt.

'Of course I do.' I manage to sound mildly outraged. 'Germany will be victorious.' I put as much conviction into my voice as I possibly can without sounding too phoney. I walk faster. I want to get home as quickly as possible, want this to be over as quickly as possible.

'Anyway, we'd better make sure you get lots of donations. I'll make sure of it,' he says. 'We are going together on Sunday. Meeting point is Café Kramer, two o'clock in the afternoon.'

'I'm meant to go with the girls in my squad.' I don't want to go with Kurt! What if Regina finds out?

'You are going with me on Sunday, and that wasn't a question.' A threatening undertone carries in his voice.

I swallow. 'All right.' I don't know what else to do. I feel like a coward.

I halt a couple of doors down from my apartment building. The last thing I want is for Ludwig to see me with Kurt. Or worse, Kurt running into Ludwig. But all the windows are blind and dark anyway. For once I'm grateful for *Verdunkelung*.

'This is me,' I say and make a beeline for the closest apartment building door, which is not mine.

'Lene, that's not where you live,' Kurt says.

I stop and turn around. He runs his hand through his slick hair, takes a step closer. It hits me that he wants to kiss me! Instinctively, I sway backwards, disgusted. The only boy I want to kiss is Ludwig! With satisfaction, I notice the hurt and humiliation of rejection spread across his face.

'Thanks for walking me home,' I say, turning, this time not wanting him to see the lie. My stomach is churning. I know I've aggravated the beast by not letting him kiss me. But imagining his lips on mine almost makes me gag.

Kurt snuffs out his cigarette. 'Any time,' he says, managing to make it sound like a threat. He turns and leaves.

I hide in the doorway of my building, watching him disappear down the street.

CHAPTER 8

For a few moments I cherish the safety of our building, the refuge of our flat an empty but impenetrable little fortress.

But the flat is cold and dark, the clock ticking on the kitchen wall the only sound, one I only ever notice when I'm home alone, and the palpable emptiness of the flat starts clawing at me.

I pull down the black-out blinds and curtains in all the rooms but when I flick the light switch in the kitchen it stays dark. The globe must have blown. I hunt for one of the special black-out light globes in the drawer. But all I can find is an empty Osram globe package. In the muted light from the corridor, I check the pot on the stove: lentil soup. I'm so hungry I could gobble the whole lot down cold, straight from the pot. But the soup has to last until my mother returns on Friday.

I warm it up, ladle about half of it into a bowl and cut myself a thin slice of rye bread. There's no speck and without it the soup tastes watery and bland. I don't care. I wolf down the first few spoons, then force myself to slow down. When I've finished I'm still hungry but there's not enough for a second serve. I eat another slice of bread with a thin smear of butter. Then I wash up and pack my schoolbag for the next day before aimlessly wandering into the sitting room. I pick up my parents' wedding photograph from the buffet where it sits between a family portrait and a photo of me taken on my tenth birthday.

My mother's face in the photo is serene and happy, a little mysterious even. My father, dashing in a dark suit, has a slightly bemused expression, as though he's looking forward to the photo session being over. My mother's white mid-calf wedding dress with a fashionable drop waist was made from silk and lace – the material gifted to my mother by Aunt Ilsa – and her veil matched the lace of her dress. Many times my mother had told me how she had to save up her modest pay for her French silk gloves and how excited she was when she found a pair that matched the dress. They both had work and my father made a little extra money, like many, buying some cheap American shares which soon miraculously ten-folded in value. They moved into this flat and bought our furniture with the money. When the Big Crash came, followed by the Depression, everything changed. The dress, the veil, my mother had to sell. But I know she kept her gloves.

I wipe a thin layer of dust off the picture frame with my sleeve and return the photo to the buffet, then slide open the drawer. It creaks in the quietness. There, at the back, wrapped in tissue paper, are my mother's wedding gloves. I unwrap them and carefully put them on, sliding them up my forearms. They are still pristine and they fit my hands almost perfectly. My mother was nineteen, only a few years older than I am now, when she married my father. I glance at the photo again, at their young, carefree and expectant faces, their chic clothes with their slightly bohemian flair, my mother in those gloves. And here they are, seventeen years later, on my hands. I touch the silken material to my face, reluctant to take them off just yet.

As I leave the sitting room to go to my bedroom the sight of my reflection in the corridor mirror gives me a jolt. Me in the detested BDM uniform, and on my hands those shiny, elegant gloves, like a relic from a time not that long ago and yet lightyears away.

I switch off the lights and go to my bedroom, slip off my shoes, lie down fully dressed on the bed. The line of luminous paint my father has drawn along the side of the door frame glows in the dark. I'll get ready for bed in a minute. But then I don't bother and just pull the eiderdown up to my chin.

The darkness is dense with absences. The absence of my father, and now, my mother. I wonder what it would be like to be alone, to be an orphan. What if my mother's train got hit by a bomb? What if my father doesn't return from the Russian front? I curl up on my side, feeling heavy with loneliness that follows me into my dreams.

I wake, minutes later it seems, because someone is pounding on the door, calling my name.

'Lene, air raid! Get up!' It's Ludwig's mother, Frau Schluck.

The air-raid siren is howling. For some reason, it didn't wake me. I'm sluggish, not fully awake. I want to ignore the siren and Ludwig's mother and just go back to sleep. But she's relentless and eventually I swing my legs out of bed, slip on my boots and grab a cardigan.

'Thanks, I'm coming, Frau Schluck,' I say as I open the door.

'Hurry up now, will you?' she warns me and turns to run. I can hear everyone clomping downstairs.

By the time I descend the first two flights I think I can hear the far-away humming of the bombers. But in the small entrance hall downstairs I pause. I'm alone in the stairwell; everyone is already in the cellar. I wonder how safe it really is down there, remembering the building in my cousins' street and how all five floors had collapsed, trapping and killing everyone in the cellar. How much had they suffered? Would it make a difference if I didn't bother going downstairs? If I stayed upstairs, death would probably be instant.

A few blocks away they are building yet another public air-raid shelter. Ludwig told me it has two-metre-thick walls and ceilings, like a vault. A vault for humans. But they haven't finished it yet. I guess they are expecting that the bombings will get much worse. Are there years of this ahead of us?

A strange sense of detachment compels me to open the front door of the building instead of going downstairs. A gust of cold night air hits me. I step outside and look up and down our street where a few hours ago Kurt had tried to kiss me. As though this were a perfectly normal world.

Everything is dark. A couple of air-raid wardens are hurrying down the street. Blackout shades are drawn everywhere and the street lights are off. I look up into the partially overcast sky. Above the bare winter branches of the few elm trees a three-quarter moon becomes visible, hangs there, casting a greenish glow. In the distance the beams of searchlights comb the sky. Everything looks strangely one-dimensional, like a set – a backdrop on a stage where nothing is real.

The humming of the bombers is definitely discernible now. I search the overcast sky. Suddenly the outline of a small squadron of enemy planes appears where the clouds are thin in the distance, high above the city, making everything come to life. An injection of fear makes my heart speed up. I watch the planes head towards us, their shapes like ships in a greenish upside-down sea. The Flak starts firing.

'Lene? What are you doing out here?' Ludwig's hand closes around my elbow, hastily pulling me inside and shutting the door. The emergency light in the cellar corridor illuminates everything weakly; on the stairwell walls arrows in luminous paint, there to guide us downstairs in the darkness, glow.

'What are you doing?' Ludwig asks again. 'The Flak is already firing. It's dangerous. You should be in the cellar with everyone else.'

'What's the point?' I say. 'If we get hit we just get buried alive anyway.'

'We won't. We'll escape through the tunnels to one of the neighbouring buildings. Try not to think worst-case scenario.'

'I've seen it with my own eyes.'

'Here.' Ludwig takes the cardigan that I still clasp in my hand and helps me put it on. 'You are wearing …' he glances down at my hands, pausing, '… white opera gloves?'

'They're my mother's wedding gloves,' I whisper.

'Let's quickly take them off,' he replies softly and starts to gently peel the silk down my forearms, pulling them off my hands. He rolls the gloves up and hastily puts them in his pocket.

His face glows pale in the semi-darkness of the stairwell. Suddenly he wraps his arms around me tightly.

I huddle in Ludwig's arms, holding on to him, the detachment and loneliness from before instantly subsiding.

'You're shivering,' Ludwig says, his mouth close to my ear.

'I'm scared,' I say. I'm not only scared of the bombers. I'm scared of tomorrow, of next month, next year. And now I'm also scared of Kurt.

'I'm scared too. Being powerless makes you feel scared.'

I bury my face on his shoulder, feel the scratchy wool of his pullover on my cheek. He smells so good. Like washing powder and biscuits and the sandy soft floor of a pine forest in summer.

'Come on now. It's probably too overcast for the bombers but let's not push our luck.' He leads me down the steep cellar stairs and along the long narrow corridor, his arm still tightly wrapped around me. It's all I want to know and feel and I wish his arm could stay there, wrapped around me, forever.

Ludwig was right. We are spared again. After the all clear comes everyone except Ludwig and me leaves the cellar and goes back upstairs, back to their beds to snatch a few more hours of sleep. Their footfalls echo on the stairs, apartment doors slam. We stay, sit in silence. Ludwig's face has a bluish tinge in the glow of the emergency lighting.

'We should go back upstairs too,' Ludwig finally says. But he doesn't move.

'I guess. I probably won't be able to go back to sleep, though,' I say. I'm tired and wide awake at the same time, like I'm stuck in some kind of semi-sleep state, incapable of moving. It's almost four o'clock in the morning and in a few hours I'll have to get up anyway. And, who knows, there might be another air raid.

'Why don't we just stay here,' I say, though I don't really want to be here, I just want to be with Ludwig.

I dread the emptiness of the flat upstairs. I dread it even more than this claustrophobic cellar space. 'My mother has gone to see my father in Hanover. He's on his way to the Eastern Front.'

'I know. Your mother has told my mother.'

Silence once more.

'Are you all right?' Ludwig asks.

'I guess so.' Suddenly I think I should tell Ludwig about Kurt and what happened today. But I don't know where to start. All I know is that I am scared of Kurt and that I am scared for Ludwig. I hate being scared. It makes me feel weak, but I don't know how to stop it.

And then Ludwig gets up and I have missed the right moment. 'Come on now, Lene. Let's get out of here.'

'You're right,' I mumble.

Upstairs, at my apartment door, Ludwig stops and I turn to face him. He reaches out and brushes a strand of my hair from my face. Then, he pulls back his hand and buries both hands in his trouser pockets.

I open the door wide and go in. I don't want to be alone. 'Ludwig …' I say. But he's already stepped over the threshold and I shut the door behind us.

In the narrow space of the corridor he wraps his arms around me again. 'I just need to make sure you are all right,' he says.

He loosens his embrace. 'Here,' he says, carefully pulling the gloves out of his pocket and handing them to me. 'I almost forgot.'

I cradle them in my hands.

'They are pretty,' Ludwig says. 'They looked pretty on you.'

'They belong to my mother. She wore them on her wedding day.'

Ludwig nods. 'Your mother will be back before you know it, Lene.' He pushes down the door handle.

'Please stay, Ludwig,' I say. 'I'm fine as long as you are here.'

'But my mother would wonder where I am.' He slips out into the dark stairwell. 'I have to go. See you soon, all right?'

I nod.

I shut the door and lean against it, listening to Ludwig's footfall on the stairs.

CHAPTER 9

My mother returns late on Friday evening. As soon as I hear the key in the lock, I race to the front door, my book falling facedown on the floor.

'You are safe,' I cry.

I feel tears rise, tears that I've held back all day, and a panic that would catch me unaware, making me gasp as my heart raced, imagining my mother on the train, vulnerable, a bomb hitting it. Finally I could let go of the thought that I might never see her again.

My mother gives me a brief firm hug. 'Any raids here?'

'Only one, on the day you left. But it wasn't anything serious. How's Vati? Tell me, is he well? Where exactly is he being sent? Did you give him my letter?'

She smiles tiredly and unbuttons her coat. 'He's fine. Give me a minute, let me get this off first.'

'Here,' I take my mother's coat and go to hang it up.

'Wait.' She pulls a piece of paper out of her pocket and gives it to me. 'From Vati for you.'

'Thank you,' I whisper.

I rush to my room. Sitting on the edge of my bed I greedily unfold the letter.

20th of November, 1942

Dear Lene,

I am on the train now and back on German soil, which is a wonderful feeling. I'm headed east as you know. However, I am reasonably confident that it is not Stalingrad.

I know that you are disappointed that I wasn't able to come home on leave and I am too. Try not to worry. All things going well, my leave should get approved soon and I will see you again. Until then, you and Mutti have to look after each other and keep each other's spirits up. Grind your teeth, Lene, and get through the things that are difficult and unpleasant. Hold on to something that allows you to look into the future with positive feelings, something that gives you hope. This will help you get through the things that you don't like and don't agree with. I know that's hard. But it is necessary. That doesn't mean you should close your eyes and look away. Remember what I told you about that last time I was on leave, when we went for our walk along the orchards?

My father's last visit comes back to me; it was late summer last year. We took the S-Bahn out to the city boundary and went for a walk in the semi-rural green. There were picturesque houses with large gardens, ponies and small apple orchards. In one of the orchards, the apples were being picked by stick-figure men, a bored-looking guard with them. The men's skinny frames, on which their striped outfits hung loosely, looked not quite real amongst the idyllic, lush greenery, the well-fed ponies and clucking chickens. I remember slowing, struck by the sight, and my father didn't urge me to keep on walking. I saw one of the men pick up a rotting apple with his twig fingers and furtively take a bite out of it when the guard was looking away.

But the guard had still seen it. He walked over and casually whacked the apple out of his prisoner's hand with his rifle butt. 'The rotten ones are for the ponies,' I heard him say. He resumed his position, leaning against a tree trunk. When the guard glanced our way, my father, who was in uniform, nodded a greeting at him and the guard ambled over and saluted. '*Sieg Heil*!'

'*Sieg Heil*,' my father said, but without the salute.

They started chatting, the guard glancing at his flock of prisoners every now and then at first, but my father, who is an exceptional storyteller, had animatedly started to recount a particularly captivating experience from the front. It was clear that the guard had not seen any battle action, so he listened, slightly open-mouthed, neglecting to look at his prisoners. My father also wasn't looking at them. But I did. Some were furtively biting into apples, wolfing down semi-chewed chunks as fast as they could. Some, who were close to the edge of the orchard where wild blackberries grew, picked them off and stuffed them into their mouths. My father was embellishing, I know when he does, because he starts gesticulating.

'All right,' he finally announced in a loud voice. 'We'd better keep moving along and enjoy the sunshine while it lasts.'

The prisoners closest to us signalled to the others, while my father added a few more morsels of front action to his story. By the time the guard turned back to the prisoners, they were at work, their shaved heads bowed.

When we were a safe distance away, my father said: 'Things don't stop happening only because you choose to not see what is truly wrong. Indifference is not a character strength. One can feel helpless overall in the face of certain things, but that doesn't mean one has to be indifferent.' He paused. 'When things have become normality they don't get noticed any longer, even though there's nothing right or normal about them.'

Oh, he knows how it is, how I feel! I close my eyes and see my father in front of me, in his uniform and I wonder if he perhaps hates it as much as I hate my BDM uniform. Because they stand for the same thing. I continue reading.

Stay true to yourself, Lene. But be sensible also, more so than you may have been in the past. Work hard at school. You do not have to relinquish your ambitions and fit into the roles that have been prescribed for your whole generation of girls. We will try to find a way so you can continue your education and perhaps go to university. Be a good daughter to Mutti and don't give her reason to worry. Keep writing to me, even though you can't write everything you want.

Your Vati

I feel breathless because of the frankness of his words. I take the letter with me and go to the kitchen where my mother is brewing a pot of substitute coffee.

'Vati gave us French cakes.' My mother indicates a tin on the table. '*Madeleines* they are called. They are, to be quite frank, out of this world.'

The scent that hits me when I open the lid of the tin is so divine that I involuntarily close my eyes, inhaling deeply the richness of butter and egg, a hint of lemon and almonds.

My mother puts a cup of milky coffee and a little plate, on which she places two *madeleines*, in front of me. A cup of black coffee and one *madeleine* for her. I take a bite. My tastebuds fly me to France, to everything I imagine France might be like. They are sweet and rich, yet airy, with intoxicating layers of all the aromas of their scent: lemon, egg, butter and almond. They taste so different to any German cake I've ever eaten.

'What did I tell you?' my mother says. 'Out of this world.' Then she tells me about Hanover, the hotel they stayed at and the photo they had taken together outside the hotel by one of my father's comrades.

'Vati is well, Lene. He hasn't changed much. He's been getting enough sleep and plenty of food. Having those reserves will help him from now on.' She pauses, indicates the letter. 'Vati wrote to you about being sensible, didn't he?'

I nod.

'That's because your Vati thinks that Germans will be turning against Germans with much more harshness. Defeat doesn't just happen on the battlefield. When things break down on the home front and morale is low, those people who contribute to that low morale, it will be treated as treason.'

'What do you mean?'

'I mean that what I got away with when the Gestapo visited, your open dislike of the BDM, things like that, could have much more serious consequences in the future.'

'I understand,' I whisper.

CHAPTER 10

Sunday and, with it, the Winter Relief collection round that Kurt has forced on me, comes around too quickly.

Kurt greets me with a self-assured wink when we meet at Café Kramer, and it makes me feel even more ill at ease. If Regina finds out about this she'll make me suffer. But if I reject Kurt it could draw attention to Ludwig. And I remember my mother's and my father's warnings too, so I clear my throat, nod a greeting and put on a smile. I must play along.

Soon we leave the tall Wilhelmine buildings and the grey façades of the tenement blocks behind. Where we end up, amongst the two-storey houses, bungalows, and the quaint family homes of the middle class, the roads are narrower and lined with young Linden trees and the sky opens up wide above. There are well-tended front yards behind low picket fences and oiled garden gates. I suspect that this is where Kurt lives.

We are both in our uniforms and I'm clutching my near-empty collection tin. Kurt carries the small box containing the pins we hand out for donations. The first house we walk up to has a disproportionally wide path, as though it's leading up to a grand villa, though the garden gnomes lining it reveal the true ilk of the inhabitants. The house itself is plain, single storey, with brown roof tiles and pine-green shutters.

Kurt rings the bell. This is not my suburb and Kurt is not my friend, but I put on my smile. I hear steps approaching inside. A woman, probably my mother's age, opens the door. She's unadorned and plain like the house, wearing an apron over a mud-coloured dress and sensible low-heeled shoes.

'*Heil Hitler*,' Kurt greets her.

'*Heil Hitler*,' I echo. 'We are collecting for the Winter Relief.' I hold my tin under her nose.

'*Heil Hitler*,' she says. 'But of course I will make a donation. Come on in. I'll have to get my purse.'

We step into the small foyer where it's warm. Above the hall table hangs a huge, ugly portrait of the Führer.

The woman returns with some coins. 'Here you are.' She feeds two *Reichsmark* into my collection tin, making sure I count.

'Thank you,' I say, astounded by the substantial donation. I hand over the latest pin.

She has focused her attention on Kurt. 'Are you off doing your defence training soon, Kurt?'

'Yes, at the end of November. I can't wait.'

I feel myself perking up at the news. I can't wait either! Surely he'll have forgotten about me by the time he gets back.

'That's the spirit,' she says. 'Your parents will be so proud of you.'

Kurt clicks his heels together. '*Sieg Heil*! And thank you for your generous donation. We'd better be off now.'

'Of course. I shouldn't have kept you.'

'Two *Reichsmark*!' I say when we are back outside. 'That's so much.' My tin weighs heavy in my hand. Normally I would have taken hours to collect such a huge amount of money. Most people in my neighbourhood only give a few *Pfennig*. And often, I think, it's not just because they can't afford to donate more. But most will give something, otherwise they risk being reported.

'Let's try here,' Kurt suggests and leads the way into another picket-fenced, gnome-guarded front yard.

Here also they know him. 'Kurt, don't you look dashing in that uniform.' This lady is like a younger version of the previous one. In the background, I hear the voices of young children. She gives us twenty *Pfennig*.

At the next house down an older man comes to the door. He uses a walking stick to prop up his lop-sided body. Medals chink on his chest.

'Our youth is Germany's future,' he roars as he deposits one *Reichsmark* in the tin.

'You,' he stabs a finger at Kurt's chest, 'are Germany's future. You will right the wrongs of the past!'

'Thank you, sir,' says Kurt. '*Heil Hitler und Sieg Heil*!'

My head is starting to hurt. This bourgeois suburb is making me feel claustrophobic.

The next house is pretty, though, almost like a little villa. There are small garden beds, no gnomes, a swing set. I notice a glazier replacing the glass in the front windows.

There are boxes on the porch as though people are just moving in.

Another young mother with a brood of toddlers clinging to her apron tails opens the door. More boxes line the hallway. When I see all the children I don't expect her to give much. But she, too, donates quite a few coins.

When we are back on the footpath, Kurt laughs and teasingly pulls one of my braids. His hand brushes my ear and I flinch. 'What a good German family they are, and they have been busy procreating, as they should, for the Fatherland and the Führer.' His hand lingers on my shoulder. I hold my breath; it takes all my willpower not to violently recoil from his touch.

'Looks like they just moved in,' I say, wanting to change the subject, distracting myself from his repulsive touch. 'There were all those boxes on the porch.'

'Ha! Filthy Jews used to live in that house,' Kurt sneers. The hatred in his voice is like a lash. His hand slides off my shoulder. 'They tried to hide their impure blood, tried to pass themselves off as Aryans. Living in that lovely house while a decent German family was cramped into a tiny one-room flat.' His voice is loaded with disgust. He shakes his head. 'Berlin is supposed to have been free of Jews ages ago.'

Free of Jews. 'And where did the Jewish family go?' The question slips out and, alarmed, I realise that my voice is bitter and reproachful.

Kurt grunts. 'What kind of a question is that? They are gone and that's all that matters. The SS and the Gestapo took care of them.' He cackles as though he made a hilarious joke. Then he looks at me funnily. 'You shouldn't be asking questions like that, Lene.'

I shrug, feeling beads of sweat break out on my top lip.

'They are nothing! They are the enemy, vermin we have to get rid of. Otherwise we mustn't concern ourselves with them.'

I'm sweating heavily all over now. It's what they tell us. What they teach us at school in *Rassenkunde*, racial studies, the subject I most abhor, and what they have drummed into us in the BDM for years. Though I will never understand how someone can cease to be a person, can become a thing without rights, because someone else decides that's the way it is going to be from now on. Like in the Dark Ages. But I can't say any of this to Kurt.

'Are you all right?' Kurt asks. 'You look kind of pale. You have to toughen up, Lene. Empathy is a sign of weakness.' He grins. 'But your secret is safe with me, little Jew lover. I think I'll have to take you under my wing a bit more.'

I can barely suppress a shudder at the thought. 'I'm fine,' I say and nod. 'And who says there's a secret?' My back is sweat soaked and I can feel my uniform blouse sticking to my skin under my climbing jacket. We keep door-knocking and I rattle my tin and keep smiling but my smile is hurting my face.

By the time we finish in the late afternoon, dusk is settling over the city. The collection tin weighs heavy, near full, in my hand. I want to go home. I feel like I'm about to crack.

'Thanks, Kurt,' I say when we walk back through a pocket of green space. 'I appreciate your help with this,' I lie, rattling the heavy tin. All I want is to get away from him. 'Bye then,' I say, and I turn to leave.

'You don't want to get rid of me already, do you?' he says. His tone is casual yet laced with threat and makes me stop. Even though that's exactly what I want.

'It's only a short walk home from here,' I say. 'I'll be all right.'

Kurt shakes his head, looking bothered. 'Last winter a girl had her collection tin stolen on her way home. We never caught the low-life who mugged her. Probably one of those disgusting foreigners. If I'd got my hands on him, I would have strangled him.' He lifts his hands and pantomimes strangling the imaginary thief, then breaking his neck, as though killing him once is not enough. 'Besides,' Kurt is suddenly very close, his chest touching my arm, 'I'm off to do my training at the end of November, away from Berlin, and I won't see you for at least three weeks. I think I deserve a little reward. Or shall we call it a farewell gift?'

I look around. It's not that late but it's almost dark, and the green space is shadowy and suddenly looks so much bigger than during bright daylight. There's no one near us.

His head hovers above me, his eyes trying to seize mine. The green specks in them are like drops of venom. His arm snakes around my back; his hand, that a second ago gripped the throat of an imaginary thief, glides up my spine. I can feel his fingers touching the clammy skin at the back of my neck. It feels as though a deadly scorpion is crawling there, ready to strike. His face is almost touching mine now. I can feel his other hand on my waist, vice-like and entitled, pulling me closer.

'And then, after I get back from defence training, I'm going to volunteer for the Waffen-SS,' he whispers in my ear. 'And you don't want to send me to the front without something to hold on to, do you?'

The full length of his body is now up against mine, his chest pressed painfully against me. I can feel his lips touching the skin just below my ear. His breath is hot, like the breath of a violent beast. Without thinking, I take a forceful step backwards and his hands slide off me.

'We are not meant to do this,' I say, putting as much authority in my voice as I can muster. 'Boys and girls are not meant to … interact … like this. It's improper and selfish.'

'Says who?' Kurt asks, stepping towards me again, undeterred. 'Your parents? Don't listen to them. Our Führer is your father and the Hitler Youth and the BDM are your family.'

'I'm only fifteen,' I blurt out. 'I don't want to do this!'

He finally backs off. 'Sure, you are right,' he says, sounding unconvinced and annoyed. 'I apologise. Are you sure that's the only reason, though?'

I nod quickly, ignoring the ringing in my ears. 'Of course it is. And I accept your apology.'

But he doesn't leave it at that. 'Perhaps there's someone else? Another boy?' He takes out a cigarette and lights it. He squints at me through the blue cloud of smoke. A predator appraising and stalking his prey. 'That boy from my squad you were with that morning a few weeks back? Ludwig Schluck. Haven't I told you to stay away from scum like him?'

Alarm bells go off deep inside my head. He probably knows why I am here with him, probably smells the truth, that I detest him. And he probably doesn't even care, perhaps he even enjoys the thought, the power he has to make me do something I don't want to do. I urgently shake my head and start moving away. 'I have to go now. It's getting late.' I slip the collection tin under my climbing jacket.

'I'll see you soon, Lene. When I get back from the training. I'll be waiting after your BDM meeting.'

I turn and quickly walk away down the path through the shadowy bushes and trees. Those alarm bells continuing to clank and bang until there's an excruciating crescendo ringing in my head. Ludwig. Whom I cannot tell about Kurt. The way Kurt just inserted himself into my life and probably thinks that I'm his girlfriend! That he thinks he has the right to take possession of me like that.

I feel weak and gutless. I know Ludwig wouldn't want me to do this for him, but I know that I have to.

Within minutes I'm in the wide canyons of familiar streets, the plain grey tenement blocks towering to my left and right, embracing and sheltering me. The only good news is that Kurt is off to do his training and I won't have to worry about him for the next few weeks. I wish I never had to see him again.

CHAPTER 11

In mid-December a thin layer of snow covers the city. Soon it will turn to slush and dirty ice, but for now, all is white and pristine. Outside our kitchen window a string of icicles has formed and sneaky rays of morning winter sunlight catch in them, making them sparkle like a crystal necklace. My mother is feeling unwell and is still asleep when I leave for school.

Ludwig's already waiting for me downstairs. 'Uh, Lene, I was wondering,' Ludwig starts as soon as we set out. He interrupts himself. 'Never mind.' But then he tries once more. 'Um, actually …' He stops again.

'Is it something you've heard on the wireless?' I ask.

It's unlike Ludwig to hum and haw like this, especially after that night when my mother was away. It feels as though we are closer than ever since then and we've been spending as much time as possible together.

'No.' He shakes his head then starts again. 'It's got nothing to do with that.'

I glance at him but his face, half hidden behind his scarf, is unreadable. He just keeps changing his schoolbook satchel from one hand to the other.

'What is it, Ludwig?' I ask. And then I very nearly catch my breath. Has he found out the secret I've been keeping from him about Kurt?

'Well, here goes,' he then says, inhaling. 'Um, on Sunday, I have two movie tickets. For the matinee …' Ludwig wavers again.

I nearly laugh out loud with nervous relief. Of course Ludwig hasn't found out about Kurt. He's still away anyway, right? Out of sight, out of mind!

But why is Ludwig so nervous about asking me to see a movie at the Sternschnuppe? We've been to the movies together in the past. But then, *he's* never invited *me*.

'So, anyway, only if you haven't got other plans, of course, like going to your cousins' or anything like that because I know you usually go there at least once a month, or perhaps you've got too much homework. I mean, I'm not that keen on the movie, though you probably are, but I really want to see the newsreel.'

A date. Ludwig is asking me out on a date!

'Me too,' I say. 'I'd love to see the newsreel. And the movie.'

'Really? That's great! It's a date then?' His nervousness is gone in an instant and he beams at me.

'It's a date.' I return his smile.

'You want to go to the cinema with Ludwig?' my mother echoes when I come home for lunch. She is stretched out on the sofa even though it's the middle of the day, a handkerchief pressed to her mouth, a cold flannelette on her forehead. Her shoes and handbag are discarded on the floor in the corridor.

'Yes, on Sunday for the matinee,' I say.

'I suppose that's fine.' She sits up with considerable effort. 'Ludwig is a good boy, like an older brother to you. How lovely to give you one of the tickets.'

I squirm. *Like a brother.* I have never thought of Ludwig like that. Even though I'm not sure how to describe my feelings for him, I do know that they are unlike anything I've ever felt for anyone before. Like protective and happy and a tiny bit jittery all at the same time.

And they have been there for as long as I can remember, ever since the Schlucks moved into the building a few years ago and Ludwig and I started walking to school together as though it had been like this our entire lives.

My mother gives me an inquisitive look and her nostrils flare. Then she sighs and slumps back down on the sofa. 'You'll have to get lunch organised, Lene. I'm too tired.'

'Sure,' I say, thinking of my date with Ludwig. It feels special, even though it's just the cinema.

My mother attempts to get up from the sofa once more, muttering something about getting some chores done. She manages to stand, then she goes all white and sways. I catch her just as her knees buckle beneath her.

'What's the matter, Mutti? Are you that unwell?' I carefully lower her back onto the sofa and adjust her limbs like a doll's. She feels so light. I prop her feet up with a couple of cushions then kneel on the floor next to her. 'Weren't you unwell yesterday too?'

'Oh, I just feel so tired all the time,' my mother says, avoiding my eyes. 'Perhaps I've caught the flu.'

'The flu?' I say. 'Are you sure?' I once had the flu and it was dreadful. I was in bed for two weeks, had a high fever, a terrible cough and my whole body ached. 'But I wasn't hungry when I had the flu, and your appetite is just fine.'

My mother sighs, then looks at me at last. 'No, Lene, you're right. I don't have the flu. I feel sick but I'm not actually *sick*.'

'What's wrong then?'

She searches for words. 'Do you remember when Aunty Ilsa was expecting baby Theo ...' She stops. 'Before she was showing, how she was so unwell?'

When Aunt Ilsa was expecting, I had a lot of questions that made my mother blush. Of course I know more now. There's a lot of talk in the girls' toilet at school, especially amongst the older girls who have boyfriends who have been drafted and a few lunatics who still dream of producing a boy-child just for Hitler.

So that's what this is. 'You're expecting a baby?' I ask.

She nods. 'I'm not very far along. But I'm certain.'

I glance at her flat belly, the loose waistband of her skirt. 'But how?' Then I remember her trip to Hanover to see my father. 'Oh,' I say. I get up, embarrassment rushing through me. 'I'd better go and get lunch ready then.'

'Thank you, Lene.' My mother seems relieved that she doesn't have to do any more explaining. I feel just as uncomfortable talking to my mother about things like that as she does.

There's little variety of food left in the kitchen cupboards so I'm not sure what I can come up with for lunch. We have some eggs, flour, milk as well as a knob of butter.

'Mutti,' I call, 'I'm making *Eierpfannkuchen*. There's no sugar though, but we have some marmalade.'

'I prefer a thin spread of marmalade rather than sprinkling them with sugar anyway. And please don't use all the flour.'

How am I supposed to do that? There is barely enough flour for *Eierpfannkuchen* as it is, and now I can't even use all of it? I get a bowl and start whisking all the ingredients together. Because there is not enough milk either I add a little water, then test the consistency of the mixture. Too runny but it will have to do. While I'm cooking, I think of the news of the baby. I'm going to be a big sister to a baby brother or sister. The thought is vague, not quite real. I don't think I even want it to be real. It's war and there are air raids and bombs. How hard will it be to keep a tiny infant safe? It doesn't bear thinking about.

My mind wanders back to my date with Ludwig on Sunday. There's a small ripple at the pit of my stomach that travels upwards.

I cast a passing glance at myself in the corridor mirror. What I see is less than thrilling. I hesitate for a moment, then undo one of my short plaits, letting my hair tumble down in messy waves. I scoop my hair up in the palm of my hand, reducing it to chin length, then sweep it back on one side and pin it behind my ear. I look my age now, fifteen, perhaps even sixteen. But I know my mother will never allow me to cut my hair and wear it like this. I sigh and re-braid it. It really makes me look like a little girl but there's nothing I can do about it now. Ludwig will be here any minute.

I pull on my wool hat, wrap my scarf three times around my neck and put on my coat. Great. The same boring old clothes I wear every day. And I can feel my toes touching the front of my beautiful boots. In a few weeks wearing them will become painful and they probably won't see me through to the end of winter.

Above me, I hear a door slam on the third floor, followed by footsteps on the stairs.

'I'm off,' I say, sticking my head in the sitting room.

'I hope you don't get interrupted by an air raid.' My mother suppresses a yawn.

'I don't think so, there haven't been any raids in quite a while.' I count to three, waiting by the front door.

I time it perfectly and open the door just as Ludwig reaches our landing. 'Morning, Lene,' he says.

'Hello, Ludwig.' Overcome by an unexpected wave of awkwardness, I close our apartment door and pull on my wool mittens with painstaking care.

Outside, the cold morning wind blows in our faces. The air feels arctic, shocking my face with an icy slap. We draw in a few sharp breaths. The sky is low and heavy with white cloud cover. Everyone is rugged up.

'Still no news from your father?' I ask.

'No. Last thing we heard was that he was headed for the Stalingrad front. That was two months ago.'

'Mail from the Eastern Front takes such a long time,' I say, but I know that after two months I'd be very worried too.

'Yes, yes, I know,' says Ludwig. He fumbles with the tickets although we haven't even reached the end of our street and are still a few blocks away from the cinema. One of the tickets slips from his gloveless fingers and drops in the snow.

'Here you are,' I quickly pick it up and hand it back to him.

'Thanks. Come on, let's run. That'll warm us up a bit.' Ludwig speeds off, kicking up a patch of snow that hadn't been cleared from the footpath. He looks back at me over his shoulder. 'What are you waiting for?'

'Hey, wait,' I call and race after him.

Ludwig laughs, toying with me by letting me get close, only to speed away again. 'What are you doing, slowcoach?' he teases. 'Come on! I don't want to sit in the worst seats of the house.'

Puffing out white clouds of breath, I only manage to catch up with Ludwig outside the Sternschnuppe. He is waiting for me, jumping up and down on the spot like a boxer. He's grinning.

'You had an unfair advantage,' I protest.

'Yes, about two metres,' laughs Ludwig.

'More like twenty.'

'Here.' Still grinning, Ludwig opens the door for me with mock courtesy.

'Uh, thank you, Ludwig,' I say.

'It's my pleasure.'

I giggle and blush, which I hope isn't noticeable as my cheeks are probably red from running and the cold. I pull off my mittens and unwind my scarf, then stomp the snow off my boots – the very last thing I want is to slip on the marble floor and fall on my bottom right in the middle of the foyer.

'Oh, hi there. *Heil Hitler.*' The young woman who caught me sneaking into the cinema last time is standing on tiptoes, pinning up a poster. She looks much like a movie star herself. Her blonde hair is set in a helmet of curls, her lips are the brightest red and somehow match the colour of her nails. The bottle green dress she's wearing shows off her figure, and the little party badge gleams on her collar.

'I see you've got company today,' she comments, studying Ludwig with narrow eyes. 'And tickets too,' she adds, returning her attention to me. 'Did you make it to your BDM meeting on time the other week?'

The other week? It was probably close to six weeks ago. Did she have an elephant's brain or just nothing better to do than spy on me? But then again one has to be prepared to be constantly observed by the likes of her. She stares at me, frozen mid-motion, waiting for an answer. I hope she can't read my mind. A sarcastic reply is on the tip of my tongue but I remember my father's words. *Be sensible.*

'I managed to get there. And thanks for reminding me that I was running late that day.' Do I sound condescending? 'I guess I just lost track of time,' I add and smile remorsefully. I shake my head as though it was beyond me now how I could have been so slack.

'We all have to make it our duty to remind others of their duties and responsibilities,' she replies coolly before continuing with her poster job.

'I think you laid it on a bit too thick,' whispers Ludwig.

I stifle a laugh. 'You reckon?'

Ludwig nods and grins too then shows the tickets to the usher.

'You might have to keep your coats on. No heating,' the usher informs us as we enter the theatre. 'We're out of coal. Go on, pick your seats, there are a few empty ones in the last row.' He winks at Ludwig, hands the ticket stubs back to him. Ludwig promptly drops them again.

'Where do you want to sit?' Ludwig asks.

The lights are already dimmed. I make out people's heads in the semi-darkness in front of us. Before I can reply, the cinema goes black, leaving just the low glow of the emergency lighting. Ludwig pulls me into a row at the back. We plonk down on our seats just as the curtain opens. Behind us, in the projector room, I can hear the faint whirring of the film reels. A moment later, the newsreel introduction blasts away.

Ludwig's attention diverts from me to the screen as the first pictures appear, showing our soldiers on a snow-covered road. The commentator shouts their exact location at us:

'Somewhere south-west of Moscow, near Kaluga.'

The next pictures are of a burning village and we are told that the fire was lit by the Soviets.

'We take Kaluga! Our soldiers comb the town and search for Soviet soldiers.'

The cinema seems to get colder by the minute. Shivering, I watch our soldiers go into the houses of the Soviet town, expecting Soviet soldiers coming out with their hands raised, surrendering. But the pictures don't come. Instead there is a cut to a new scene and more commentary.

'Our troops are unstoppable and so are our Luftwaffe Stukas! They have destroyed supply routes and Soviet cargo trains. Soviet prisoners are captured in the big battles near Moscow!'

I blow into my hands and rub them together. It's freezing in here. Where did I put my mittens?

'The Battle of Stalingrad!'

This battle is on everyone's mind, but information about it is so scarce, conflicting and vague. Ludwig leans forward, tenses up. And I know Ludwig fears his father is there somewhere. I keep rubbing my hands, trying to make as little sound as possible.

'Give them here,' Ludwig suddenly whispers and grabs both my hands, closing his fingers around them. 'I'll warm them.' His eyes don't divert from the screen where our soldiers are shown fighting in the city of Stalingrad, a battle which has gone on forever now.

'Soviet snipers could lurk anywhere. The losses of the enemy are enormous!'

There is another cut to a new scene but the pictures blur in front of me. All I can think of are Ludwig's hands, warm and comforting, around mine, and the way it feels when his thumb strokes the back of my hand and my wrist.

CHAPTER 12

After the movie we take the long way home, walking slowly, hand in hand. It feels like early evening even though it is only mid-afternoon. It's snowing now: snow falling heavy and dense, earth and sky, the street, the whole city merging into one big snowdome, Ludwig and me invisible inside it, concealed and protected by the whirling snowflakes.

Then that illusion of invisibility shatters.

'Hey, Schluck, you lying swine. Stop! That's a bloody order!' a harsh voice snarls. Someone has invaded our snowdome.

I recognise that voice immediately and so does Ludwig.

'Horst,' I whisper.

Ludwig starts running, like an animal sensing danger, and pulls me along. Instinctively I start running, following him into the wall of snow.

'You've been missing the Hitler Youth drills again, haven't you?' I pant, struggling to keep up with him.

'Just run, Lene,' Ludwig wheezes, letting go of my hand now so we can sprint faster. 'Run!' His voice is thin and frantic.

We must have got a good head start because I can't hear anyone following us. Or are our pursuer's footsteps just muffled by the snow, by the pounding of our boots and our sharp, hacking breaths echoing in our ears?

We run almost blind, the thick dance of the snowflakes reducing visibility to next to nothing. I've lost my orientation. We dodge people appearing out of nowhere and they stop and swear at us. We zigzag around them, narrowly avoiding the trees lining the footpath, more sensing than seeing them.

Hidden underneath the fresh snow, patches of ice have formed since this morning. It's on one of those patches that I slip, my foot kicking out from underneath me. I lose my balance and hit the frozen ground, hard. But the pain is drowned out by the rush of fear and adrenaline. Ludwig instantly pulls me up again. We have lost ground and I'm sure I can now clearly hear the thud of boots behind us. There's more than one person chasing us and our pursuers are closing in.

Stumbling, with Ludwig dragging me, we regain momentum. The footsteps recede in that veil of snow once more. Did we shake them off for good?

A shadow emerges from the wall of white in front of us. Another pedestrian we have to dodge. We swerve to avoid a collision. But the shadow comes right for us, cutting us off. Then, to my horror, it solidifies into the uniform of the SS. The fear that engulfs me is like nothing I have ever felt before. It knocks the air out of me, makes my bones and muscles weak, makes a scream rise in my throat.

'Stop!' the SS soldier shouts. He's young, almost baby-faced, probably only a few years older than Ludwig, but his expression is hostile and his eyes appraise us without the slightest sign of emotion. There's a gun in his hand. He's waving it, pointing it at us.

'You two, stop. That's an order. Up against the wall!' His voice is commanding, cold, loaded with impatient aggression that could turn into violence at any moment. We stop immediately but we still both receive a hard push in the back and it knocks what little air is left out of my lungs. I can now clearly hear the footfall of our pursuers. They have almost reached us.

There's two of them. The first is Horst, the short bulky Hitler Youth squad leader whose voice I recognised outside the cinema. Behind him the second figure appears.

Kurt.

I gasp. *Oh God*, I didn't know he was back already.

When he sees me disbelief flashes across his face, then it turns into an angry grimace as he looks at Ludwig, full of hatred, triumph. But in an instant, his face goes all blank and hard, like the SS soldier's. He has got himself under control again.

'Horst, get them!' the SS soldier orders, and the squad leader pins us up against the wall with such enormous strength, I fear my spine will snap. The cold, rough sandstone scrapes my face.

'I got them, *Sturmscharführer*,' Horst sneers.

'Then let's go,' the *SS-Sturmscharführer* barks.

Let's go? Let's go where? My heart is racing, I feel my body shaking. I've never been so afraid in my life.

'Kurt,' I say, twisting my head to look at him. 'What's going on? I don't understand.'

Kurt doesn't reply.

'Shut up!' Horst bellows.

I can see a muscle in Kurt's jaw twitching hard.

Horst grabs my arm and yanks me away from the wall. Kurt takes Ludwig's arm and we are marched off behind the *SS-Sturmscharführer* who's leading the way, the gun dangling in his hand.

They drag us down the street. Ludwig manages to look at me and his mouth silently form the words 'I'm sorry'.

'Shut up!' Horst immediately shouts again and punches Ludwig in the ribs. Ludwig sucks his breath in sharply.

It feels as though we are lugged through the streets forever. Where are we going? The falling snow makes everything look the same. Eventually we are pushed through a wide gate. At that moment, the snow eases and I can make out the concrete *Reichsadler* perching on the gate's posts, and a low u-shaped grey building behind a huge quadrangle.

In the middle of the quadrangle stands the most horrific structure I have ever seen.

Makeshift gallows.

For a moment the clouds open and the sun breaks through, and I can make out every grotesque detail. The noose swinging from the gallows; a group of SS soldiers standing next to it, casual, as though this was a perfectly normal day for them, smoking, talking and laughing; a unit of SS soldiers marching off in formation and disappearing behind the building at the other end of the quadrangle.

Horst lets go of my arm, but he and Kurt grab Ludwig even harder, jamming him in between them.

Everything slows. I turn my head, which feels like it takes forever to rotate, by forty-five degrees. I'm watching a film, see the *SS-Sturmscharführer* talking to another soldier, a superior, conferring with him. I can't hear them; I can see their mouths move, but all I hear is a roaring silence, as loud as an avalanche in my head. The *Sturmscharführer* salutes, whips around on the heel of his shiny black boot. He sharply nods at Kurt and Horst and they start dragging Ludwig towards the gallows.

'*NO!*' I scream. The sound of my voice makes the silence in my head burst. For a second or two I'm anchored to the ground, rendered immobile by the sheer horror of what is unfolding.

Ludwig is trying to yank his arms free, fights, digging his heels into the snow. But he doesn't stand a chance. His face is waxen and hollow.

I exist solely in this horrible, endless moment.

'*NO!*' I scream again, then I beg. 'Kurt, please don't do this. You have to stop this! Please!' I stumble forward, am right behind them, reaching for Ludwig, clasping his cold hand. Kurt glances back at me and it hits me how much he's enjoying this, how much he wants to be part of this.

'Shut up!' Horst screams at me.

Kurt says nothing. He coils his upper body around, so fast and fluidly that I don't see it coming, and punches me in the shoulder. A single punch that fells me. I clamber up again, not even feeling any pain. Ludwig is now only a few metres from the gallows.

Suddenly there is a burst of commotion at the set of doors closest to us. The *Sturmscharführer* raises his hand, and Kurt and Horst halt, Ludwig still wedged between them.

More SS soldiers spill out into the quadrangle from the building. In the midst of the group is a figure who is in civilian clothes, standing out because of it. A boy like Ludwig, sixteen, perhaps only fifteen years old. He's been beaten up badly. He has a black eye, his nose looks broken and his face is smeared with fresh blood. He is hauled along by two SS soldiers. His face, like Ludwig's, is a mask of terror underneath the blood. But he doesn't scream or fight. Around his neck hangs a placard that reads: *I am a coward and a traitor of the German Reich*. The boy's legs flop as he is dragged along, without any strength, only pure fear.

The moment goes on. Horribly slow and too fast all at once. The cluster of soldiers, the fresh blood on the boy's bruised and beaten face.

The boy is dragged to the gallows where he is lifted up onto a crate. One SS man props him up, another slings the noose around his neck. I can hear them laughing. And suddenly the fear is gone from the boy's face. He stands upright, his shoulders pulled back, his legs straight.

This is wrong, so wrong. Surely they just want to scare him! People are executed for treason, for refusing to follow orders, for many things, I know this, but there are always trials first, aren't there? And they are adults, not kids!

They tighten the noose around the boy's neck. Next, without warning, one of the SS soldiers kicks the crate from underneath the boy's feet, casually, as though it were a football. I hear Ludwig gasp. A hoarse scream escapes from somewhere deep inside my throat. And in that short span of time, between the boot of the SS soldier hitting the crate and it flying out from beneath the boy's feet, the boy shouts: 'Down with the madman Hitler!'

'You defeatist shit,' the executioner mutters. 'How dare you!' He kicks the boy.

The boy swings on the rope. Spasms make his body convulse. I avert my eyes, my throat tight with horror and tears, but I'm grabbed and pushed closer.

'Watch,' the *SS-Sturmscharführer* hisses into my ear. 'You just watch.' He yanks my hair and forces me to look.

The boy's struggle is over. His lifeless body hangs from the gallows, broken.

Oh God, will Ludwig be next? Hoarse, alien whimpers come from somewhere deep in my core.

The *SS-Sturmscharführer* returns his attention to Ludwig, releasing me again. 'This is what happens to boys who wag Hitler Youth drills, who lie and deceive and don't prepare for their heroic duties as German soldiers. They are traitors and traitors must die.' He stops and appraises Ludwig grimly. 'Miss another drill or duty and it'll be you up there next time, Schluck. Got that?'

When Ludwig doesn't answer immediately Horst dishes out a couple of kicks to his calves. 'And we might string up your little girlfriend along with you!' he snarls.

'I won't miss another drill,' Ludwig manages to say, his voice faltering.

'You have to be a little more convincing if you want us to let you go,' says Horst.

Ludwig stands to attention, salutes. 'Yes, understood, *Sturmscharführer*! It won't ever happen again. *Heil Hitler*!' Ludwig flings his arm up. It's shaking. But only ever so slightly.

'That's better.' The *SS-Sturmscharführer* nods and grins, looking pleased.

Horst is grinning too, aping the *SS-Stumscharführer*. Kurt's face is stony, his eyes icy and furious when they brush me. Then they grasp Ludwig with absolute hatred.

'Let them go,' the *SS-Stumscharführer* orders Kurt and Horst. He seems to have lost interest, as though what just happened is of no significance to him. He's about to turn around, walk off, busy.

Horst instantly lets go of Ludwig's arm but Kurt doesn't. 'Let them go?' he asks. 'Both of them? This traitor doesn't deserve to live.' He pushes Ludwig towards the gallows.

The *SS-Stumscharführer* stops mid-motion, takes a quick step towards Kurt. 'When I give an order, you follow that order like a *reflex*. No matter what I'm asking you to do. Let him *go*!'

Kurt drops his hand. 'Yes, *Sturmscharführer*.' His teeth are clenched. He salutes. 'I'm proud to have done my duty and reported him!'

For a second Ludwig doesn't move.

'You heard it. Piss off,' Kurt hisses. He looks at me while he says it.

'You'd better listen to him,' the *SS-Sturmscharführer* says. 'You can go. Both of you.' He pauses, a malicious smile flashing across his face. 'Before someone changes their mind.'

I turn and tear out of the quadrangle, Ludwig behind me. The distance to the gate stretches forever. But just outside I stop.

'What are you doing, Lene?' Ludwig gasps. 'Keep going. Run. Don't stop!'

But I look back. I have to. I owe it to the boy on the gallows. The quadrangle has emptied. Kurt, Horst and the SS soldiers are gone. Only the boy's body with the placard around his neck remains. Outside the gate, pedestrians hurry past, avoiding the sight of the dead boy up on the gallows, a traitor, an enemy of the mighty German Reich.

CHAPTER 13

'I knew him,' Ludwig whispers. He has stopped running and slows to a near standstill. His face is so white, as white as the snow. It's not the shade of a living human.

Leaning against a tree, he sucks in sharp breaths. 'He was in my Hitler Youth squad. Kurt and Horst always had it in for him. Worse than for me. I thought it was because he was missing drills and military athletics. I never asked, I never even tried to talk to him, Lene.'

I wrap my arm around him and briefly touch my face to his. 'Come on, Ludwig. Let's not stop here.' I want to get as far away from the quadrangle and the barracks as quickly as possible. We stumble down the street, poisoned by the bitterness of our impotence, inebriated by the knowledge that we have escaped death.

A bus halts the moment we pass a bus stop and without thinking, without paying, we get on, not knowing, not caring where it will take us. We stand at the back upstairs, huddling amongst the other passengers, the windows fogged solid. My heart is still racing and as the pounding recedes back into the depth of my chest, I feel my body turn into a gelatinous softness, like a cold jelly flopping, a mass without bones, from its mould onto a plate.

With my sleeve, I wipe the foggy window, creating a small periscope-like look-through into the world outside. There, below me, my periscope shows the quadrangle. On the ground, in the thin layer of fresh snow, a middle-aged man in civilian clothes has fallen to his knees in front of the gallows. A river of red is streaming from one eye, making dark holes in the snow. As he stumbles to his feet, attempting to reach the boy on the gallows, an SS soldier brings him down again with his rifle butt. There's something familiar in the sleek, fluent movement, the precision of the blows.

Gradually, the periscope look-through fogs over again.

'I'm so sorry, Lene,' Ludwig mutters over and over as we walk home from the bus stop. 'I'm so sorry for dragging you into this, for putting your life at risk.'

'Stop it, Ludwig.'

'I'm so sorry,' he says again.

'It's not your fault. You didn't drag me into anything.' My whole body still feels strange and weak. The roaring in my ears has returned. I wonder if Ludwig feels the same. But I don't have the strength to ask. I just want to get home.

'L-Lene,' Ludwig stammers when I stop outside my front door.

I grab his hand and try to squeeze it but my muscles don't seem to find the strength.

He nods, his hand returning the squeeze weakly.

'Tomorrow. I'll see you tomorrow,' I say before shutting the door.

I walk past the sitting room where my mother is and go to my room, sit down on the bed. For a moment I just stay there, my hand brushing across the familiar texture of the taut blanket, the perfectly folded sheets tucked in at the corners.

The events in the quadrangle are replaying over and over in my head, but at the same time it feels as though this afternoon happened to another person, not to me, not to Ludwig. I see Ludwig being dragged towards the gallows. Then I see the boy on the gallows. I see it again and again. I touch my shoulder which I now realise is throbbing, and I remember the smug expression on Kurt's face, the vile fervour when he punched me. He got me right on the bone. I take off my coat and unbutton my blouse to reveal a purple and blue bruise. I quickly cover it again. The fact that Kurt has left a mark on my body makes me feel nauseous.

The uniform. The uniform Kurt wore. It wasn't the Hitler Youth uniform but the uniform of the SS.

And then I hear the boy's voice just before he was gone. '*Down with the madman Hitler!*' And in that moment I realise he was more alive than any of us. Those words, his voice saying them, that is the only truth, the only reality that I must let affect me.

The next day after school I silently follow Ludwig upstairs. His mother isn't home. Ludwig paces in the sitting room in front of the silent radio.

'What's the boy's name?' I ask. 'You said he was in your squad.'

Ludwig nods but doesn't say anything.

'Don't you remember?'

'I do. I know his name.' He massages his temples. 'Hans-Peter, that's his name. Hans-Peter Zoller. His name was always last when they did the rollcall.'

'Hans-Peter,' I repeat slowly. The most ordinary of German names. 'What about his family?'

Ludwig looks down, shakes his head. 'No, Lene. It's too dangerous. We've escaped death this once. They will be under Gestapo surveillance for sure. Or worse.'

'Ludwig, I don't know if I can live with myself.'

Ludwig solemnly shakes his head. 'Hans-Peter is dead. There's nothing we can do to change that.'

In my mind's eye, through the periscope, I see the man kneeling in front of the gallows, being knocked down trying to get to the boy, without doubt his son.

Is Ludwig right? What if it were my mother or father, and Ludwig's, next time, kneeling there?

I catch Ludwig looking at me in a funny way, his face all closed off, his jawline set in resolve. 'We can't be seen together any longer, Lene,' he says. His voice is different and unfamiliar. 'It's too dangerous.'

'Ludwig!'

He's turned his back on me, doesn't let me see his face, looking out the window at the city below.

My mind closes in on itself, a deep, ugly hole opening up. 'Ludwig, we can be careful, no one has to know that we are still seeing each other,' I plead.

He shakes his head, his back still turned. 'No. We are not taking that risk. I don't want to talk about it any longer. You have to leave.'

'Ludwig, you don't mean it! I know you don't really want me to leave!'

Ludwig has found out about Kurt and me! That's what this is, that's the real reason for what he's doing.

'Please go, Lene. Now.'

The hole swallows me. I get up and flee, embarrassed, hurt, stunned.

CHAPTER 14

It's the New Year and I go through the loathsome routine of getting ready for my BDM duties. I struggle with my neckerchief, struggle braiding my hair; strands keep slipping from my fingers which are slightly shaky. I feel uncoordinated, my whole body seems unbalanced, wonky. Will 1943 be the last year of war?

The German Sixth Army under Field Marshall Paulus are now encircled at Stalingrad. Over ninety thousand soldiers still remain there out of the three hundred thousand strong Sixth Army. Our leaders admitted the encirclement days after everyone knew anyway because it had been broadcast by all the foreign stations and people were talking everywhere, hushed. There was a silent outrage, one could feel it, about the fact that the encirclement was not confirmed by our government for days, as though those men, whom Hitler had forbidden to retreat, whom he had simply sacrificed, suddenly didn't exist.

Walking out of my room I bump my shoulder on the doorframe. Pain shoots up my shoulder and down my arm and Kurt jumps out of the shadows of my mind like a hideous hobgoblin. The bruise from his punch is still clearly visible, the flesh sore and painful almost three weeks after the day of the hanging. The fear of him is a constant companion. Every time I set foot outside I fear that he'll be there, ready to pounce and do damage. I often feel as though someone is shadowing me. But when I turn around there's never anyone there. Outside, a light powdery snow has started falling and the sky is low and oppressing, everything is white and grey and bare, like it is going to be like this for the rest of our days. I hurry along when, ahead of me, I spot Annalisa and know there's safety in her company.

She curtly nods at me when I join her. But after that she doesn't look at me again and we don't talk. I guess I've become a pariah of some sort. That's fine by me, all I want is to not walk alone. We have almost reached the hall when Annalisa unexpectedly breaks the silence.

'I've heard what happened,' she quietly says under her breath.

For an instant it feels as though we are close again, like we once were. We glance at each other for no longer than it takes for the snowflakes that land on her cheek to melt, but long enough for me to see her fear. She lowers her eyes and hurries along. It's clear that she's panicked, worried that she has revealed too much just by saying this, and realising that she couldn't hide her fear.

'Annalisa, wait,' I call. But she doesn't.

She enters the hall a few steps ahead of me. We take our spots at the sewing machines as Regina dumps a couple of Luftwaffe uniforms on my table that need mending as well as a few caps that need to have the piping replaced. I pick up a cap. The eagle depicted on it is in full flight, and looks lifelike, almost beautiful. If it wasn't for what it was carrying in its talons.

'What are you waiting for, Lene? Stop daydreaming and get on with it,' Regina reprimands me and nudges me in the back.

I bow my head and start working on a jacket sleeve that has come undone as the hall fills with the busy sound of dozens of sewing machine needles stitching away.

The vestibule door slams.

'*Heil Hitler*!'

I'd recognise that voice anywhere.

'*Heil Hitler*,' Regina replies.

I lower my head even more. I want to shrink, collapse onto myself. My heart starts racing.

'We'll need those uniforms back tonight.' I hear something being dumped on a table.

'Well, we can certainly try, Horst,' Regina replies.

I lower my head even further. Where's Kurt? If Horst is here, then he can't be too far away. Had he secretly been watching me on my way to the hall? Thank God I walked with Annalisa.

'Tonight. It's an order,' Horst growls.

The noise of the sewing machines has dimmed. A few girls have stopped working.

'Sure. I'll see what I can do', Regina says.

'Good. I'd really hate to repeat myself.'

'Is Kurt still around?' Regina then asks, her voice too casual.

I stop sewing, my ears ringing.

Horst lets out a short snort-like laugh. 'He's always around.'

'So he hasn't started his training yet then?' Regina asks.

Another Frankenstein laugh from Horst. 'He sure has.'

I cautiously glance up when his receding footsteps tell me he's leaving. I catch a glimpse of his back. A younger boy is following on his tails.

Regina claps her hands. 'Back to work, stop gawking at the boys.' On the table next to her sewing machine is a huge pile of Hitler Youth uniforms. She picks up about half of them and dumps them on my table.

Regina is still folding uniforms when she releases me almost an hour later than the others. I leave the hall, looking for Annalisa, or one of the other girls. But most of them have long scattered, rushing home to help with dinner and chores. It's nearly dark outside. The snow has stopped and what has fallen in the afternoon has melted.

I gasp as Horst's ugly pancake face appears out of the shadows. He glowers at me, his eyes narrow and viciously excited. 'Don't you think for one second that Kurt is finished with you!'

His young sidekick next to him laughs. Horst gives him a hard shove. 'Get the hell inside and get the uniforms, you moron.' The boy scrambles away.

For a second I'm frozen, my heart high in my throat. Horst comes closer. 'Shaking in your boots, are you?' He grins his dead grin.

The schoolyard suddenly looks like the quadrangle where Hans-Peter was hung. The building's windows reflect nothing but the emptiness of death. There's a roar in my ears again and then the flight reflex kicks in. I bolt down the street, Horst's vile laugh echoing in my ears, following me home.

That night the nightmare comes. In it, exact rows of BDM girls on sewing machines fill every corner of the schoolyard, rows and rows of them, mending and stitching away at uniforms, one homogenous mass, their heads bowed, feet treading feverishly. From the school's windows, vast red, white and black banners cascade and wave. And in the centre of it all, Hans-Peter hangs from the gallows. I don't know where Ludwig is but I know he's in danger. There is silence. There is always silence in dreams, and I can't scream, no matter how hard I try.

I wake with the crisp thought that I will see Ludwig later today, that I will perhaps tell him about the nightmare, that, in a stolen moment, the touch of his arm around me, his hand holding mine, will take the horror of it away.

But then I remember that Ludwig doesn't want anything to do with me any longer. And that thought is worse than the nightmare.

On my way to school I see Ludwig walking ahead of me in our street. He's in his Hitler Youth uniform, his shirt tail poking out from underneath his jacket. At the sight of his familiar frame I feel a sharp pain of longing. I want to speed up and catch up to him, to have things back to the way they were. Ludwig's steps are heavy as though he's dragging himself along. For a moment I observe him from a safe distance, then I fall back even further.

On the way home I scan the street ahead of me, the footpath on the other side of Schönhauser Allee. Nothing. I turn into our street and hurry home. No sight of Ludwig. Inside our flat I lean on the door, listen for familiar footsteps. I don't know how long I've been standing there when my forehead, pressed against the wood, goes numb. My satchel has long dropped to the floor like a dead weight.

When I hear the door slam downstairs, I press my ear to the door again. It's Ludwig. I easily recognise his footfall, like I've done for years. When he walks past our apartment I reach for the doorhandle. How desperately I want to push it down and open the door! Do his footsteps slow down a little? I can't tell. I feel my throat go tight with tears.

I kick at my school satchel and leave it there. I don't care about my homework. What's the point of it all?

CHAPTER 15

A couple of weeks later, I walk home from school slowly, dawdling, looking out for Ludwig. But in vain. I feel numb, simply going through the motions every day, like a machine. I don't know how much longer I can keep doing this. How much longer Ludwig can avoid me. I have come to believe that he is taking a different, longer route home. It hurts every time I think about it.

As expected my mother isn't home. She's at an obstetrician appointment and won't be back for another couple of hours. I dump my schoolwork on the kitchen table. I'm behind with everything. Biology, Latin. Chemistry is the worst. Has it always been this challenging? I think of my parents, how disappointed they'll be in me if I fail. How disappointed my father will be.

I go to my room and pull my father's last letter from the box in my wardrobe.

Stay true to yourself ... But be sensible also ... Work hard at school ... do not have to relinquish your ambitions ...

My father's handwriting blurs. I lie back on the bed and close my eyes. This is not how it's going to be! I have to pull myself together. And Ludwig cannot keep hiding from me forever. Surely, if someone has been watching us, they would have stopped now? Wouldn't they have more important things to do?

With fresh resolve, I get up and return to the kitchen. I spread out across the table, open my books, neatly line up my pencils, my ruler, a copy of the periodic table. And I start working.

When there's a knock on the door I jump. I check the clock. It's too early for my mother to be back and she'd have a key anyway. The knocking becomes more persistent, demanding.

Annoyed, I march down the corridor. Dust particles of that complicated equation still loiter in my brain. But a second later, just as it occurs to me that maybe I shouldn't open the door at all, chemistry is the last thing on my mind. Perhaps it is the last intelligent thing I will ever think.

The second I push down the handle the door flies in my face. I jump out of the way, only just avoiding being whacked in the head. The next thing I know, the door is shut again and I'm not alone in our flat any longer.

A male, dressed in a Hitler Youth uniform, looms above me.

'Thanks for letting me in, Lene.' Kurt smiles his poisonous smile that never reaches his eyes.

'Get out!' I gasp. 'My mother will be back any second.'

'No, she won't,' he says, his voice so controlled that his lips barely move. He looks me up and down slowly and deliberately, his eyes stabbing at me like greedy, angry claws. I cross my arms over my chest as he flicks his tongue across his lips.

'Get out,' I say again. I know my voice is shaking. 'You have no right to be here.'

He takes a step closer to me. 'I decide what rights I have.' He comes closer still and I recoil backwards into the kitchen. There is only the table between us.

'You have been two-timing me, Lene. With that traitor Ludwig Schluck.' Kurt moves around the table, panther-like, casual and furious.

'Stay away from me!'

For a second he halts.

'And I haven't been two-timing you with anyone!' I say as firmly as I can.

'I don't believe you.' In one fluent movement he grabs me by the wrist and pushes me into the far corner next to the kitchen buffet. His other hand clamps hard around my sore shoulder where a phantom pain still remains. I wince.

'Does it still hurt?' he taunts. 'I'm so sorry I had to do that. But it was your own fault.' His hands tighten even more, but this time I don't wince. I won't give him the satisfaction.

'You know,' his grip on my shoulder loosens, 'when Ludwig gets called up, and believe me, he will, I'll make sure he gets sent to the Eastern Front.' He laughs. 'Although that's where all the weaklings who don't volunteer get sent anyway!'

Ludwig is not even seventeen yet, he can't get drafted! 'I haven't been two-timing you, Kurt, I swear!' I call in desperation.

Kurt's hand crawls up my shoulder and his fingers reach the bare skin on both sides of my neck. For a moment his hand clamps around my throat as though he wants to choke me. He smiles, tightening his grip ever so slightly. Then his hand slides down my neck and into my blouse. His breathing goes ragged. 'There's no coming back from the Eastern Front, not for someone as useless as him. He won't even survive the first week.'

'I haven't seen Ludwig in weeks! I've been waiting for you to come back from training.' A truth and a lie.

I try to push his hand away but I'm mashed into the corner like a soft, useless potato dumpling while he is like a block of concrete pressing against me, flattening me. I don't even get my hands anywhere near his to fight them off.

'Really?' Kurt's hand slides underneath the strap of my petticoat. It pauses there.

I nod vehemently.

'Well, I am here now.' Then he brings his mouth close to my ear and whispers: 'But I'm not sure I believe you. Prove it! Prove that you have been waiting for me and that weak defeatist means nothing to you!' His mouth moves away from my ear and his face is centimetres from mine. His eyes are glassy and have a feverish glaze. He looks like he hasn't slept in days.

I crane my neck backwards, my mind spinning. How am I going to get out of this?

'You have to give me now what you denied me last time. I'm off doing my duty for the Führer tomorrow. I've only just managed to squeeze in this little visit.' The pressure of Kurt's body on mine has eased off slightly.

'Are you going to the front?' I ask. Perhaps if I get him to talk all of this will stop.

'I am going to an *SS-Junkerschule* in Bavaria for officer training. And then, who knows?'

Bavaria. Hundreds of kilometres from Berlin. It takes all my self-control to not show my elation.

'Make this one of the best moments of my life, Lene, will you?' He pauses. 'Actually do you know what *would* have been the best moment of my life?' His face is so close to mine, his mouth so close to my lips; it's as though he wants to infect me.

I shake my head.

'Well, that *would* have been if Schluck had hung alongside that traitor I denounced.'

'What a miserable life you must lead!' I spit it out before I can stop myself.

Kurt's face turns red. 'My life is dedicated to the Führer and all that he stands for and the eradication of everything that undermines him and his greatness.' His voice is quiet but loaded with rage. 'And now my life is about to get a whole lot better.' His leg pushes between my knees. He tries to kiss me but I manage to turn my head in time and his lips just miss my mouth.

'No! Get off me! You're vile!' I wriggle back, somehow managing to retreat further into the corner. I press my knees together, trying to push his leg away. Suddenly his whole weight bears down on me and I lose my balance, my knees buckle and I'm pushed down on the floor, my back against the wall. With one quick motion Kurt pulls me towards him by my ankles. Then he falls on top of me, pressing me down with his body. This is it. There's nothing I can do. I close my eyes, sinking through darkness.

A key turns in the lock.

Kurt swears and backs off me, stands. He pulls me up, then straightens his uniform and runs his hand through his blond hair. 'Don't mention one word about any of this or else,' he hisses.

'Lene?' my mother calls from the corridor. 'Are you home?'

'In the kitchen,' I rasp.

'Oh, you have a visitor?' Surprised, my mother stops in the doorway.

'*Heil Hitler*!' Kurt says. 'I'm collecting scrap metal. Can you spare anything, a pot or pan?'

Suddenly I understand why he's in his Hitler Youth uniform, instead of showing off his new SS uniform!

'We can't spare anything,' I say. 'I've already told him. He was just about to leave.'

My mother looks from me to Kurt, suspicious, her forehead furrowed.

'It is your duty to support the war effort and make sacrifices,' Kurt says. 'I will report any non-contribution.'

'Is that so?' my mother replies sharply and opens the pot cupboard. She pulls out a metal strainer and hands it to Kurt. 'We can do without that one. Is there anything else? Otherwise I'll show you out.'

'*Sieg Heil*!' Kurt wedges our sieve under one arm. As the other arm shoots up, he arrows one last glare at me without my mother noticing.

Alone in the kitchen, I lower myself on a chair. My heart feels as though it's wheezing, like it can't quite keep up with how fast it needs to beat. I bow my head over my chemistry book. Furtively I touch my neck. Are there marks there?

When my mother comes back to the kitchen, I sit up quickly, dropping my hand. She shakes her head a little at me. 'They are such a nuisance. Just give them something, anything when they turn up and send them on their way as quickly as you can.'

'Yes, Mutti.'

'Are you all right?' my mother asks. 'Is there something else going on here?'

I shake my head.

'You seem very quiet these days.'

'I'm fine. It's just chemistry. I don't think it's my cup of tea after all.'

'Hmm. That's not the end of the world. But you'd better see it through to the end of the school year now.'

'I will.' But chemistry is the very last thing on my mind. All I'm thinking is: Kurt's gone. Let him get sent to the front as soon as he finishes his officer's training. I want him to get killed the minute he sets foot on the front line. No, let him fight, let him live in the mud and trenches for a few months, let him be miserable and filthy and lice-ridden, let him be petrified. And then, let him get killed. Let him get taken out clean by an enemy bullet.

'Is all well with the … pregnancy?' I ask, realising that I've gone quiet again.

'Yes, all seems to be fine. The nurse suggested to get ready for the baby soon, before I feel too heavy.'

'Perhaps I could go and get some of the things that Theo doesn't need any longer?' I say.

'Perhaps.' My mother looks doubtful, concerned, sensing perhaps that there's something going on with me she doesn't know about.

She cups her hand underneath her belly which has the slightest suggestion of a curve. 'But let's wait until the days start getting longer again.'

CHAPTER 16

In late March the nights are still cold but during the day there are twinkles of spring sunshine and milder temperatures. My mother is now around five months pregnant, so well in the safe zone. I've finally convinced her to let me go and collect Theo's baby clothes from my aunt in Charlottenburg.

'I really shouldn't let you go,' my mother says, hovering behind me as I get ready. 'I'll be fine.' I button my coat and hook my father's old backpack across one shoulder. 'Theo's clothes are beautiful, much better than anything we could afford.'

My mother nods. 'You are right, of course. With the fabric shortage they are a godsend indeed. I'm so glad Ilsa hasn't donated them.'

I can't wait to get out of the house, to get a break from the drudgery of routine, even from school which I'll be missing today, a distraction from constantly thinking about Ludwig. The other day I ran into him in the stairwell, and he slowed and whispered: 'Horst's gone'. Before I could reply anything about Kurt, Ludwig had hurried past me and out the door, signalling for me not to follow him.

As if she can read my mind, Mutti says, 'I know something has been going on with you, Lene. With you and Ludwig.'

I shake my head. 'Don't worry about me, Mutti. I'm absolutely fine.'

My mother is still reluctant to let me go. Although it's been quiet, there's always the risk of an air raid. Berlin hasn't been the enemy's priority, like the Ruhr area with its steelworks industry, or Germany's major port cities. And in Berlin we are fortified with Flak defence and most of the enemy's bombers don't have the reach to carry out large-scale area bombings here. But for how much longer?

'Ilsa could try to send the clothes in the parcel mail,' my mother deliberates.

I shake my head and I hug her. I feel excited about the baby now; it started kicking a little while ago. My mother put my hand on her belly and underneath my palm I could just make out the faintest movement. 'I will get them and that's the end of it.' I know it's a dilemma for my mother and I don't want her to get too upset and worried as her blood pressure is quite high. 'It will be good to see my aunt and cousins. I haven't seen Gertie, Ophelia and Theo in such a long time. I'll be as quick as possible.'

'I will phone through in a couple of hours to check if you have arrived safely.' She cups my face in the palm of her hand. 'Last year I was at my wit's end, but you have become such a responsible girl, Lene. I really wouldn't know what I'd do without you.'

The tram and underground are more or less operating on schedule and I make it to Charlottenburg without major hiccup. As I walk from the station to my cousins' apartment, I slow. A block of buildings has been ripped in half, with one side turned to pulverised rubble, crumbling onto the street below, the other side still standing with its flats exposed. There's clean-up activity underway with the POWs doing the most dangerous work. Clusters of onlookers stand around, talking in hushed voices.

'The bombs were meant for Siemensstadt. But it was too overcast.'

'Yes, it was another targeted bombing. The bombs should have never been dropped here.'

'But it could have been so much worse.'

But when an unexploded bomb is discovered and one of the POWs is ordered to disarm it, everyone scatters and I quicken my steps too.

There's a foreboding feeling somewhere deep in my belly, telling me that these occasional raids in the last few months are just a prelude, a tiny taste of things to come. Any tentative hope I had that 1943 might be the year that the war would be over has been diminished to no more than a weak glimmer, especially since Herr Propaganda Minister Goebbels announced to the world on our behalf that we were at total war. Apparently the fifteen thousand people who cheered during his speech at the Berlin Sportpalast, which was broadcast on the wireless, were a true representation of all of us.

I turn into my cousins' street and here, apart from the empty block where the building was hit last year, nothing has changed. Their apartment building looks as grand as ever.

I take the portal steps in one big leap and push open the heavy front door. I pause, catching my breath. It's like a time warp in here, like life outside is taking place in a different universe. The black-and-white chequerboard marble floor is clean and polished, the huge gilt mirrors are spotless. Only the ruby carpet that used to be on the stairs is gone. I suspect it has been turned into uniforms.

The back door that leads to the rear building opens and the caretaker comes in carrying a dustbin and a rag.

She knows me. '*Heil Hitler*, Fräulein Lene. My, you are a young lady now. Are you visiting your aunt?'

'*Guten Tag*,' I reply and nod. 'I'm sorry, I'm in a rush.' I scramble upstairs but not before noticing the shadow of disapproval on the caretaker's face.

I ring the bell and Gertie lets me in. She's changed since I last saw her. She looks older than her fourteen years, her violet blue eyes serious. We hug each other. 'Your mother telephoned already to see if you had arrived safely yet,' Gertie says.

'I got through fine.' I say. 'Why aren't you at school?'

'I've been recruited to help out at the local kindergarten a few hours every week. I have to be there soon. They are short-staffed. Some of the woman who used to work there have to work at a drug manufacturing factory out south now. Apparently they can't keep up with the huge *Wehrmacht* orders.'

She looks at me, her eyes large and round. 'I hope I can catch up on what I'm missing at school ... when the war is over.'

I feel fury rising deep inside me on hearing that, at fourteen, Gertie, who's exceptionally bright, is forced to miss school. 'Yes, when the war is over,' I repeat. There now seems to be only one way the war can end. The only question is: when will that end come? Though everything is going its normal way here in this lovely apartment. What a fragile, false normality it is.

'Is your mother not here?' I ask. I have to focus, collect those clothes and return home.

'No, you just missed her. But she'll be back shortly,' says Gertie. 'Only Ophelia and Theo are here. They are in the bathroom. Ophelia is potty-training him.' Gertie lowers her voice. 'He's taking such a long time to get the hang of it. He's almost three! But Mama has packed all the clothes and a couple of small blankets for the baby. She said to take the pram too.'

'The pram?' I'm not sure I want to be burdened with it. The thought of dragging it across the city seems simply ludicrous! I pick up the substantial parcel of baby clothes and blankets from the hall table. It's heavy.

'Take the pram,' Gertie insists. 'Theo doesn't need it any more. He's much too big for it.'

Uncertain, I stare at the bulky pram.

'It can double as a bassinet for the first twelve months,' Gertie says.

Absurd! Everything is falling apart, the whole of Europe, our lives, people are dying everywhere, and I have to lug a pram across Berlin. But I know that once I'm back home, I will regret it if I don't take it.

The lavatory flushes and a moment later the bathroom door down the hallway opens. Ophelia followed by my little cousin Theo come out. Theo makes a proud face. He runs down the hallway and I bend down to give him a quick hug.

'He finally did it,' Ophelia says and rolls her eyes. 'Took him long enough.'

'Well done, Theo,' Gertie praises him and pats the top of his head.

'Well done,' I echo. But all that's going around in my head is the dilemma with the pram.

'Right, I'm off,' says Ophelia. 'I'm already running late.'

She's in her BDM uniform and despite my exasperation about the pram I notice the squad lanyard on the breast pocket of her jacket, and there's also a new insignia on her sleeve. She reminds me of Regina. Her hair is done exactly the same way, though it is not blonde but light brown and she has inherited her father's hazel eyes. How it must bug her that Gertie looks like a BDM poster girl with her blonde curls and violet blue eyes!

'What are you late for?' I irritably ask. 'A BDM meeting at this time of the day?'

Ophelia points at her lanyard. 'I worked hard enough to make leader. I'm not going to stuff it up by missing the leader meetings now. We are introducing a whole new system in our borough on how we can support the war effort more effectively.'

The war effort! A new system?! Wordlessly I grab Ophelia by the arm and roughly drag her to the kitchen. There I open the balcony doors and pull her outside. Taken by surprise, Ophelia doesn't resist.

Beyond the backyard and the bare branches of the chestnut tree, the bombed section of buildings that I have just passed on my way here are clearly visible. From up here on the second floor the destruction is even more evident. It looks like the structures have just fallen away, scooped untidily out of the cityscape. Black smoke hangs over the area and the smell of fire is still strong and pungent.

'Did you notice this?' I shout at her, pointing at the ruins across the top of the tree. 'Have you noticed what's been happening around you? And all this will get much, much worse, I'm sure. This is just a taste of what's to come! Berlin will be destroyed just like other cities in the rest of Germany. Your so-called war effort will only prolong all of this. There is no final victory!'

Downstairs in the yard a door slams.

'Are you insane?' Ophelia hisses. And now she is the one who yanks me back inside by the arm. She quietly shuts the balcony doors.

'You must be barking mad screaming around defamatory lies like this. Only a lunatic would do such a thing.'

'You are the lunatic,' I reply. 'Wake up, for goodness sake. These are not lies! This is real, the truth. You are the one who believes in lies. We have to stop and start thinking for ourselves again and accept reality. Your father is already dead, mine might be soon, and they pretend that the hundred thousand German soldiers taken prisoner at Stalingrad don't even exist. German cities are being erased by the Americans and the British and soon it'll be Berlin's turn. And the Russians will have their revenge too.'

My cousin looks at me coldly, detached, and with utter distaste. 'You know, Lene, people hang for saying things like that. Lies they might have heard on enemy stations. And good Germans consider it their duty to report people who spread defamatory lies to undermine the spirit of the German community. No matter who that person is. Even if it's their own family.'

My breath catches in my throat. I see Ludwig being dragged to the gallows, Hans-Peter's lifeless body with the horrible placard around his neck. I suck in a sharp breath at the split-second memory flash of that horrible day.

'Stop it, Ophelia,' Gertie says, standing between us. 'What are you talking about?'

'Perhaps I need to remind Lene of what *really* is reality,' Ophelia replies.

'All of it is reality,' Gertie says quietly and calmly. 'People who don't believe in final victory and total war hang, but all of those things Lene just said are true too.'

Ophelia stares at her sister, the expression in her eyes just short of abhorrence. 'The enemy will never get to Berlin. That's an outrageous thought! The Führer would never let this happen.' Her voice trembles. 'And Vati died a hero's death for the Führer. I will not give up believing in this, will never stop believing in the Führer. It's the only choice. His will is all that matters. Do you two understand?' Ophelia's voice is about to tip.

Gertie and I look at each other. Could it be that Ophelia is struggling with it all just like we are? That she is even more scared? But chooses to keep believing the lies, to cling to them for dear life, to possibly even sacrifice her own family for those lies?

'We do understand,' I say. Once though, Ophelia had thought her father was a coward for considering to ask for a transfer from the Eastern Front for some of his men. And the word 'hero' leaves such a bitter aftertaste. What does it mean to be a hero? Was Hans-Peter who was hung by the SS a hero? There's no doubt in my mind that he was. He hadn't agreed with the way things were, had spoken his mind, had the courage even at the moment before death, and he had paid the ultimate price.

'I have to go to the meeting now,' Ophelia says. 'You two can just stay here and keep talking your defamatory talk. But don't expect me to shed any tears for you if you get caught.'

She turns around and heads for the door. But there she stops in the open doorway and glances back at us one last time. 'When we have won the war with our new miracle weapons and live in a vast Germany with the Führer our leader and glorious new buildings replacing the few old ones that have been destroyed, I will look back on today and I will know that I was right and you two were wrong.' The door clicks shut behind her.

'She's going to tell on us,' Gertie whispers. 'She's going to blab to one of the other lunatic BDM leaders and then they are going to report us to the Gestapo.'

'She won't,' I say. 'She's just scared.' Perhaps it's the only hope she is capable of, the belief in Hitler and his ruthless and megalomaniac plans for Germany.

'How can you be so sure? I feel like I don't know her any more. My own sister! Why would she scare me like this? She must have completely lost her mind.'

I take the heavy parcel of clothes and drop it in the pram. 'I should go,' I say. 'It's getting late.' I pause. 'Be careful what you say around Ophelia, Gertie. Just to be safe.'

My cousin nods.

'Gertie,' a small voice squeaks. Gertie spins around. We have completely forgotten about Theo who must have been standing there, listening, the whole time.

'What is it, Theo?'

'Toilet,' he demands and points at the bathroom door.

Gertie stares at him with incomprehension. Then she turns back to me. 'The world is going to hell and I have to potty-train my little brother,' she says. 'I feel like I'm losing my mind as well.'

I hurriedly hug my cousins goodbye, then wheel the pram to the door and lug it down the stairs, not bothering to wait for the lift. The caretaker is standing on a stepladder, shining the gilt frame of the mirror with a rag.

'*Heil Hitler*, Lene. You take care now,' she says without interrupting her task.

I don't reply.

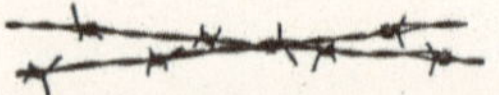

The air-raid siren starts howling shortly after I get off the underground at Alexanderplatz. I fall into a trot, following the rush of people to the public shelter. The expensive pram with the precious parcel of clothes clatters and bounces on the cobblestoned road, slowing me down. I clench the handle of the pram and speed up.

When I get to the shelter there's a large crowd of people lining up already to get in.

'Move, hurry up, everyone, we have to close the doors,' the wardens shout and urge us on.

But we can't move quickly because the doors are clogged by too many people wanting to get to safety. I look up to the slightly overcast late afternoon sky. There is no sound or sight of any bombers. But once our Flak starts firing, it'll be suicide out here with all the shell splinters raining out of the sky.

People are pushing from behind. The handle of the pram digs into my stomach. I manage to move forward a bit and I finally make it to the entrance. The crowd shifts again and I'm through the door, but then I'm stuck there for ages without any progress. At last the people ahead of me disperse a little and I realise the upper levels are full, so are the rooms with the bunk beds, and there are people already hunkering down on the stairs. I'm directed to one of the below ground levels where, I'm told by the warden, there's still room. But there's no way I can take the pram down there with me. I take out the bulky parcel of baby clothes and try pushing it into my backpack. It doesn't fit; it's too wide and way too thick. I drop it back into the pram and drag it to a luggage area where I leave it next to a large suitcase and a child's scooter.

Wedged between a mother with two young children, a middle-aged couple and a group of junior Hitler Youth boys with their scared-looking squad leader who's not much older than they are, I slowly descend the flight of stairs and make my way along the crowded corridor past a first-aid room and some restrooms. In the first-aid room, a nurse is comforting a pregnant woman who is doubled over in pain.

The air is damp and foul smelling. It's so crowded. There are several hundred people on this level alone and more are coming down the stairs behind me. I fight a wave of claustrophobia, telling myself that it's much safer in here than down in our cellar; the walls here are much thicker and the doors are gas and fire proof. I take a deep breath of the foul air to calm myself. But it helps a little.

I move along the narrow aisles, deeper into the shelter, apologising as I squeeze past people, dodging legs, bags and small children crawling on the floor until I find a spot on the bench right by the wall. I could be here for hours. I think of my mother who'd be beside herself worrying about me right now. I wish there were a way I could let her know I was in a safe place.

I put my empty rucksack down next to me and rest the side of my body against it, close my eyes and feel, in my mind, the touch of Ludwig's shoulder on mine. I dive away into a semi-sleep.

'Lene!'

My eyes spring open. I blink, confused. There's no Ludwig, only strangers wherever I look.

'Lene, it's me.'

I turn around to someone pushing in through from behind.

'Annalisa!' I call. 'Here, sit next to me.' I move my backpack to make a little more room and she squishes next to me, apologising to the woman on her other side, who begrudgingly shifts a couple of centimetres.

'I was behind you before, when we were lining up to get in but you didn't see me. Then you were gone.'

'I had to put something in the luggage rack, then I was told to go to the lower level.'

Annalisa nods. 'The lower levels are safer. If there's a direct hit. Which won't happen anyway. But, you know, just in case.' Annalisa talks rapidly.

'Sure.' I haven't seen Annalisa for a few weeks. 'Where have you been?' I ask. 'You've dropped out of school? And I haven't seen you at BDM either.'

She nods. 'We've moved in with my grandparents. They have a small house out in Weissensee. I was about to get on the S-Bahn when the alarm sounded.'

'Weissensee is nice,' I say. And probably safer.

Annalisa looks down at her scuffed shoes. 'We don't have to pay rent there either.' She pulls on her loose-fitting jumper.

There's something different about Annalisa. I'm not sure what it is. 'Are you all right?' I ask. 'You seem different.'

'Never been better. I believe with my body, heart and soul in the Führer. And I know that he loves me.'

I have no reply.

She leans in closer. 'My body is doing its duty for the Fatherland and the Führer!' she whispers in my ear.

What a strange thing to say! Before I can ask her what she means, the all clear comes and Annalise jumps up, climbs over the bench and disappears amongst the crowd of people gathering their belongings.

I shoulder my backpack and retrace my steps back to the exit. Past the first-aid room where the woman's labour is now so far along that she's unable to leave, past the rooms with the bunk beds.

Word travels down from the upper level that it was a handful of Russian bombers that caused the air raid, but they never made it to Berlin as they were attacked by our *Luftwaffe Messerschmitts*.

I creep up the stairs with hundreds of others, finally nearing the exit and let out a sigh of relief that there were no bombs. I can't wait to get home and show Mutti the pram. Thank goodness I listened to Gertie and decided to take it!

I squeeze through a too-small gap in the thinning crowd, ignoring reprimands.

'Sorry, sorry, just trying to get to the luggage area.'

'So are we!' someone complains.

Finally, I'm almost there. A sunken-cheeked soldier in front of me shoulders his pack and I peer past him to where another man retrieves a large suitcase. I crane my neck, confused.

The pram isn't there! And neither is the parcel of clothes. I stare at the empty spot. Am I in the wrong place?

'Do you need any help?' the soldier asks.

I shake my head.

He shrugs and moves away from the luggage area towards the exit. Perhaps I am lost. But then I notice the child's scooter next to the empty spot where my pram should be. Frantically, I rush around the luggage area, looking around feverishly. I catch sight of the soldier who's now almost at the exit. I push past people to reach him. 'Wait!' I call.

'Yes, do you need help with anything after all?'

'Did you see a pram?' I ask. 'When you got your backpack? Did you see anyone take a pram with a large parcel in it?'

'I don't think I did, but I wasn't really paying attention. Maybe? I haven't slept in three days. Sorry, I hope you find it.'

He turns away and asks the person ahead of him where the nearest pharmacy is. I fall back, let people nudge me out of their path.

I wait in the luggage area with my empty backpack. I wait after a boy has collected the scooter. I still wait long after it is clear that the pram and the parcel will not be returned.

All those lovely clothes we so urgently need for the baby. Gone.

CHAPTER 17

There is a new photograph on the buffet in our living room. It shows my parents outside the hotel they stayed at in Hanover. It took such a long time to arrive that my mother had almost forgotten about it. It was sent to us from the photo studio in Hanover where the film had been left and developed, on the eve of my father's departure for the Eastern Front. In the photo my parents look sombre, though there is a transient happiness in their eyes, as though they are desperately trying to grasp and hold on to their time together, to cherish every single minute. My father looks handsome, though he doesn't quite match the picture of him in my memory. He has aged, is a little thinner. A new far-away expression is there and I can tell he's trying to control it. It's as though a little bit of his soul is not present any longer.

I hear my mother's footfall coming down the corridor and I quickly avert my eyes from the photo. Though my mother's belly is not very big yet, she moves around carefully as though she's balancing a tray of expensive crockery. She's just been to see the doctor again and her blood pressure is still high. It's worrisome, especially since she's got more than three months to go.

'What do you think the baby is, a boy or a girl?' I ask.

'I think it's a boy.'

I nod. 'I think so too.' I pause. 'How I wish we had all those lovely clothes from Theo.' I still can't believe what happened. That I didn't open the parcel and put at least some of the clothes in my backpack. 'I wasn't thinking,' I say.

'Lene, it's not your fault. Stop beating yourself up. It was an air raid! You were scared. Let's not talk about it any longer.'

I sigh. 'Have you thought of a name for the baby yet?'

'What do you think of the name Gustav if it is a boy?' my mother asks. 'Vati's middle name.'

I nod. 'Yes, I like that name.' Gustav. The baby becomes more real with every passing day.

The downstairs door slams loudly, in a familiar way. 'I think that's the post.' I jump up, nearly tripping over the laundry basket, then race downstairs, taking two and three steps at a time. My father's letters have been coming fairly regularly, about once a week. They have been bringing little news of significance, other than confirming that my father is alive. The postwoman is feeding letters through the door slots in the ground floor flats.

'News from the front by the looks of it.' She hands me a single letter then continues on up the stairs.

The front door opens again and Frau Schluck comes in carrying a near-empty shopping bag. 'How are you, Lene? It's been a while since I've seen you.'

'Good morning, Frau Schluck. Yes, it's been a while since I've seen you, too.' I hesitate. 'How is Ludwig?' I then ask.

She regards me for a moment. 'I think he misses you, Lene.' She indicates the letter in my hand. 'News?' she asks.

'Yes,' I hold up the treasured *Feldpost* letter as the postwoman comes back downstairs.

She has two envelopes for Frau Schluck. 'I'll need you to sign for this one,' she says, indicating one of the envelopes. She hands Frau Schluck a pencil, avoiding her eyes.

Frau Schluck's fingers are shaking as she signs the form. She clasps her mail in one hand, her knuckles white. The letter at the top must have come from the front too. I quickly glance at it and recognise the *Feldpost* stamps. The other one I can't see. The house door slams behind the postwoman.

'This one is not from my husband,' Frau Schluck says. 'It's from his commanding officer. Why would he be writing to me?' her voice is trembling and her face is strangely white.

'Oh,' I say, swallowing away a lump in my throat. There's only one reason for such a letter.

Frau Schluck presses the envelopes to her chest, closes her eyes. 'Dear God,' she mumbles. 'Please, I hope he's just wounded.'

'Come on, I'll walk up with you,' I say. I feel helpless and don't know what else to do. I guide Frau Schluck upstairs by her arm. 'Is Ludwig home?' My heart is pumping hard suddenly as though it wants to be seen. *He misses me.*

'I don't know,' Frau Schluck says. 'I've been out queuing for meat.'

'Lene, what is taking you so long?' my mother calls impatiently from inside our flat when we reach the second floor.

'I'm coming, Mutti.'

Frau Schluck stops like a sleepwalker, the letters still pressed to her chest.

'Would you like to come in for a moment?' I offer. But she shakes her head and I watch her shuffle upstairs to the third floor.

'Who were you talking to?' My mother appears in the doorway.

'Frau Schluck,' I say. 'I think it's Ludwig's father,' I whisper, closing the door. 'I think there is bad news.'

'Let's hope you are wrong. It would be a heartbreaking tragedy if there were, especially after his unit never made it to Stalingrad and avoided that horrible fate of our soldiers there. I will check on Frau Schluck later.' She indicates the letter I'm holding. 'From your father, thank God. Please open it for me.'

There is just one sheet of paper. Disappointed, because there is no separate letter for me, I hand it to my mother. Her eyes drink the words. The letter is short, which I can tell by looking at the back of the sheet. A faint smile appears on my mother's face.

'Here,' she says and hands me the letter, 'read for yourself.'

My eyes fly over the few words my father has written.

24th of April, 1943

My beloved family,

I apologise for the shortness of this letter. I am very pleased to report that I have been promoted to Oberfeldwebel. There's more good news – I'll be able to come home on leave for a few days soon. This is due to recent developments. I'll tell you more when I see you very soon, hopefully in time for the birth. I am sending my love to you, my beloved Christa, to Lene, and to the baby too.

Anton

It has been such a long time since I've seen my father. His leave has been postponed again and again since last December and now it's early May. I know he wouldn't write about it in his letter if it wasn't as good as approved this time around. My legs feel shaky with the joy of knowing that he is all right, that he will be here soon.

'This is wonderful. Your father might be here for the birth and get to see the baby!' My mother's cheeks are flushed, her eyes glisten with tears. 'Perhaps this means that the war will soon be over.'

'Yes, perhaps.' I don't believe that the war will be over soon. But what I believe I can't say to my mother.

'I'd better go and check on Frau Schluck.' My mother stands.

'Should I come?' I ask.

'Give me a few minutes, then perhaps you should come up too.' She nods at me. 'I heard Ludwig come home earlier when you were up in the attic hanging up the washing.'

I swallow. *Ludwig misses me.* 'I will come up soon then.'

Once my mother has left I re-read the letter. My father is sending his love to me, Mutti and the unborn baby. My eyes wander to the family photos on the buffet and I wonder if there will ever be one of the four of us. I check the kitchen clock and watch the minute hand go round and round. My mother has been gone for about ten minutes. Suddenly, I'm uncertain. What if Ludwig doesn't want to see me? I get up, my palm flat on the letter, as though having a silent conversation with it. If Ludwig doesn't want to see me I'll have to deal with it, but that means I have to find out first! I don't want him to be alone if there's devastating news. I want to be there for him!

I leave Vati's letter on the coffee table and go upstairs.

The Schluck's apartment door is ajar and I close it behind me. I find Ludwig at the kitchen table. His back is hunched as though he is in physical pain and his hands are white, hard fists. In front of him are the two letters.

'Ludwig,' I whisper and slide onto the chair next to him. 'What is it? What's wrong?' I can hear Frau Schluck crying in the sitting room. Every now and then my mother says something soothing but the crying doesn't stop.

Ludwig pushes the letters across the table. 'Father has fallen.'

'Oh, Ludwig, I am so sorry.' I touch his wrist and in an instant his hand clamps around mine as though he's been waiting to do that for a long time. Under his touch the last few lonely months fall away, disappear and our lives relink.

'And I ...' Ludwig starts. His voice is hoarse and choked sounding. '... I have been called up.' His face is hollow with disbelief.

The other letter.

It's as though those words, what they mean, are taking everything from me, from us. The news I had been dreading more than anything.

'It can't be true. It can't be. There must be some mistake. You are only just seventeen. And you haven't even finished school!' This had to be wrong.

'Do you think they care?' Ludwig is shouting suddenly, deep anguish lacing his voice. He slams his fist down on the table, once, twice, while his other hand still holds tight around mine. 'They do not care about school and academia any more. They never have. They do not care about people learning, wanting to go to university. All they care about is turning us into soldiers so we can invade countries we have no entitlement to and die in the muck like all the others and the less we think the better. God, how I hate this war, how I hate Hitler, what he's turned Germany into—'

'Ludwig!' Frau Schluck barges in, her face tear-streaked and pale with shock. 'You have to keep your voice down. The whole house can hear you.'

'I'm sorry, Mutti. But it's the truth. And I'm sure I'm not the only one in this building, in this whole damn street, this whole city who thinks exactly like me.'

'That may well be, but there are others, many others, who don't think like you and who will denounce anyone they suspect of anything untoward. And they will do it with a smile on their face.'

Ludwig lets out a bitter laugh. 'So true it is. But have they just been drafted and will they have their life squandered, the life of their father?' he replies. But his voice is much quieter now.

His mother takes a shuddery breath and presses her handkerchief to her mouth to stifle another sob.

'There has to be a way out,' I say when we are alone in the kitchen again. I pick up the call-up notification, looking for an indication that it is all a mistake. 'There has to be!' I repeat, stupefied, numb. I refuse to accept this.

'You mean desertion?' asks Ludwig. He voice is toneless. 'People hang for far less.'

'I know,' I whisper.

'On the other hand,' Ludwig says, glancing over his shoulder to make sure his mother is out of earshot, 'perhaps I'd rather get executed like Hans-Peter, I'd rather die for something I believe in than fight and die for something I condemn.'

'Don't say that. I won't let you do that.' But I also think, what if everyone refused to fight? You can't shoot or imprison millions of men and boys. It's a naïve, idealist thought. And who really knows how many more are willing to fight? What power do we, two kids, have against an overwhelming war machine? All we can do is refuse to be part of it and bear the consequences: a certain death.

'What do we fight for?' Ludwig mutters, as though debating with himself now. 'For Hitler, for victory …' He shakes his head, snorts in disgust. 'So wrong. There will be no victory. There will be a slow, horrendous, torturous end to this war. It's all so wrong!'

I don't know what to say. There is only the feeling that the ground is slowly slipping away beneath me. And there is absolutely nothing I can do about it.

'Do you know what's been happening to the Jews? First the German Jews and now those in the occupied territories?' Ludwig suddenly asks. There is a rawness in his eyes, a burning intensity.

I avoid looking at him. Everyone knows something horrendous is going on but no one really talks about it. People don't care. Or approve. Or are scared. And we are all too busy worrying about ourselves.

'They get murdered.' Ludwig talks so quietly now I can hardly hear him. 'I overheard my father telling my mother the last time he was on leave. He has seen concentration camps the size of cities, out east. They get sent there from all over Europe. They get murdered in extermination camps. Hundreds of thousands, perhaps even millions of men, women and children get murdered there. Jews, Communists, and all the people the Nazis consider inferior, unworthy. Some of them have to work for the German war machine first, and then, when they can't stand up any longer they get sent to the camps and get murdered. Do you understand what all that means? Extermination! Camps built for the sole purpose of murder. The captured territories get *cleansed*. Is that what I'll be fighting for? My father, your father?'

This doesn't make sense. I shake my head. 'No,' I whisper. 'No one should be fighting for that.'

Ludwig lowers his voice even more. 'Do you think after getting rid of all the German Jews the Nazis would allow them to just go on with their lives in those countries we have invaded?' He shakes his head. 'What are we going to do, pretend not to know or not to care? We Germans, unable to put two and two together? I don't think so. Everyone knows. Everyone sees. Everyone's indifferent.'

I don't want something so horrible to be true, though deep down I know that it is. 'But you are not responsible for this, Ludwig,' I say.

'We are all responsible. We are all Germans. We are complicit because we all play our horrible little part in this, we've all been going along, in the Hitler Youth, the BDM, and I'm going to be out there on the front fighting for Germany, for Hitler, for this twisted ideology. Like my father, like your father. Don't you see that it's all connected? It's what we will all be remembered for when all of this is over. Our association with this, that we are responsible for this, that we fought for this, that we were part of this. That we *let* this happen. And this is why we will keep fighting until the bitter end, because we are already too guilty, so what difference does it make!'

'You are right,' I whisper. 'You haven't hurt anyone, I haven't, but we are still part of this unless we make a stand against it. Like Hans-Peter.' But in me there's something that eclipses that principle of courage. It is the will to live, for Ludwig to live. Perhaps I am ashamed of it but it is the truth.

'Have I done anything good? Have I helped anyone? Have I stood up for what I thought is right, fought against something I thought was wrong? No, because I'm a coward,' Ludwig says.

I'm overcome by a sense of helplessness. 'You are not a coward. What could you have done? And if you desert you will get executed,' I say. It is all I can think of at this moment. It is all that matters to me.

'Yes, and how could I do that to my parents? Their son: a deserter, a traitor. Just imagine the shame! The repercussion! At least if I go and fight I have a small chance of coming back.' He lets out a cynical laugh that sounds so much older than he is, that says that he doesn't believe for one second that he will be coming home.

'I don't think your parents would ever be ashamed of you,' I say.

Ludwig shakes his head, overcome.

'You will get training,' I say. 'They'll teach you how to stay alive.'

Ludwig stares at me. 'Lene, they train us to fight and kill. They started training us for it the minute we had to join the Hitler Youth when we were ten years old. They don't care if we live or die as long as the battle is won in the end.'

Impulsively, I lean close and I wrap my arms around Ludwig and put my cheek up against his. I don't care that my mother and Frau Schluck are in the room next door.

'I want you to stay alive,' I whisper. 'I want to live, I want you to live. It's all I want.'

I feel Ludwig's arms holding me, his breath warm and gentle on my skin. And for a moment it is all I am aware of, all I am, all I want, to be like this with Ludwig forever. I want to be without this war that destroys everyone and everything. Ludwig moves closer and his embrace grows tighter. 'I've missed you so much, Lene,' he whispers. 'But these last few weeks I've been thinking that perhaps now you don't want anything to do with me any longer.'

Heat rushes to my face as I soak in the feeling of his body against mine, his smell, his breath touching my skin.

'I want to stay alive and come back. I want to come back to you and to Berlin. It is all I want.' Ludwig shifts away a little and looks at me, his arms still around me. A crooked grin appears on his face. 'I'll just have to shoot the enemy before they shoot me – it's quite simple when you think about it.'

I manage a weak grin as well. 'Simple,' I say and nod, though I find it impossible to picture Ludwig with a rifle or *Panzerfaust* in his hand.

'At least I went to those dreadful Hitler Youth drills these last few months.' Ludwig clears his throat and now takes his hands off my waist. 'They might have been good for something after all.'

'When are you leaving?' I ask.

'I have to report to the barracks at the start of next week. For the training.'

Two days. 'So soon,' I whisper.

'I suppose I'm urgently needed.' The hard, cynical edge has crept back into his voice.

CHAPTER 18

From the moment we step out onto the street, the tram stop is like a force field, mercilessly pulling us in. There is no escape. Such little time remains; soon the tram will take Ludwig away. Minutes are slipping away fast. I try to hold on to them, like I have held on to the precious last few days with Ludwig, trying to shut out the enormity and inevitability of what's looming. I also told Ludwig about Kurt. About my fear that Kurt could have something to do with Ludwig's call up. But he dismissed it in a flash as he'd learnt that most in his class at school had also been mobilised.

'Do you know where you'll be posted, do any of the others know?' I ask as we cross the road underneath the S-Bahn overpass.

Ludwig shakes his head. 'Training and then maybe Flak somewhere or straight to the front. I guess we will all soon find out.'

So that's what 'total war' looks like? Pulling boys out of classrooms, sending them to the front, tens of thousands, perhaps hundreds of thousands of them. Because our leaders think boys can win the war for them. Will Ludwig be sent to the Eastern Front? I remember Kurt's threat. Does he really have influence over who gets sent where?

'Where is your mother?' I ask. 'I thought she would be with us.'

'She couldn't bear coming to the tram. She nearly collapsed when we said our goodbyes. The cruelty of it! Her husband has fallen and now she will lose her son as well.' Ludwig seems to be in a kind of trance.

'Don't say that.' It's a fairly long walk to the tram stop but today it feels like the shortest walk I've ever taken. I reach for Ludwig's hand.

The weather gods are making a mockery of us. The day is glorious. The sky is blue, dotted with frivolous, fluffy clouds. And yet everything is a blur. The sun in the sky, the field grey uniforms everywhere, the shop windows displaying meagre wares, the cinema.

And then we've reached the tram stop and Ludwig just stands there, frozen, one white knuckled hand clasping the straps of his rucksack. His other hand clasping mine.

This is tougher than anything I've ever had to do. There are boys like Ludwig, from our suburb, from his school, waiting for the same tram, probably going to the same barracks, and Ludwig nods at them stony-faced. Some look much like Ludwig: frozen, ash-coloured. Others, I'm guessing the ones who have volunteered, look upbeat and excited. I don't know which is worse.

'I wish that tram would never come,' I whisper.

'But it will,' says Ludwig. 'And if it doesn't I'll have to walk to the barrack. There's no way out of this.'

'Ludwig, stop it now, stop being like this!' I must have shouted because people are turning to look at us. Some understanding, some full of suspicion and disapproval. But it works. Ludwig seems to wake from his trance-like state.

I grab both his hands. I don't care about the other people watching us. My mouth is close to Ludwig's ear. 'You will come back,' I say with more conviction than I've ever mustered in my life. 'I believe that you will come back and if you believe in it too, it will happen. Your life is not lost just yet.'

Ludwig stares at me. The small line has formed on his forehead just above his eyebrow. Then he nods with resolve. 'I will believe in it. I promise. Every single day, out there, that will be my goal. To come home.'

He suddenly pulls me away with urgency, away from the prying eyes, behind a newspaper kiosk. He drops his rucksack on the ground and faces me. The small line on his forehead is still there. I reach out and touch it and I feel Ludwig's head leaning into my hand as though it is the last time he will ever feel a caring touch. Gently I trace over his face with my fingertips, then rest my hand on his shoulder. Faintly, in the distance, carrying over the other city sounds, I can hear the tram approaching.

I close my eyes and it amplifies the feeling of Ludwig's lips on mine. The kiss is soft and warm and sweet and so full of that promise, that promise of a future together. The moment seems fleeting and yet infinite.

Our lips separate.

Ludwig picks up his rucksack. 'I have to go now.'

'I love you, Ludwig,' I say. The feeling had been there with me for so long that I can hardly remember how I felt before it.

'I love you too, Lene. Always have.' He jumps onto the rear platform of the already moving tram and I run alongside it as it gains speed. I run for as long as I can, for once finding the right rhythm, dodging people and traffic. But soon the tram becomes too fast and I have to stop and just stand there. I can still see Ludwig's face. He's smiling and I wave a last goodbye. The tram turns the corner and he is gone.

'Ludwig and Lene,' I whisper, relishing the sound of our names together. The promise they hold.

PART TWO

1946

CHAPTER 19

I'm here again, in my city, Berlin. Broken, blood-sodden, disgraced, conquered, beautiful Berlin. It's May. Almost a year since I left, a year since the war ended. Outside the train window the sameness of rubble and ruins are a never-ending landscape of annihilation. This is my Berlin now.

At last the train pulls into the station.

When I'm on the platform and have both feet firmly planted on that Berlin soil again, Ludwig instantly becomes more real. As though he is still here, like I am again, in my city. The long ago memory of us standing at the tram station is alive, more present, more real, and so is our promise to keep believing in Ludwig's return.

I let the mass of people sweep me down into the city, down the crumbling station steps where my eyes catch on a barefoot man in a tattered German uniform sitting there. An old young man, his insides spilling out of his eyes. I look away. But even though the train was packed with returnees, the image has brought back the moment my father came home this spring, released from an American POW camp. He was also wearing the remnants of his uniform, though stripped of everything that made it distinguishable as German.

Everything was strange. Us, little Gustav, my mother and me, re-united with my father, standing outside a small cottage in a place that held none of our history. A clean slate. My father there like a shadowy imitation of his old self, a civilian suddenly, someone who had been a soldier almost his entire adult life. But nonetheless, it was him. And then, after he'd slept for a long time, he was a little bit less like an imitation.

I walk past the ruined Kaiser Wilhelm Memorial Church and down the Ku'damm. Ruins, fragments of walls, remains of once grand façades of glorious apartment buildings are silent monuments, waiting to be dismantled or, one day, restored. I look up, blinking into the brightness of the day. Half a room hangs in the sky, a petite gilt chair, a bedside table, a rug flapping.

I leave the Ku'damm and turn into the Charlottenburg side streets. Rubble removal and clean-up is underway everywhere. Hopper cars are lined up on tracks and hundreds of women form human chains from the ruins, filling the hopper cars with rubble or hammer mortar off intact, reusable bricks. Neat stacks of perfect bricks are loaded onto the beds of trucks. One drives off purposefully and I feel an irrational surge of something that resembles happiness.

'Lene! We were getting so worried.' Aunt Ilsa hugs me tight. 'How long did it take you to get here?'

I'm not even sure how much time has passed since I left the cottage, walked to the village station and boarded the first of many completely overcrowded trains. 'Around twenty hours, I think.' I suddenly realise how delirious I am. I lean on my aunt, who is bony but familiar. Already, the journey is a blur. Those countless hours I spent waiting for trains at stations I'd never been to before, anxious that I might not be able to get on the packed trains or that I would be stopped, as travel for civilians is still restricted.

'Goodness me, you can hardly stand up and you probably haven't eaten in ages,' says my aunt. Her voice comes to me through a tunnel of tiredness.

I'm almost constantly hungry but I know here in Berlin it's about to get worse. 'I had some bread yesterday,' I say. 'And some potatoes.'

My aunt gives me a slice of bread with a piece of herring, then a shrivelled apple. I wolf everything down, including the pips and the apple core, slumped at the kitchen table. Next thing I know I stagger down the hallway to my cousins' bedroom and fall down on a bed. 'I'll just rest for a little while.' My words are slurred like those of a drunk.

'You poor dear,' Aunt Ilsa says. She sounds far away.

'There is a sack of potatoes in my backpack,' I mumble. 'From my mother.'

The last thing I notice is my aunt removing my shoes. My eyes are already closed and I tumble into the vortex of sleep.

When I wake up it's almost dark outside and I'm covered with a blanket. The apartment is quiet. I sit up and reach for my jacket. In its pocket is a letter I have been carrying with me everywhere for the last two and half years.

Ludwig's only letter to me.

I move closer to the window and, even though I know it by heart, I read it once again, like a ritual, in the remaining light.

23rd of October, 1943

Dear Lene,

The months since I left feel like a whole lifetime of someone else's life. I knew most boys in my unit from school. There are not many of them left.

It is quiet where I am right now. I never thought I'd say this, but I've never felt so glad to be in a cemetery where we are hiding out amongst the headstones. Every night I remember what we talked about that day I left and what you said to me about coming back. Though it is all I want, the truth is, it has been hard to keep believing in it. Here at the front things are pretty much what I thought they would be like.

Only a thousand times worse.

I wish I could be more upbeat but I just can't lie to you. There are too many lies already.

Lene, I would like to write so much more but the light is fading and time is running out. I will try to catch a few hours' sleep in a minute, before the next attack.

I'm thinking of you. I love you. Always and forever.

I promise.

Ludwig

I remember a sensation like sea-sickness in my stomach when I first received the letter which miraculously had made it through the censoring back then.

Alway and forever. How I thought there would be no forever, that Ludwig was saying goodbye. A farewell letter. That's what I thought this letter was.

Time is running out. I will try to catch a few hours of sleep before the next attack. When he was writing those words, Ludwig didn't think he was going to survive the night, the next attack.

And perhaps that's what happened. Because, almost six months later, Ludwig's mother received the notification informing her that Ludwig was missing in action. There's always hope when a notification says 'missing in action', the smallest glimmer, a straw to cling to, a straw that only just keeps you from drowning.

I put the letter back in my pocket, get up and make the bed. Then I open my backpack and carefully slide out another sheet of paper. I smooth it then prop it on the bedside table. It's a drawing my little brother Gustav gave me when I left. Four figures with funny long fingers and wild hair above smiling faces stand in front of a house with disproportionally large flowers in the front yard. Underneath the drawing, my father's handwriting: *Mutti, Vati, Lene und Gustav.* Just that, our names. I smile and adjust the drawing on the bedside table, then walk out into the corridor.

The light is on in my aunt's bedroom and there's someone walking around inside. I knock on the door which is ajar.

'Come in, come in.'

I enter the room expecting my aunt, but instead I find my cousin. For a moment I just stare.

Ophelia is posing in front of the bedroom mirror, turning and twisting her neck, looking at herself from all angles. The floral summer dress she wears is cinched at the waist with a thin belt, the neckline is low, exposing skin that glows pearly white, and she's balancing on high heel, peep-toe shoes.

'Do you think I should go one tighter?' Ophelia asks, indicating her belt. She puckers her lips and pushes her chest out. Her lips are painted bright poppy red and her eyes look dark and seductive, done like a movie star's.

'I don't know,' I say. 'It looks like it's pretty tight already.'

'You think?' Ophelia is unconvinced. I don't think she's really interested in my opinion. She tightens the belt but now her hipbones are protruding through the fabric of the dress and she decides against it. She drops a lipstick into a small handbag, then slings the bag over her arm.

'Are you going out?' I ask.

Ophelia laughs. It sounds tinny and forced. 'Of course I am, silly. What do you reckon? Do I look a treat or what?' One last glance at her reflection.

I nod politely. 'I guess you do.'

I catch my own reflection in the mirror, standing next to her. Two girls, both nineteen years old, couldn't be more different. I look tired and pale, almost grey, in dusty, creased clothes, with limp oily hair. In comparison, Ophelia is a freshly hatched tropical butterfly, her colours too dazzling to be real, the smile on her face too bright.

'Honestly, I don't know why you came back to this dump of a city,' Ophelia says. Her smile darkens. 'We even have to share our apartment with strangers, can you believe it? That's what it has come to. There are three people living in our dining room! And they don't even have the decency to talk to us, treat us as though *we* are the ones who have been taken in.'

I didn't know about the strangers who shared the apartment. But it makes sense, of course, with the shortage of housing. Why should there be an exemption for my aunt? But there's no time to inquire about the others who live here.

'Don't wait up for me!' Ophelia brushes past me and a moment later the apartment door closes behind her.

I walk through the rooms but there doesn't seem to be anyone else home. The dining room door is shut and for a moment I pause and listen, but I can't determine whether the room is empty or if there are people asleep behind the door.

Yes, why did I come back to Berlin, to this ruined, starving city, and alone, without my family who reluctantly let me go? It's a question my parents also asked. For them, this shattered city holds no future. It represents the past they want to forget. They want to start over in that little village near Hanover that was hardly touched by the war.

The opposite is true for me. I had to come back. To delve into the past in order to go on with my life. I will never forget the past. Because the past is never just about the past, it's always also about the present, and the future too.

CHAPTER 20

The next morning there is a packet of Camel cigarettes, a block of Hershey's chocolate and half a pound of coffee on the kitchen table. Theo is ogling the goods.

'Welcome back, Lene,' he says very seriously, his eyes only diverting for a fraction of a second.

He endures my hugs and grimaces when I plant kisses on both his cheeks. 'Am I taller than my cousin Gustav?' he asks, wiping his face with the back of his hand.

'You are six, three years older than Gustav, so of course you are taller,' I say.

Relief washes over his face.

'The kids at school are picking on him.' My aunt emerges from the walk-in pantry. 'They say he's short.'

'You look just fine to me,' I say. 'There will always be kids who look for someone they can pester and harass.'

Theo picks up the block of chocolate and starts to peel off the wrapper.

'Theo!' My aunt shakes her head and he quickly puts the chocolate back on the table.

'Where is everyone else?' I ask.

'Gertie is trying to get eggs and bread. She's probably gone to the Tiergarten.'

I nod. The black market had been thriving even before the war ended.

'Ophelia is still in bed.' Aunt Ilsa pauses and her lips curl as though she's tasted something bitter. She doesn't mention the strangers who live in her dining room.

I remember Ophelia in front of the mirror last night. Her brassy brightness. My eyes return to the goods on the table. American cigarettes and American chocolate.

'Ophelia has an American boyfriend,' Theo pipes up.

'Theo, be quiet!' my aunt reprimands him.

'But it's true,' he insists. 'It's her second American boyfriend. She didn't like the first one any more because …'

My aunt shuffles Theo out of the kitchen. 'Enough of that, I said, it is none of your business,' she says under her breath. 'Another word and there will be absolutely none of that chocolate for you. Understood?'

'Ouch, that hurts,' Theo says and lets out a pretend squeal. 'Why isn't Lene allowed to know? And I hardly ever get any chocolate anyway.'

'Scoot off and get ready for school.' My aunt slides the goods out of sight into the buffet drawer which she locks. 'Lene, can you wake up Ophelia, please? Or she will sleep away the whole day again.'

It's dark in Ophelia's bedroom. I quietly cross the room and draw back the curtains.

'No need to be quiet. I'm already awake.' Ophelia scrunches up her face and squeezes her eyes shut as daylight pours into the room. Her hair is a tangled mess and her face looks pale and puffy. There are black smudges all around her eyes and traces of red lipstick smeared around her mouth.

'God, don't you hate mornings?' she says and yawns.

'Not particularly,' I say. At least it's a morning without war.

'The beginning of another day which will be just as depressing as the one gone by. I like the night. At least everything disappears then,' Ophelia declares. 'Everything, including myself.'

I don't want to start on the wrong foot with Ophelia. I want to start afresh, leave behind what has happened between us, what I thought of her back then. 'Was it a late night?' I ask.

Ophelia laughs. It's the same dark, put-on laugh I heard yesterday. 'Who cares about time? I certainly don't,' she says.

I give up. 'Are you getting up then? Your mother said Gertie might be able to get some eggs and bread.'

'Now, isn't Gertie a good girl going to the Tiergarten!' Ophelia swings her legs out of bed and stretches. 'She'd better be careful. We wouldn't want her tainted by the seediness and immorality of the place.'

Ophelia is still wearing the lacy slip she must have had on under her low-cut dress last night. 'Another day in beautiful Berlin,' she mutters. She rubs her eyes with her fists and for a moment she looks like the girl from our childhood who has fallen asleep in dress-up clothes. But then she reaches for the packet of cigarettes on the bedside table and lights one. As she deeply inhales the smoke, lines around her mouth appear and make her look much older; the illusion of youth and innocence is gone.

Ophelia repeats the question she asked me last night. 'So why did you come back to Berlin, Lene? Surely life is better in that little rural paradise where your parents are resettling.'

'It's hardly paradise, but, yes, things are better there for my parents. They have a nice place to stay with a garden and my father has found work.'

'And you?'

'I belong here. And I have to find out what happened to Ludwig.'

'Ludwig?'

'An old friend. The boy who lived on the third floor in our building.'

'I didn't know you had a boyfriend.'

I blush. 'He isn't really my boyfriend.' He is so much more than that.

'So, what happened to this Ludwig? No, wait, let me guess. He fell in Russia?'

'Missing in action on the Eastern Front.'

Ophelia rolls her eyes. 'Same thing. Lene, listen, you've got to let go of the past and move on. He's not coming back. None of them are. There are graveyards as big as Berlin over there,' she vaguely points east, 'with hundreds of thousands of soldiers buried there. Hundreds of thousands more whose exact fate, whether dead or alive, will never be known.'

She comes over to me, cigarette in hand. She swipes my hair back and studies my face, then grabs a lipstick from the dressing table. Before I can stop her, she has dabbed bright red colour on my lips. 'We can spruce you up a bit and find you a new boyfriend in no time. One who is alive.'

I slap her hand away. 'No!' How dare she write off Ludwig like he is no more than a name, a number, a past crush who is easily replaced!

Ophelia shrugs. 'Fine.' For a moment we stare at each other. Contempt glimmers in her eyes. I wonder what my eyes display at that moment. I look away.

'You just hold on to the past then, like everyone else in this city,' says Ophelia. 'Like all those prematurely aged mothers, the widows who hold on to the hope that their sons or husbands have, by some stroke of luck, survived. But it won't do you any good,' she says. 'It's time to move on. There's a new era on the horizon and it's time for living.'

But there's little expression in her eyes or her face now, just the pale, puffy mask of it. The contempt in her eyes is gone, they are just blank, like she herself is not alive at all. Ophelia plonks back down on the bed, pulling the quilt tight around her shoulders.

'God, I'm so sick of the same old stories,' she mutters. 'And everyone's got another version of the same sad tale.'

'You have to get up,' I say. I turn and leave the room, wondering if there is a germ of truth in my cousin's words.

Suddenly the thought of returning to my old neighbourhood and contacting Ludwig's mother terrifies me. Was I holding on to something that held no hope whatsoever?

Breakfast is meagre. But we have coffee, *real* coffee, its smell and taste intoxicating. Gertie slices the bread and spreads gauzy smears of margarine.

'Thank you.' I take the slice that Gertie hands me.

'Couldn't get any eggs,' Gertie says and bites into her own slice of bread, her eyes closed.

Gertie is seventeen now but she has remained a full head shorter than Ophelia. She wears her hair in a short boy's haircut and her violet blue eyes seem even more striking than I remember them – they have taken on a permanently hard and determined expression.

The French doors to the kitchen balcony are open and in the backyard the chestnut tree has visibly grown since the last time I was here almost a year ago. The morning sun makes the umbrella of leaves look rich and green, as though they were edible.

When I came here with my mother and brother, after the *Kapitulation*, when the battle in the city was over, the tree was singed, dusty and wilted, and I thought that it was a miracle it had even survived. That it didn't explode in a rain of sawdust, didn't burn to a stump or be felled for firewood. Just like this building, with the glorious marble, mirrors and gilt in the foyer downstairs and vast apartments, is still here. That it was somehow, by some stroke of luck, spared and has survived almost undamaged, and with it my cousins and aunt. In fact, I think it's a miracle that we are all still here. Me, my mother, my brother Gustav, especially my father. What if there hadn't been a pilot who took pity on my father's unit and flew them out of that encirclement at Kharkov against orders and saved them from sure death on the Eastern Front?

Ophelia comes in. She has thrown on a dressing-gown but hasn't bothered cleaning her face. The black smudges of mascara are still there. They are like charred skin under her eyes. She wolfs down a slice of bread with margarine then goes out on the balcony where she lights another cigarette. Smoke drifts into the kitchen.

'I wish you wouldn't smoke all those cigarettes yourself,' Gertie says. 'We need them for bartering.'

'Oh, shut up, Gertie,' Ophelia replies, but there is little malice in her voice.

Aunt Ilsa doesn't reprimand Ophelia for her language, just looks away as though she hasn't heard. She turns to me instead. 'Lene, will you register for rubble clearing?'

'I will do it today.'

'Good.' She nods shortly. I know that it's an imposition that I came here to stay with them and the last thing I want is to be a burden. Doing reconstruction work and receiving the highest rations is what I'll have to do to earn my keep.

'Can you take Theo to school for me beforehand? It's quite a walk now as the local school was destroyed.'

'Of course.'

'Why does Lene have to take him? Can't Ophelia do it for a change?' Gertie snaps. 'She does nothing all day. Nothing! Doesn't lift a finger! Never mind that reconstruction work is meant to be mandatory!'

'Aren't you forgetting that I did get us the chocolate and the cigarettes, and that coffee that you are slurping at this very moment?' Ophelia replies from the balcony. 'If I hadn't managed to get any of this we would be doing it a lot tougher.'

'Oh, well done, but it's not like you have to work for it like the rest of us! We work like dogs in the ruins all day. All you do is smile and pout and preen, and who knows what else?'

The back of my aunt's hand whips across Gertie's face. There's a brief moment of complete stillness, of shock. Gertie doesn't move, hasn't even flinched. A red mark spreads across her cheek. Gertie's face hardens.

'Take Theo to school, Lene.' My aunt's voice trembles. 'And you, Gertie, apologise to your sister. Now!'

'No! Why should I apologise for telling how it is? I'm allowed to do that now, I can say whatever I want.' And then she looks straight at Ophelia who stands in the balcony doorway, her face waxen and dead looking. She's silent, her eyes downcast, enduring the assault, Gertie's deliberate cruelty.

And Gertie isn't finished yet. 'The days when we had to watch our mouths and had to control our thoughts so we wouldn't risk getting reported and executed are over, and thank God for that!' she hisses at her sister.

I take Theo by the hand and we scramble out of the kitchen. Behind the dining room doors, I can hear people moving about.

'Why does Ophelia have to pout and preen and what does that even mean?' Theo asks me on our way to his school.

I blush, horrified, and quickly look over my shoulder to check that there's no one walking right behind us. 'That was just a silly thing your sister said. She didn't mean anything by it.'

Theo isn't fobbed off that easily. 'But what does it mean? It has to mean something because why would Gertie say it otherwise?'

'I'm not sure,' I lie. I'm mortified that I have to have this conversation with my six-year-old cousin.

'And it has to be something bad or Mutti wouldn't have slapped Gertie,' Theo ascertains. 'She never ever slaps us,' he adds. 'Pouting doesn't sound that hard,' he continues to think out loud. 'And she gets all that stuff for something that easy?'

Oh God, why won't he shut up! I speed towards the school, following the students walking around us in the same direction.

'If *you* don't know what it means, I can ask my teacher,' Theo offers. 'She knows everything. And then I can tell you.'

'Don't you dare! If you do, your mother will slap you too, I can guarantee it.'

'Geez, don't get your knickers in knot,' Theo replies.

'Theo! Talk to me like this again and I will personally smack you.'

'Pffft, you wouldn't.'

'Try me.'

'Oh, fine.'

He's right, though, I would never lay a hand on him.

'You can drop me off at the gate,' Theo says when we arrive at school. 'I'm old enough to walk to school by myself anyway. I don't know why you had to take me.'

'Because it's too far,' I answer weakly. 'And too dangerous with all the ruins everywhere.'

'I don't care about the ruins. They've always been there and they are great fun to play in.' He trots off through the gate into the yard without looking back, muttering: 'Girls are so stupid. I wish I had brothers and not sisters.'

But if Gertie and Ophelia had been boys, I can't help but think, they most likely wouldn't be alive now. Chances are they would have become cannon fodder. Or boys of violence. For a moment I remain at the school gate and watch Theo disappear into the throngs of happily chatting six- and seven-year-olds.

CHAPTER 21

The site I get deployed to is in one of Charlottenburg's neighbouring suburbs, Wilmersdorf, and in its final stages of being cleared. I take my designated spot in one of the human chains of women and spend the next hours passing buckets filled with rubble down the chain. It's the same motion over and over and the bucket comes down the chain more and more slowly as the sun rises higher in the sky and our arms tire. We work mostly in silence. I think we simply don't have the energy to talk.

Human chains just like ours wind all the way up and down the street. There are hundreds of us in this street alone, but in the light of the task at hand we are no more than a few ants in the midst of a giant ruined anthill. A city of ruined anthills. The destruction is even worse in many other parts of Berlin. Still, even clearing and rebuilding this single street seems like an insurmountable task. A few men wearing tool belts and overalls are busy doing surveying and have started repairing mains on the road and the cleared sites. Another small group of tradesmen are replacing timber frames and glass in one of the less damaged buildings.

As blisters start forming on my palms and fingers and my arms and shoulders start burning and throbbing, the bucket starts slipping from my grip. When I drop it, rubble spills out as it hits the ground and everyone stops, grateful for the unexpected interruption.

Once I notice an American camera crew slowly driving past in a jeep, filming us, and I wonder if this footage will be shown in a newsreel in the cinemas in America. The thought is discomforting and makes me feel ashamed.

At midday, we are allowed to take a brief break. It's hot and dusty and the piles of smashed concrete and rubble radiate heat. There's not a tree or shrub anywhere, so I sit down in the shade of a hopper car. I'm completely unprepared for the punishing work in the ruins. My eyes feel gritty with dust, my head is throbbing and my face is sunburned. I'm famished, already completely exhausted, and I don't have any food. Yet, that tentative feeling of near happiness eclipses all of that.

'There's a fountain and a working water pump one street over.'

The girl who sits down next to me is about my age.

'It's right on the square. You can't miss it.'

'Thanks,' I say. I'm incredibly thirsty but so exhausted that I just want to sit down and not move for a while.

'Here.' The girl hands me her thermos. 'I can refill it later.'

'Thank you.' I greedily take a big gulp of water and hand the thermos back.

'First day?' the girl asks.

I nod.

'I'm Heidi.'

'Lene.' I glance at her. Unlike me, she's perfectly prepared for the work in the ruins, and the heat. She wears a lightweight, faded orange and green cotton dress which is of good quality but has seen better days, a scarf is tied around her hair, and on her feet are sturdy leather lace-up hiking boots. Her arms and legs are brown from the sun.

Heidi is beautiful. It is plain obvious despite the unflattering scarf and the layer of dust on her face. Her eyes are dark grey like the North Sea on a stormy day. Her neck is long and elegant and her cheekbones high and defined. Her lips are almost as red as Ophelia's last night, only Heidi's look like they are that colour naturally.

Heidi now takes off her scarf and shakes out thick curls the colour of oak. 'Look,' she says and reaches into the pocket of her dress. She pulls out a pair of sunglasses. 'Aren't they amazing?' She puts them on.

The sunglasses are shaped like a cat's eyes with dark brown lenses and a gold metal frame. They look like they came from a world far away, like a movie set or the French Riviera.

'That way I don't have to squint my eyes, which will give me wrinkles. And they look pretty glamorous too. Not with this outfit of course.'

I can't help but laugh. Even though her comment is slightly grotesque. There's absolutely nothing glamorous about where we are and what we are doing. And getting wrinkles is the last thing anyone seems to be worried about.

She pushes her sunglasses up onto her forehead and winks at me with a smile. 'No point in being gloomy all the time. Things are what they are.'

'I guess,' I say.

'When we first started clearing the site,' Heidi chatters on, 'we were told that there were still dozens of bodies buried under every single ruin in the street. They hadn't been able to get to them. Apparently they got bombed at the very end of it all, in March or April '45.'

There's something slightly odd about the chatty manner Heidi talks about this.

I nod. 'I remember those bombings.' It's not something I will ever forget. 'They seemed to go on nonstop, weeks on end. We didn't leave the cellar or air-raid shelter for days and days.' I pause. 'It's all a bit of a blur, though,' I then add quickly before my mind can take me back to that time.

Heidi looks at me with a strange, somewhat bewildered expression. 'Right,' she says. Then she is silent for a moment. 'I'm sorry. I shouldn't have brought it up.' She puts her hand on my arm. 'I guess one gets desensitised doing this job for so many months. Don't worry, we probably won't find any more bodies on this site.'

'You don't have to apologise. Everyone knows the facts,' I say. In the end, when there were nonstop bombings, and then when the Russians stood at the gates of Berlin and the battle for Berlin roared around us, there were dead everywhere, civilian and soldiers, young and old. Everyone in the city has been living with the dead.

'Some talk about those facts, others don't. I, for one, believe that talking about things is healthier than bottling it all up,' Heidi keeps on. She shakes her head as though suddenly realising something. 'Oh, just listen to me.'

'It's all right,' I say. It's true, I don't mind talking.

'I've applied to get into a medicine course at the University of Berlin,' Heidi says. 'I guess that explains it, doesn't it? I'm planning on specialising in psychology. Though now I'm having second thoughts. I think I might do neurology instead.'

I feel wave of envy. Once, I had planned to go to university too. But by the end of 1943 there simply was no school any more. It was obliterated and we just tried to survive. It was a long shot anyway, me going to university. Now I would probably never get a degree as I was still three years away from sitting the school leaving exam that would have allowed me to study at university. It seems like an unrealistic ambition from a different life now. I wonder how Heidi managed to finish school.

Heidi looks at me with almost clinical interest. 'Are you all right? You seem off with the fairies suddenly.'

I'm weighing up whether or not to share my thoughts. I search for the right words, somehow feeling comfortable with this girl I've only just met. She's right, mostly people just bottle things up and want to forget, as though nothing has ever happened in this, our country, even though we all know about all the things that have happened, the things we were part of. And the evidence is all around us. And each day the papers report an avalanche of newly uncovered horrors. How insignificant my own small aspirations are compared to all of it. How unimportant they seem now in the light of everything.

The supervisor calling out to us interrupts my thoughts. Our break is over and we must get on with the work.

As we walk back and take up our posts again, Heidi says: 'Perhaps we can talk some other time.'

'Sure.'

As she smiles at me, I see the kindness in her eyes, but also a glimpse of something else for a moment, something that is sad and painful through and through.

Heidi quickly puts her sunglasses back on, obscuring her eyes with the dark lenses.

When we finish work in the late afternoon I look for Heidi but can't see her anywhere. I crave talking to her. I ask one of the other women if they've seen her, but she tells me that Heidi has already left. I turn to leave but there's an unexpected hand on my shoulder.

It's Heidi. 'See you tomorrow, Lene.'

I smile. 'Bye, Heidi. See you tomorrow.' And suddenly, with Heidi there, the prospect of clearing rubble in the ruins every day seems less daunting.

On the way back home I stop at the water pump. When it's my turn I gulp down cold handfuls of water, filling my empty stomach with it. I wash my face and splash cold water on my sunburned neck and arms. I sit down on the crumbling wall of the dry fountain for a moment, looking around, pausing, letting it sink in that I'm back in Berlin.

Many of the buildings facing the square only have a few battle scars, and if I don't let my eyes wander too far and ignore the destroyed shrubs and flowerbeds and smashed sculptures, it looks almost like it did before the war.

Almost.

When an open jeep with half-a-dozen American GIs drives past behind a half-track, the soldiers whistle and shout greetings at me and the other women and girls standing by the water pump.

Some of the girls laugh and wave back, returning their greetings. I look away. I have no interest in getting an American boyfriend.

I get home at the same time as Gertie. Like me, she's dust covered, sweaty and red from sunburn.

'Look,' she says and opens the bag she's carrying. 'Eggs.' She carefully takes them out and places them in a bowl.

Five beautiful brown eggs. Large ones too.

'Four cigarettes for an egg. It's absolute insanity!' Gertie says.

After a dinner of fried potatoes and eggs, I wash the dishes while Theo sits at the kitchen table, practising his alphabet. Suddenly he interrupts his careful efforts and glances up at me as though something important has just crossed his mind. I just know what that might be. I finish the dishes in a hurry, hang the tea towel out on the balcony to dry and leave the kitchen. I have no desire to continue the conversation we had this morning on the way to school!

My arms and shoulders ache and I feel every single muscle in them. Blisters cover my hands. I'm bone-tired. It's only eight o'clock, not even dark yet, but I kick off my shoes and stretch out on the bed.

In the semi-state before sleep I think I see Ludwig, tangible and real, in the twilight of the room.

CHAPTER 22

The next morning, I dig the 1941 Berlin phone directory out of the hallway table next to the now useless telephone. I open the directory under the letter 'Z', trawl down the columns of names and scribble down addresses on a tiny piece of scrap paper which I tuck into my jacket pocket next to Ludwig's letter.

I leave the apartment together with Gertie, but this morning I'm not heading to the site in Wilmersdorf. I hadn't planned on telling anyone where I'm going, but at the last moment I change my mind.

'Gertie, wait.'

'What?' Gertie turns around impatiently. She doesn't want to be held up.

'I'm going back to my old apartment. I have to visit someone there. It's important.'

'To find out about this Ludwig?' She pauses. 'Ophelia told me about him.'

I nod. 'Yes.' That and someone else if I find the strength for it.

'Be careful. And make sure you are back before dark,' Gertie warns me. 'Remember, things are different in the Soviet sector.'

I nod. 'Please don't tell your mother where I'm going.'

'Why should I? She's got enough on her plate as it is. She doesn't need any more worries,' Gertie says curtly, already walking off, full of aim and purpose. It's clear that she thinks that trying to find out about Ludwig is a frivolous waste of time.

Getting on the train feels like getting into a time machine. So many times I have made this trip across the city. But it is so different this time. The train slowly rattles along eastwards through Berlin, swaying slightly. As it emerges from a tunnel I remember how I used to love the train going along this particularly narrow viaduct between houses. I would catch a glimpse inside the apartments, before the war, before the black outs. In winter, in the early evening, lights had just been switched on but curtains hadn't been drawn yet, and I would see families sitting down at dining tables, a woman and children in a kitchen, a student at a desk. In my mind's eye, I can still see them, those apartments and the people in them.

This city is full of the ghosts of the premature dead, ghosts of people whose lives were cheap and meant nothing to those who squandered them. Ludwig might be one of those ghosts; I'm scared of what I might find out.

Around me, on the train, people are facing away from the windows. They are not new to the city again, they don't see what I see. I look at the men, trying to read their faces, the few, amongst the women and children. One is sitting across from me, absorbed in today's paper. The Trials are on the front page again. So are the quarrels about the shared administration of Berlin between the Western Allies and the Soviets. Tensions between them are rising. The fear that the city will fall under the Communist regime after all has everyone in its grip.

I change trains. Soon I will be leaving the Western Allies' sector.

When we are below ground again the train abruptly slows and halts in the middle of nowhere. We sit in the dark and wait for a few long minutes before the train starts moving again. But we have to get off one stop before the Potsdamer Platz terminus. The line ends because of the reconstruction work on the tracks and shafts. We are told to disembark.

I climb the station steps into daylight. I blink, dazed, at the ruins, the crumbling buildings, the empty spaces, the strangely uniform tall rubble mounds, the paths zigzagging through them. The ruins and the dust make everything look unfamiliar and the same. Everything is the same strange rubble colour. With many streets not passable, I've got no idea what the shortest way from here to Alexanderplatz is, if there's another underground or S-Bahn that's operating. Feeling rattled, I make my way through the crowds milling about in what I think is the right direction.

Ahead of me a focal point emerges. The blackened hull of the Reichstag, the skeleton of its collapsed dome, comes into view. It looks so pitiful, and yet the old building exudes a solidity, a pride, even from a distance. I'm drawn to the Reichstag even though I know I should turn right about where I am now.

Evidence of the ferocious battle that took place here just over a year ago is still everywhere. Rusting barrels of Flak guns point skywards, burned-out half-tracks lie tipped on their sides. The wasteland nearby has been turned into communal farmland and there are people tending to it. Beyond, the Spree river glistens in the sun. Children play on the sandy banks and bathe in the shallows.

I approach the desolate Reichstag building which hasn't been used for its purpose for so many years now, ever since that fateful, dubious fire that destroyed it in 1933, long before the war, paving the way for one man alone to hold all the power in the palm of his hand.

Parts of the ruined front of the building have been fenced off. A few people are milling about. I, too, stop in front of the broken portal steps. The façade towers over me, blackened, scarred and bruised but not destroyed. I look up, and above that once grand entrance, the inscription is still there, put there decades ago by the *Kaiser* in the middle of another war, another time. The metal cast letters are blackened but otherwise hardly damaged. They are still legible.

'Dem Deutschen Volke' – To the German People.

Look what we have done. Do we even deserve to have a parliament, to run our own country again?

I turn the corner of the building where it's suddenly deserted, and walk along the side, as though in a small way seizing it for myself. I go right up close to it, stop and touch the blackened bullet and artillery-riddled masonry, wanting for the building to come back to life again.

Where I am, the wall is covered all over in Cyrillic words. The footprints of the Russian soldiers who conquered the city and took the Reichstag. With my fingertips, I trace a short message, wondering what it says.

'"Stalingrad – Berlin",' an unfamiliar voice says behind me.

I spin around and my eyes catch on a man standing atop a pile of rubble mashed in with ash, rubbish and clumps of earth.

A Soviet soldier.

'"Stalingrad – Berlin", is saying there,' he repeats in broken German. He leaps down from the rubble mound and lands right in front of me. Dust flies.

I take a step back but there's only the wall behind me.

The soldier on the other hand doesn't move; he stands right in the middle of the narrow path where he landed, his feet apart: the stance of a victor. I try not to meet his eyes. The rough masonry is pressing into my shoulder blades; my heart is pounding.

Gertie's words are echoing in my ears. *Things are different in the Soviet sector.* Of course they are. Everyone remembers what it was like when the Red Army surged into Berlin, how it all belonged to them until the Western Allies arrived.

I am not actually in the Soviet sector now, though. But there's no one else close by. Only the children on the river banks and the people tending the potato fields.

'You understand?' the Soviet soldier asks me. 'You understand meaning?' He still doesn't move.

I'm compelled to look up into his face. He's young. Older than me, but still young. The rank insignia on his uniform tells me he's probably an officer, which explains why he is allowed to leave the Soviet sector. I force my eyes to meet his.

'Yes.' I nod. 'I understand what it means.'

Two words, the names of two cities, his city and mine, both in ruins now. First his, then mine.

He acknowledges with a nod what I said. 'Good,' he replies. 'Not forget that.' He points at himself and then at me. 'Both we not forget that.' Then he turns around and strolls away, trailing blue cigarette smoke.

I'm running, but my heart is drumming in my chest and my legs feel gelatinous, forcing me to slow to a walk. I suck in sharp breaths. I'm still shaking from the encounter with the Soviet soldier. And I have wasted so much time. It seemed like minutes, but the sun is high up in the sky and I realise I must have spent hours staring at the Reichstag, walking around it, touching it. And now it's well past noon.

I get on the S-Bahn near Alexanderplatz and collapse on a grimy seat. The jelly feeling spreads from my legs to the rest of my body and I'm glad that I'm sitting down. I wipe my sweat-slippery hands on my less-than-clean skirt, but it doesn't help much. The jelly feeling gets worse the closer I get to my old neighbourhood.

What am I about to find out?

The ruins and battle damages are much like I remember them, still hardly touched by clean-up activity and reconstruction work, and when I walk through the rubble down my street it is as though I never left. There it is, the building I used to live in, the building Ludwig used to live in. Most of the balconies have been blown off, the façade is pitted, windows are boarded up and the roof has caved in or is partially blown off.

I climb the stairs, and stop outside the makeshift door of our old apartment which was barely habitable when we left. There was a gaping hole in the outside wall where my room used to be and no glass in any of the windows; the furniture was smashed and most of our belongings were taken when the apartment was ransacked by Russian soldiers while we were hiding in the public air-raid shelter.

On the third floor, I lean on the Schluck family's apartment door and knock and knock, keeping my eyes closed. I'm not prepared for what I might find out and I'm not prepared for being here again. But I will never be prepared.

The door suddenly swings open and I stumble into the flat, collapsing into Frau Schluck's arms, hugging her.

'Lene!'

Tears claw at my throat. 'I'm so sorry for barging in on you like this out of the blue,' I burst out, struggling to talk. Eventually I regain my composure and I let go of Frau Schluck who hasn't stopped hugging me tight.

'Don't apologise, Lene. I've been thinking of you a lot,' she says. 'How is your mother and little Gustav?'

'They are all right. My father has come home.'

'God bless him.'

We sit down. Frau Schluck is still clasping my hand. She knows what I am about to ask.

There's nothing else but that one question.

'Ludwig?' I say. My voice sounds hoarse. 'Is there any news?'

Frau Schluck sinks away, eyes looking but not seeing me any longer.

'I keep inquiring,' she finally says, 'about whether he could have been captured by the Soviets and is detained in a camp somewhere. But the Soviets are not cooperating with the inquiries about prisoners of war. The Red Cross is trying to trace him. It can take many months, if not years, they say. There are so many missing in action, like Ludwig, hundreds of thousands. Most are simply presumed dead. I also tried contacting his commanding officer, but he fell.' She chokes, tearing up. 'I'm sorry, Lene. I know this is not what you wanted to hear. I really don't know if there's any hope.'

'I'm so sorry too,' I whisper.

'There's no one left to ask,' Frau Schluck says. 'Most of the boys from our borough are gone. They were all mobilised when Ludwig was. All those clever boys in his class who could have done anything. Instead …'

'There was no choice,' I say. But many, then and even later in 1944 and 1945, didn't go reluctantly. Many still believed in it all like a religion that had been drummed into them for more than a decade, prepared to fight and die for Hitler and final victory, thinking that they would forever be remembered as heroes if they did. Yes, the truth is that they didn't have a choice, whether they believed in it or not, and neither did Ludwig. The truth is also that there is always a choice, even when, in the end, the choices we make might make little or no difference. Does it matter that we didn't want to go and fight but still did, whether we believed in final victory or not?

I remember the last time I sat at this table. With Ludwig. I remember his despair about courage and how he wanted to be executed for something he believed in rather than fight for something he abhorred. I think of Hans-Peter whose execution we witnessed. An extraordinary boy who opposed Hitler and whose violent killing was used to teach us a lesson.

'Those boys we lost, they could have done so many things with their lives. They could have had a life, could have had families, some might have even gone to university. Like Ludwig wanted to. Ludwig could have done anything. Such a waste. And what for? Look at us now. We are in ruins. Look what they've done to us, the Americans, the British, and the Russians.'

Self-pity.

'Did they have to raze our cities to the ground like this?' Ludwig's mum asks.

'I don't know,' I say. 'Perhaps not, perhaps there might have been another way. But perhaps it was necessary to liberate us,' I say.

I'm silent for a moment, unsure if I should say out loud to Ludwig's mother, who is suffering so much at this moment, what I think. But I do.

'What about the other cities, those cities to the east we invaded, why did we raze them to the ground *first* without mercy?' I whisper. Yes, we are in ruins and we are allowed to feel misery and sadness, but should we allow ourselves to feel only sorry for ourselves, to let that misery and sadness turn into victimhood? Germany was the aggressor.

'I didn't make those decision, Lene. Neither did you.' Frau Schluck pats my hand. 'Nothing is ever as clear cut and black and white as people want it to be.'

'No, it isn't.' In the eyes of the world we are all guilty.

'I'm not an educated woman, Lene. But I know one thing which we mustn't forget, something you are too young to remember. Hitler and the Nazis took advantage of a loophole in our constitution to dismantle democracy. And they were not voted into power by the majority of Germans.'

I nod and ask for a pencil and a piece of paper. I write down my aunt's address. 'If you hear anything,' I say, 'Or … if Ludwig should …' I can't finish the sentence. Saying it out loud reinforces the unlikeliness of it. I don't have to anyway. 'Please let me know. Anything.'

I push the piece of paper across the table and get up.

'Stay, Lene. Please.'

'I can't.' I feel void, like my insides have been ransacked. But somewhere, somehow, I manage to find some filament of hope and cling to it for dear life.

The moment I leave the building I get the feeling that I'm being watched. The feeling attaches itself to me like a ghoul. I shake it off, thinking that it's just the familiarity of the place, every street, every corner, every building so saturated with the past, everything steeped in memories. I keep glancing back over my shoulder though I can't see anything unusual, just people going about their business, children playing in the rubble, people queuing for food, chains of people clearing rubble.

I'm walking in the opposite direction now, to an S-Bahn station in the neighbouring borough, from where Frau Schluck has told me I can catch a train that will get me almost all the way back home to Charlottenburg.

I'm almost there when I hear footsteps right behind me, so close I can feel them on my skin. I spin around, unable to restrain myself any longer.

I draw in a sharp breath as time collapses. The recognition is like a punch in my gut. 'I guess old habits die hard,' I say. My voice is icy and it sounds exactly the way I feel.

'I wasn't sure that it was really you.' The lie comes out of his mouth effortlessly.

'Of course you knew.'

For some reason this makes him laugh. He relaxes and hooks one hand into his trouser pocket. 'You haven't changed, Lene.'

I'm gradually recovering from the shock of seeing him and rage starts to gather like a red-hot wave, making me seethe. 'You haven't changed either, Kurt. And that's not a good thing.' My teeth feel as though they are about to crack I'm clenching them that hard.

'Look at us,' Kurt says. 'This must be fate. I guess we are just meant for each other after all. Did you come looking for me, is that why you came back here?'

'I'm trying to find out what happened to Ludwig.'

'Ludwig!' He laughs in my face. 'He's gone, Lene. Get over him.'

My anger and fury laces with such a powerful loathing for Kurt; I never thought I'd be capable of feeling anything so ferocious. The taste of bile sloshes around in my mouth. 'I wish you were gone instead. In fact, that was my only thought whenever I thought of you – that you were dead.'

'The best always survive,' Kurt replies.

'Those in the SS! Ruthless Hitler Youth leaders!'

'That's exactly what I'm saying. Only the cream of the crop survived.' He's suddenly uneasy, glancing around nervously.

'What's the matter, Kurt? Don't want anyone to know about your past?' I stare at him, overcome by the bitter taste in my mouth.

It looks like I've hit the nail on the head. Kurt changes his tune. He's still a manipulator. 'I guess I was just lucky,' he says. The hardness in his face lessens. 'Oh, Lene, come on, let's forget about the past. That's all finished. Let's start afresh. What do you say?'

Finished? His audacity is like another insult. It might be finished for him. But I will never forget what he did to Ludwig and me. What he did to Hans-Peter, to his family. And I know how close Ludwig came to being executed as well that afternoon in 1942. The unfairness of it! Ludwig gone, perhaps buried somewhere in the muck of the Eastern Front, and Kurt here, chasing after me as though the last few years never happened.

I look in his face, into those green-flecked poisonous eyes. 'You and me,' I say calmly, 'are never going to happen. Even if you were the last person on the planet.'

For a short moment he seems taken aback, almost hurt by my bluntness. And his expression makes me wickedly happy.

But then, his face changes, and goes from relaxed to hard again. 'Don't fool yourself, Lene,' he says coolly.

I turn around and walk away. He doesn't follow me this time. When I look back over my shoulder he's still standing in the same spot, watching me. But when another jeep with Soviet soldiers approaches, he furtively slinks away.

'You bastard,' I mutter under my breath.

Suddenly, the past is alive, as though it happened yesterday, and I know with an acute certainty what I have to do before I get on the train. I have to see Hans-Peter's family. We didn't contact them back then out of fear, but it would be wrong to leave it any longer. The rage of seeing Kurt has given me a boost of strength, of resolve, so I pull out the list of addresses from my jacket pocket.

When I get to the first address there's no building, only ruins and rubble. My heart sinks. But then I spot a makeshift noticeboard: notes stuck to an intact section of the brick wall. Relieved that some or all who used to live here have survived the bombing, I look for the Zoller name amongst the new addresses. It's there! And their forwarding address matches the second one I copied down from the phone directory this morning. My guess is they moved in with other family members, like most who got bombed.

Another jeep with Soviet soldiers drives past as I make my way there. They don't wave or call out greetings, but I can feel their eyes seizing me. They speed past without slowing and I exhale deeply. Another encounter with a Soviet soldier might not end as well as it did this morning. It is a risk, but one I have to take. It's already late in the afternoon and I remember Gertie's warning to be back before dark; I need to hurry.

I walk fast, just stopping short of running, which would draw attention. When I arrive at a grey working-class tenement block, much like the one I used to live in, not too far from where my old school used to be, I let out a sigh of relief. It still stands and so do many in this street – badly damaged, pitted from shells and bullets, most windows gone, but upright nevertheless. The front door is gone and I walk in, quickly working my way up the stairs, reading the name signs next to each door. I find the sign *Zoller* on the fourth floor and knock without hesitation.

A child opens the door, a girl, perhaps five or six years old.

'Good afternoon,' I say. 'I'm looking for Herr Zoller.'

She shakes her head. 'He's not here.'

'Not here?' I echo in disbelief. What now? 'Will he be back soon?'

'I'm Herr Zoller.'

I turn around. Behind me, on the stairs, stands the man I last saw on his knees in front of the gallows over three years ago. He's wearing dusty overalls over a dirty work shirt, its sleeves rolled up, with a canvas bag grasped in his calloused hand.

I step aside to let him pass.

'How can I help you?' he asks, pausing to glance at me then motioning for me to follow him.

Inside, in a small kitchen, Herr Zoller puts his canvas sack down on a chair and turns to face me.

The moment feels surreal and real, mundane and yet momentous, past merging with present. I feel a tightness in my throat at the realisation that stars had to align just a little for it to happen.

I clear my throat and swallow hard. 'Are you Hans-Peter's father?' I ask after introducing myself.

He stands there, his arms slack, sad surprise on his face. 'Yes. Hans-Peter was my son. You knew him?'

I shake my head. 'I didn't know him.' I take a deep breath. 'But I was there,' I say. 'When he died.'

'You were?' he whispers.

I nod. 'Your son was incredibly courageous.'

'Yes, he was.' Herr Zoller pauses for a moment. 'Please tell me about that day, Lene. The day of the execution.'

'Are you sure?' I ask.

He nods.

I take a deep breath. 'Hans-Peter and my friend Ludwig were in the same Hitler Youth squad. Ludwig was there too when it happened.' As the pictures of that afternoon flood back, my heartbeat rises into my throat. With some effort I push it all away. And then I tell him everything, and those horrible pictures rolling around in my head start to clear. 'We thought they would hang us too, but we were spared. I'm so very sorry that your son wasn't.'

'My son stood up for what he believed was right and he paid for it with his life,' Herr Zoller says. His eyes are proud but full of sorrow.

'He stood up for what he believed in until the very last moment,' I say.

'When Hans-Peter was seven years old, in the winter of 1934,' Herr Zoller starts, then stops and closes his eyes for moment, 'I was taken away and held at the Prenzlauer Berg water tower with others: Communists and Social Democrats. Hans-Peter witnessed that. I never talked in front of the children about what happened there but I guess they figured it out. It was fairly obvious when I came back.' He pauses. 'I was lucky that I did come back. I worked as a printer for a publication that was banned after 1933. We tried to keep going underground but …' He shrugs. 'None of us, those who came back that is, were game afterwards.'

'That's understandable,' I whisper.

'We went silent and we went along with everything. All I was thinking of was my family, how to keep them safe. But Hans-Peter …' He stops and shakes his head. 'When he had to join the Hitler Youth he just didn't go. He didn't get away with it for long, though. They came tearing up the stairs to our flat, all those eleven-year-olds in their brand new uniforms, shouting and chanting, and they just scooped Hans-Peter up and took him away with them to whatever drill they were doing that day.' For a moment he smiles a little. 'After that he called the other boys a bunch of mops, eagerly soaking up all the dribble that came out of the leader's mouth. But he kept going. Didn't take it serious, though.'

I tentatively smile, too.

'Of course things got more complicated when he got older.' He looks at me, sad and resigned.

'We should have come and talked to you straight after. But we were scared. Horst and Kurt were still threatening us.'

'Kurt Jenschke? Hans-Peter told me how he was harassed by him.' Herr Zoller's breath catches a little and his eyes harden.

'Yes, one of his squad leaders. He's the one who denounced your son! And he's back now, lurking around in our old neighbourhood.'

'You most definitely did the sensible thing by not contacting me back then,' Herr Zoller says firmly after a brief moment of silence. 'The Gestapo was watching me. They threw me in prison again for six months eventually.'

'But there's something else you must know, Herr Zoller. I'm so sorry for what happened. I'm so ashamed. We didn't do anything to help your son. Didn't even try.' And, after all these years, I still feel ashamed for having been a coward, years and years of cowardice. And

I know that shame and guilt will never quite go away. And neither will the admiration for someone like Hans-Peter who fought against what was wrong without any regard for his own life.

'Don't punish yourself,' Herr Zoller says. 'I can tell you probably have less reason to feel guilty than many others.'

'Perhaps,' I reply. 'But how guilty one feels and how guilty one is – each thing has little to do with the other.'

'Will you remember Hans-Peter for being courageous?' Herr Zoller asks me. 'That's one thing you can do.'

'I promise,' I say. 'I will always remember him.'

'You know,' Herr Zoller says before I leave, placing his hand on my forearm with quiet insistence. 'I had two sons. One went and fought for Hitler. One opposed Hitler. Both are dead now.'

CHAPTER 23

Dust flies as I empty another pail of rubble into the hopper car and the warm summer wind blows it in my face. A dull ache has settled in my shoulders and upper arms. I'm hanging out for the midday break.

'Where were you yesterday?' Heidi asks, sitting down next to me in the shade when our break comes. 'I thought they'd transferred you somewhere else already. But the supervisor didn't know anything about it. She wasn't happy you weren't here, that's for sure.'

'It's a bit complicated,' I utter, feeling embarrassed about missing a day.

'Sick?' Heidi raises an eyebrow.

'No. Just trying to find out something about someone. An old family friend.'

'That's not complicated. Everyone is doing that.'

'No, I guess it isn't that complicated,' I admit. 'I had to go to Prenzlauer Berg, where I used to live.'

'Oh, I used to live there too,' Heidi says. 'A long time ago. Later we moved to the Grunewald.' She bites her lip as though this has just slipped out, as though she regrets sharing this information about herself and her past.

'Do you still live there?'

She shakes her head.

'You found a place somewhere around here?' I ask.

'Yes. In Wilmersdorf.'

I wait for more but Heidi is silent.

'With family?'

'I haven't got any family left,' Heidi says. There's a tiny tremble in her voice but also a hint of something else that I can't quite pinpoint.

'I'm very sorry,' I say.

'Don't be. You didn't kill them.' Heidi gets up and dusts off her skirt with violent slaps.

'I'm sorry, I shouldn't have asked,' I say.

'No, don't be silly. It's just one of those days. When things catch up with you. I'll see you later.' She walks off.

This Heidi is not like the Heidi I met the day before yesterday.

The next day Heidi and I are given the job of refilling everyone's thermos bottles with water at the pump. We each carry a sack containing the empty bottles. Heat and dust hang over the city. Heidi puts her sunglasses on and hums to herself as we walk. She appears to be altogether more buoyant than yesterday.

'Do you know when you will start your course at university?' I ask.

'Perhaps in October. The department isn't up and running yet. No lecturers. Especially in psychology. Dead, or managed to flee in time. And most who were put there by the Nazis have been dismissed, are imprisoned or banned from teaching.'

I swallow, digesting what Heidi said. Putting facts into words like this is not what most people do. Suddenly there are bright colourful dots dancing in front of my eyes, ambushing me. Dizzy, I stop and lean on the wall for a moment before sitting down heavily in the dust. I haven't eaten much. A piece of bread is all I had this morning. It's that time of the month too.

Heidi crouches down next to me. Of course she knows what's wrong because it happens all the time. Girls fainting from exhaustion and lack of food. She reaches into her dress pocket and pulls out a small parcel. 'Open your mouth,' she tells me and unwraps it.

I do as I'm told and she pops a lolly into my mouth. Sugar rushes through me like white water, cherry flavour floods my tastebuds. I wonder how she can afford to give such a valuable rarity to me, a virtual stranger. But the dizziness subsides and the bright dots disappear.

'Better?' Heidi asks.

I nod, grab her hand and she pulls me up. I suck on the lolly until it's only a sliver on my tongue. When that melts away too, sweet cherry flavour remains before it slowly fades like a delicious memory. I feel awful for causing the delay. We hurry filling the bottles with water, then head back. The heavy sack cuts into the blisters on my hand, but the sugar and Heidi's kindness have given me a boost and I ignore the pain.

The supervisor reprimands us for taking too long. Our troupe of women has fallen behind schedule; we should have finished clearing the site days ago. She splits our group of around twenty women into two smaller groups. Half of us, including Heidi and me and most of the younger women, move on to the next site where we merge with another group.

The ruin we have been assigned to is a towering mangled mess of pulverised bricks, glass, twisted, partially melted steel and large chunks of reinforced concrete. The rubble mess is contained by a fragile parapet of bricks. A monumental task. I look at our wheelbarrows, buckets, picks and shovels. How?

'Right, listen up,' the supervisor says. 'We'll get a winch tomorrow and some help from the Americans or British. Most of you know the drill. We'll start today, bring down anything that's worth salvaging, sort it, and it will be collected later.'

I scan the ruin. Not everything that's meant to be salvaged and collected will make it down from the ruin. Pots, cutlery or wood for cooking, or heating in winter, will disappear in rucksacks and large pockets. Easily visible things would have probably been taken a long time ago, but once the first layer of rubble has been removed there might be more.

'Lene, if you come across any timber, grab it,' Heidi whispers. 'And be quick or it'll all be gone.'

Working in the ruin is hazardous. Heidi and I claw our way up to what used to be the first floor but which has now caved in under the weight of the collapsed storeys above. We try shifting a slab of concrete that sits precariously on top of some unstable looking rubble. In the cavity beneath I glimpse a wooden beam, some of it smashed into smaller pieces. But the concrete chunk doesn't budge. Two other girls scramble up to give us a hand. The rough surface of the concrete digs into my blister-covered palms.

'Are there any gloves?' I ask.

One of the girls shakes her head. 'The supervisor is trying to organise some. She's not here.'

We exchange quick glances. All of us have seen the prized wood beneath. We draw in sharp breaths, tearing at the chunk of concrete. On my palms, blisters burst. Finally, employing all the strength we can muster, the four of us manage to lift the concrete. Carefully we make our way down the slippery slope of rubble with it and dump it in a hopper car. There's no sight of the supervisor yet and we clamber back up, reach into the cavity and retrieve the pieces of wood from the shattered beam, furtively stuffing them into our pockets and backpacks.

By the time the supervisor returns and hands me a pair of gloves, we have formed a chain and have started removing the first layer of loose debris. It's my job to fill the pails with rubble and then pass them to Heidi. I work with concentration, hunkered down, carefully checking my foothold as I change positions.

The face is staring at me, empty-eyed, from the rubble tomb.

I reel backwards, the ground beneath me shifts under my weight and I slide down, only just catching hold of a twisted steel girder to stop my fall. I clamber back up. Heidi is already there, digging with her bare hands, her arms flying. Within seconds her hands start to bleed.

'Heidi, stop!' I call.

But she keeps going, hasn't heard me. The other girls come climbing up as well to see what is going on.

I try to grab hold of Heidi's arms and hands which are like human shovels.

'Heidi, please stop,' I cry, louder.

Heidi frantically shakes her head, pulls her hands away. 'But they need help!'

I kneel down behind her and wrap my arms around her, pressing hers down by her flanks, preventing them from moving, her hands from digging. 'They are dead,' I say. 'They have been dead for more than a year.' Heidi's shoulders and arms keep jerking and shuddering like a robot that is running out of power. 'More than a year, Heidi, a whole year. At least.'

The supervisor climbs up to us and glances into the crater. 'Take Heidi away and give her some water. Calm her down,' she instructs me. She sounds annoyed. For her this is just another hold-up.

Heidi has started shivering and is taking sharp, rapid breaths. She is close to hyperventilating. I carefully guide her down to level ground and help her sit in the shade, her back resting against a stack of bricks. She's floppy, like a ragdoll. I wet my handkerchief with cold water from my thermos and dab her face, her neck and the insides of her wrists with it. The supervisor keeps signalling me to hurry up.

'Get back to work,' Heidi says. She breathes more normally now and has stopped shaking and jerking her arms. 'I'm fine. I'll be there in a moment.'

The other women have freed the body from the rubble and bring it down. It is no more than a skeleton with some shredded rags that once were clothes. They lay the body by the roadside.

I leave Heidi in the shade and clamber up the ruin again.

'There are more down there,' one of the other girls says. She points into the hole. I can see a leg and a dusty ponytail. They don't belong to the same person.

I try not to look at them while filling bucket after bucket and shifting and removing clumps of concrete and bricks. Though the sight of the dead is something everyone, even the youngest children, got used to in the last year of the war. There's little smell from the bodies, just an airless, musty, cellar-like odour. When we've freed the next body, we lift it out too. There's just bones beneath the trouser leg. I carry it down with another girl and lay it next to the first body. We have nothing to cover them with.

'I'll walk you home,' I say to Heidi after our shift. 'It's not far, is it?'

She shakes her head, doesn't protest. She's still pale and shaky looking.

'Thanks for doing this,' Heidi says. She shifts her pack, heavy with the filched wood, to her other shoulder. She rested for a few minutes after we found the bodies, then she got on with her task, clearing rubble for the rest of the day, pallid-faced, silent, avoiding looking at the bodies until they were taken away in the late afternoon.

Heidi lives in a one-room ground-floor flat in a *Hinterhaus* just off the Hohenzollerndamm. The roofs of both the front and the rear building have caved in and the façade facing the street has been ripped open. Inside Heidi's tiny flat there's a single bed and a small table with a chair. Tucked away in a recess is an old wood-burning stove. I see a large open suitcase with neatly folded clothes sticking out from underneath the bed.

'The toilet is two flights up. It's working,' Heidi says.

'Thanks,' I say, rushing away. A working toilet is a luxury as not all water mains or the sewage system have been repaired yet. I have become used to not going all day.

When I come back, Heidi has pulled out a box from underneath the bed and is sifting through its contents. The box, to my amazement, is filled with food. I can see cans of beans and soup, sugar, flour, dried fruit, nuts and sweets. My eyes return to the suitcase on the ground. The clothes in it are ironed and clean, of good quality.

While Heidi has her back to me I give the sparse room another, closer inspection. There's not much else to see, though. A hairbrush, a book and a candle on the upturned box that serves as a bedside table. On the windowsill an aluminium pot, a plate, a few cups, some cutlery and a couple of photos.

'Pea soup?' Heidi turns around, holding up a can. She sees me looking at the photos but doesn't comment. 'We'll have it cold though.'

I nod. I'm ravenous.

When she divvies up the soup, I get another chance to look at the photos, taking a step closer. One is of a woman with two girls. The woman looks so much like Heidi; she has the same oak-coloured hair and pronounced cheekbones, and I realise that she must be her mother. One of the girls is unmistakably Heidi: serious looking, perhaps eleven years old, beautiful already. The other girl is a few years younger, sweet and a little chubby still with baby fat.

Silently, Heidi gets two spoons and glances at me looking at the photos.

The other photo shows a man. He's handsome, but there is something impenetrable and harsh in his eyes. He wears the uniform of the SS. I swallow hard, look away, then look back. I can see Heidi in his face.

Heidi hands me a plateful of soup and a spoon. Instantly my mouth starts to water.

'Take a seat,' she says and points at the single chair.

'Thank you.' With my eyes closed I eat the first spoonful. Ham, peas and potatoes. The most delicious taste.

We eat in silence. Heidi has settled down on the bed, eating the soup straight from the can. She finishes first; she's given me the bigger serve. She wipes out the can with her finger, licking it and I do the same with my plate. When every little trace of soup is gone, Heidi places the can on the windowsill.

'That's my father,' she says, indicating the photo of the man and sitting back on her bed. 'He became a Nazi with all his heart and soul. If he had a heart and a soul, that is. He divorced my mother in 1937, even before the racial laws were passed. Then he sent me to Switzerland to stay with some distant relatives of his. That's my mother and my little sister in the other photo. So far I've found out that they were sent to the Theresienstadt concentration camp in late 1941, then from there they were transferred to Auschwitz.'

I scrape the last bit of soup from the plate.

'My sister's name was Charlotte.' Heidi smiles. 'I was always jealous of that name. I thought it was so pretty, a little exotic. My mother picked it.' Heidi slips her shoes off and stretches out on the bed. 'Heidi on the other hand, my father's pick, named after that distant aunt in Switzerland I stayed with. So sound and wholesome, like a little lump.'

I sit motionless at the table, the empty plate in front of me. I have no words.

Heidi has the words for me, asks the questions for me. 'Why did he choose to save me?' she asks. 'Why? I spent the war in Switzerland. While on the other side of the border … I lived in a beautiful house, I went to school.' She turns her head and looks at me. Her face is hollow, her eyes broken into tiny shards of something far beyond pain. 'While my mother and my little sister were sent to the gas chambers.' She closes her eyes, her body sinks into the bed. 'I don't even know when they died, not even the year. There are no proper records. As though my sister and my mother never even existed.'

I get up and cover her with the white, beautifully embroidered quilt that's folded neatly at the foot of the bed.

'I'm not asleep,' Heidi whispers.

'I know.'

'I'm so cold,' Heidi says.

I tuck the quilt in around her body, despite the fact that it's the middle of summer.

I want to ask her about her father. I want to ask her why she came back to Berlin. Why she left that beautiful house in Switzerland and lives in this shabby room in a bombed house in a ruined city, in a country that betrayed her and destroyed her family. But now Heidi is asleep. I leave, shutting the door quietly behind me. Perhaps one day I will ask her those questions.

I walk home slowly. My feet feel like lead weights and this story I've just heard whirls around in my head. It's a different story altogether, different from those stories that we, the perpetrators, carry around with us.

CHAPTER 24

The next day, Gertie and I meet up at the Kurfürstendamm after work. 'We have to go to the Tiergarten,' she says and starts walking. A bulky satchel is slung over her shoulder.

I nod. The Tiergarten is one of the places where goods change hands, where anything can be obtained with the right currency.

'I don't like going there by myself,' Gertie says and grimaces. 'It's shady. But it has to be done.'

'What have you got?' I ask, pointing at the satchel.

'The usual. Cigarettes and coffee. It's about the only thing that's worth anything. And we've already traded all of Mutti's jewellery.' Gertie says it matter of fact, without bitterness. 'I guess we were lucky that we had all that jewellery to barter with. It got us through the worst.' She frowns a little. 'I imagine that most of it will end up being worn by some lucky housewife on the other side of the Atlantic.'

I remember my aunt's jewellery. On rare occasions she would get out her jewellery box and we girls were allowed to try on a few pieces. There was a diamond and ruby brooch in the shape of a panther, a double-strand pearl necklace with a sapphire-encrusted clasp, a diamond-studded Cartier watch bought in Paris and a bracelet set with emeralds the size of small beetles. Most of it Aunt Ilsa wore with her evening gowns when she went off to a party or the opera with my uncle.

'They were such beautiful pieces,' I say.

'All gone now. All but the wedding ring.' Gertie shrugs. 'They are just things at the end of the day.'

We are at the edge of the Tiergarten. At once the crowd of people thickens around us.

'We have to stay together, all right,' Gertie warns me. 'And don't talk to anyone.'

I nod, pausing mid-step. There are all sorts of people here: refugees and displaced people from all over Europe; returnees, some still wearing bits and pieces of their uniforms; crooks and hustlers; women young and old; even young children by themselves, some with backpacks and walking sticks and lost empty expressions on their faces. There are plenty of Allied soldiers, a few Soviet officers too.

Gertie grabs hold of my arm. 'Don't worry,' she says. 'I know where to go, we'll be out of here real quick.' She sounds so assertive, like she knows exactly what she's doing; her confidence reassures me.

We are swallowed up by the crowd as we make our way deeper into the black market. There are people bartering and trading everywhere. I see a Soviet officer inspecting a watch, shaking his head, rejecting it. An American soldier looks at a Leica camera offered to him by a small, hollow-looking man. The American quickly slides it under his coat and hands over a packet of cigarettes. Another man has a whole wheelbarrow full of paintings and sketches on offer. The American who's bought the Leica briefly stops and flicks through them. The man's lips are moving fast, pleading with him to buy one, but the American looks at him indifferently. He leaves, without buying anything. I can see a painting, small but striking, modern, bizarre, nothing that would have been allowed under the Nazis. It's as though it came from the world before. I move closer. But the peddler, noticing my interest, throws a rag over the wares and hastily wheels his cart away.

I look after the man, wondering how he came to own the paintings. He has disappeared and his spot has been taken by a woman showing off an expensive fur coat which she is wearing despite the early summer evening. A quick exchange of words with another

American soldier prompts her to take it off. The coat disappears in his backpack, a pound of coffee in her purse. A moment later she has melted into the crowd.

I suddenly realise that Gertie has let go of my arm. I glance around but I can't see her. Pins and needles flutter up my spine. I failed to listen to her and stick together! I search for her more frantically. She's gone. My façade of confidence cracks and in an instant I can feel eyes gliding over me. I start walking purposefully as though I know exactly where I'm going and what I'm doing, at the same time furtively searching the crowd for Gertie. I hope I don't look as lost as I am.

Near a cluster of singed, dusty shrubs I catch sight of a group of girls and women. Their skirts are a little too short and the first two or three top buttons of their blouses and dresses are undone, exposing sharp collarbones and the softer flesh beneath. Lips are bright red in thin faces, drawn into smiles. Then I see her. It is no more than a glimpse. My cousin Ophelia. I blink, people move about in front of me, obstructing my view and when I look again she's no longer there.

'Goodness me, where have you been?' Gertie appears out of nowhere and grabs hold of my arm. 'Didn't I tell you to stay together?'

I feel like a child who hasn't paid attention to the teacher's instructions. 'Sorry, but you were suddenly gone.' I look back over my shoulder for the girl I thought was Ophelia but Gertie pulls me along. Did my mind play a trick on me? I know that Ophelia has some sort of a liaison with an American soldier, and I know that it wasn't her first liaison of that kind either.

'Come on, let's go.' Gertie yanks my arm angrily. 'I'm finished here and I don't want to get caught in a police raid.' She has lost all patience with me. 'You are a real liability, you know. Hard to believe you are actually two years older than me. You used to look after me!'

We walk quickly back through the Tiergarten until the crowd thins. 'You can let go now,' I say and free my arm from Gertie's grip, rubbing at the white marks left there by her fingers.

'I'm sorry.' Gertie draws in a long breath and lets it out slowly again.

I realise her confidence is no more than pretence.

'I'm glad that's done,' she says.

'What were you able to get?

'Margarine, some onions, oats and carrots.'

'I think I saw …' I stop.

'What? What did you see?'

'Nothing.' I shouldn't tell Gertie about Ophelia. And what if I'm wrong and it wasn't her? I want my eyes to have betrayed me.

'What were you going to say?' Gertie persists.

'Someone selling these paintings. Like really amazing ones, that could have been in a gallery or museum. Before,' I quickly say.

'Really? Oh well, I guess you can find anything and everything here. Even something from the ancient past.'

I'm glad she hasn't noticed my cover up. I wonder if she's seen her sister too.

Only my aunt and Theo are home when we get back.

'Where's Ophelia?' Gertie asks. 'Isn't it a bit early for her to have gone out already? The sun hasn't even set.'

I flinch and wonder if she is being deliberately cruel.

My aunt ignores the comment. She looks completely spent. I can tell she doesn't have the energy to reprimand Gertie, so I do it instead. 'I think you ought to stop talking about your sister like this now,' I say sharply.

Surprised, Gertie glowers at me. 'Why do you care all of a sudden?' she mutters.

I shake my head. 'Never mind. There's no need to talk like this, that's all. It doesn't help things. Why don't you put the food on? Your brother is famished.'

Aunt Ilsa smiles at me weakly. 'I've got good news,' she says. 'I've found work at the American officers' mess.'

'Oh, Aunt, that is wonderful.' I spontaneously hug her.

Even Gertie comes over and silently hugs her mother.

'Does that mean we will get sweets and chocolate?' Theo asks.

'I'm not sure about sweets and chocolate, but it means we might get more food.'

Later, my aunt helps Theo wash up in the bathroom while Gertie and I prepare dinner.

'You know, I will never forgive Ophelia for what she did, back then,' Gertie suddenly says.

I immediately know what Gertie is talking about.

'That day when she threatened us, remember? When you picked up the clothes for Gustav and the pram. And all the things she said about our father, that he was a coward. How could she!' Gertie says. 'How she worked so hard to become a leader in the damn BDM! How she took to it all like a duck to water.'

'Gertie, she was swept up in it all, like many others. You have to forgive her,' I say. 'Those were just words. She never did anything to hurt you, or me, or anyone else.' Unlike others I knew back then, I add silently in my head.

'How can I forgive her? I was so scared of her. Scared of what my own sister could do to me.'

'But she didn't act on her threats and that's all that matters. Believe me, Ophelia is atoning for it now.'

'All she does is go out with the Americans and have a good time.'

'Gertie, do you really think she's having such a good time? I think you know that she probably doesn't.'

Gertie is silent, her eyes lowered.

'Just try to forgive her,' I say. 'There's nothing any of us can do to change the past.'

I sit up until late, mending Theo's socks, waiting for Ophelia. We all have secrets and hopes and the past is the present and it's threatening to drown us.

I catch my breath as, unexpectedly, someone scurries past the kitchen and down the corridor. A moment later the dining room door opens and shuts again.

Ophelia comes home at midnight.

'You're still up,' she says, sticking her head into the kitchen. She comes in, opens her purse and puts a pound of coffee and a packet of cigarettes on the table.

'I wanted to finish those,' I say, indicating the mended socks. 'Did you eat?' I ask.

Ophelia sits down, crosses her legs. 'Jasper took me out for dinner.'

'Your boyfriend?'

She nods. 'He's nice. From California.' Her fingers play with a cigarette, she picks it up and puts it between her lips. She looks for matches in her purse but then changes her mind and places the cigarette back on the table. Her foot in the black high-heel sling-backs is seesawing fretfully.

'Your mother has found work at the American mess,' I say. 'In the kitchen there.'

For a moment Ophelia says nothing, then she takes one of the cigarettes after all. With shaking hands, she manages to light it after the third attempt. 'Oh wow,' she says, blowing out smoke. She blinks and rubs her eyes.

'Everything will be better now,' I say.

Ophelia stares at me.

'Ophelia, you don't have to pretend with me.'

'You saw me today, didn't you?'

I nod.

'Don't you see how it makes sense to be flirty with the Americans. How else would I get us coffee, or cigarettes?' Ophelia offers her cigarette to me. Hesitantly, I take a few puffs, then hand it back to her.

'But Jasper is a steady boyfriend,' she continues. 'I really like him and I think he likes me. He helps as much as he can.'

'That's good.'

'Found out anything about your Ludwig?' she then asks.

'No.'

'Not all may be lost, you know,' she says. It sounds half-hearted, like she's trying to say something nice.

'I'm not sure that I still believe in some kind of miracle.' I realise that this is true. It's the first time I've put the thought into words. Since finding out there is no news about Ludwig's fate, the promise we gave to each other feels paler, and the promise of a future together feels more and more like a naïve fantasy. 'But I'm not ready to let go of hope entirely, or perhaps it won't let go of me.'

'You can't keep hoping forever,' Ophelia says. 'If you haven't found out anything in, I don't know, six or twelve months, you should draw a finishing line.'

It sounds very practical and easy but I know it isn't. 'I don't think I can do that.'

'Lene,' Ophelia hands me the cigarette again, 'I know this sounds harsh, but this is your life too. Don't waste it. Even if Ludwig has survived and he is in Soviet captivity somewhere, it could be many years before he comes home. If he ever does. No one knows how long the Soviets keep them for or if they will ever let them go. Or if he will even survive those years.'

I draw the smoke deep into my lungs now without even coughing. I know Ophelia is right.

CHAPTER 25

But a few days later, my reluctant deliberation of perhaps drawing a finishing line is proven premature. My fingers are shaking like brittle branches in an autumn storm. I'm holding a small parcel wrapped in newspaper, and a letter. Both arrived in the mail for me today. From Frau Schluck. I tear open the letter first. *Please*, I pray, *let it be good news*.

Berlin, 9th of June, 1946

Dear Lene,

This was given to me by the mother of one of the boys in Ludwig's unit who has returned. He found it in the field hospital near the Romanian border in the spring of 1944 where Ludwig was treated for a head wound. He said the hospital suffered a heavy air and artillery attack and, after that, Ludwig was gone. They presumed he was killed in the blast along with many others.

The young man said that he wasn't sure that information was accurate, but his mother did not elaborate – though it is, of course, not hard to understand what he's hinting at. I was never even told about Ludwig's injury or that he was in the field hospital! All I ever got was the notification that Ludwig was missing in action. The way they treated us mothers in the end!

Can there still be hope after all this time? I think perhaps there is.

Warm wishes,

Hilde Schluck

I greedily tear away the newspaper. The package contains a journal, crudely made, thin, containing no more than a dozen pages which are bound between two pieces of thin, grey cardboard. The cardboard is splattered with mud and dirt. It's bent, cracked and distended by moisture.

My hands shake violently as I glide my fingertips across the rough cardboard cover again and again. This is Ludwig's. He touched it, made it; he wrote in it.

For a moment I just sit, my palm on it, letting the shaking subside. Then I open it.

Written in the top left corner on the inside of the cover are Ludwig's initials. The pages are filled back and front. Ludwig's handwriting. Seeing it, recognising it, is like the most powerful sunbeam filled with hope and exhilaration. I start reading, gulping the words like air. My heart is racing; the first entry is about me.

10th of October, 1943

When we said goodbye and I had to get on the tram I could hardly bear to look at Lene, but I knew if I didn't, then that moment would be a moment lost forever. Her desperate and futile attempt to keep up with the tram. I almost can't endure recalling that look in her eyes, that heartbreaking interlocking of despair and hope. I feel as though I betrayed her by giving her that promise that I will believe in coming home. The truth is I don't believe in it. I'm not a romantic. I'm a realist. But I didn't lie about loving her. That is real. The only thing that is real and true.

It now feels wrong that I kept us apart for months after what happened to Hans-Peter. It must have been a horrible time for Lene, just as it was for me. But I couldn't think of anything else to do. I felt as though everything was frozen with thin ice over an ugly depth, one wrong step and we would crash through the ice into endless coldness.

When Lene couldn't keep up with the tram any longer and she fell behind and her face became more and more indiscernible, I felt nothing, as though I was dead already, and at the same time I felt everything. On the inside, I screamed and cried and thrashed; for everything we would never have.

12th of October, 1943

I know I shouldn't be writing this but if I don't I will go mad. I'm beyond caring if someone who shouldn't reads this!

Back in mid-May, when we assembled in the barracks' quadrangle, there were familiar faces all around me. Boys from school, most of them my age. The older ones had already left after sitting their emergency school-leaving exam. We were counted like sheep, to the slaughterhouse we go, our worth not measured in the meat we would produce but how many tanks we could blow up, how many enemy soldiers we could take out, how long we would stay alive. When we were kitted out in mismatched uniforms, it all became so much more real and all I could think of was that I didn't want to be here.

But I must. We all must.

These are the times we live in. We belong to the Führer. The Eastern Front is the destiny that has been chosen for us. Did anyone volunteer for this?

The rifle, when I first held it, felt as cold as death in my hand. But, of course, what else should it feel like? I've held one before, in the Hitler Youth. I know how to use it. Rifle, hand grenade, anti-tank gun, bayonet knife, gas mask.

When I ran I was barely able to breathe, perhaps I was not meant to. The training took place under battle-like conditions and I learnt quickly, adapted quickly. In the evening sleep came the second my head hit the pillow in the quarters. A couple of months of this. Why delay it any longer? We are ready.

I stop reading for a moment, trying to grasp what's in front of me. The despair, the fatalism, how alone and lost Ludwig must have felt. With a heavy heart, I turn the page.

13th of October, 1943

I'm writing this entry on the train as we are crossing Poland. Night is falling. I've just finished playing cards with Hubert who has volunteered. So, yes, there are some who still believe in all of this. But only criminals would allow a not yet sixteen-year-old to volunteer for the front. Perhaps he has lied about his age, though it is obvious how young he is. He is as tall as a baby giant and his cheeks are soft and chubby like a child's.

Hubert is excited. I know he is, even though he doesn't say as much. The others in our carriage slumber, stretched out on the straw-covered floor, heads resting on rucksacks and straw pillows, or on hands folded as though in prayer.

Pray, oh comrades, pray, perhaps it will save you . . .

One or two still write letters in the dying light. I know it's what I should be doing. I keep composing them in my head, those letters, to Lene and to my mother, but then I can't bring myself to write those words that come from the nowhere land between truth and lie. Instead I'm writing this.

Hubert is sleeping now. He is stretched out on the straw, his gangly limbs neatly arranged alongside the soldier next to him. 'We should all try to get some shut-eye', he said, sounding a bit like an old battle horse, 'because it might be the last chance we get for a while.'

Yes, I will try to get some sleep too, as soon as I finish writing. Hubert can't wait to blow those Ruski bastards to pieces. He's told me this at least half-a-dozen times in the last few weeks when all we did was dig anti-tank trenches. He really does not know what he is in for. Has he not listened to his father's stories, like I did? I told him that he might get his chance sooner than he might think. He didn't like this and said that I sounded like I'd rather not get my chance.

I have to be careful. A measured degree of enthusiasm is still required. I like Hubert and I don't think there was any malice in his words, but one never knows. So I gave him a speech about doing my duty like everyone else, about final victory and total war. And I will do my duty. I'm here now, I've made my choice.

I'm writing with my back resting against the wall of the railway car. I can feel the cold of the night rushing past outside. The wagon has no windows, just air vents, but I've opened the door a crack to let in some more fresh air, and the twilight. When I look out I can see the dark shapes of trees flying by, open fields. The moon is blue. It is autumn but trailing behind it is its big scary buddy, winter.

Looking up into the sky I worry about this big blue moon. There's so much light that our train would be clearly visible for any enemy reconnaissance plane. But we are still in occupied Polish territory so I guess we are probably safe for now. Soon we will be crossing into occupied Russian territory and if the rumours are to be believed, the Wehrmacht is in steady retreat. 'Tactical retreat' they call it. I think there's only one kind of retreat. It doesn't matter what you call it. Calling it something else is just another lie.

When I stick my head out of the door I can see the endless centipede of cars that make up our troop train. At its head is the locomotive, hauling us along at a slow but determined speed. So far we have only stopped once to stock up on coal and water. We are high priority. New troops to replenish the diminished divisions at the front.

15th of October, 1943

When I opened my eyes this morning, daylight was pouring into the railcar through the wide-open door and we were not moving any longer. I quickly grabbed my rifle and slung it over my shoulder. I asked if anyone knew what was going on, but no one did. They sat there like me, clasping their rifles. Everyone was edgy. Someone suggested that we had reached the railhead, but I knew that it was too early for that. We were too far from the frontlines still, of which there was no sign or sound.

I pushed my way through to the door of the wagon and looked outside. The commander and some of the officers were standing around in groups, talking. That's when I heard the roaring. I instinctively ducked because I thought it was an air attack, but the officers outside didn't even flinch. The roaring got louder and a moment later, a train that looked like a railroad battleship appeared next to us. It was a self-propelled armoured train, a monster, a fortress of steel shields, rivets and guns, both futuristic and medieval looking at the same time. I spied an enormous howitzer gun mounted on it. The rolling fortress dwarfed our train, swallowing the morning sun as it roared past. We had been diverted onto a sideline to let it through. The armoured train was even higher priority than us, fresh troops. Suddenly the group of officers outside disbanded and I knew something was happening when the armoured train slowed.

A sergeant told us to disembark. Everyone in our wagon jumped up. Hubert elbowed me because I didn't move immediately. He shouted excitedly that we had been given an order. I was one of the last ones to get off the train and the sergeant pointed at me and yelled to get a move on and that his grandmother was faster than me. In the meantime, the armoured train had come to a complete standstill next to us.

We were ordered to follow the sergeant and about fifty of us did, hustling to keep up in full gear, our aluminium canteens, ammo pouches, rifles, helmets and gas masks clanking and clattering, our boots stomping on the ground still hard from last night's frost. We ran alongside the armoured train and up close it looked even more intimidating. A steel monster towering above us. Parts of the train were painted in camouflage green, others were grey and greenish steel and looked more crudely made, no more than riveted together steel sheets like dented and battered shields.

So this is where I am now. In one of the infantry railcars of the armoured train. Hubert is here as well. We spent most of the day crouching with our rifles behind the armoured flanks of the infantry car, searching the countryside for partisans, ready to shoot at any movement. There's no roof or cover so we are exposed to attacks from the air but there's always at least one man keeping watch with binoculars.

The others who stayed on the troop transporter have gone straight to the front. I guess my chances, at this point, of staying alive are definitely higher than those on the train destined for the frontlines.

It's the end of the entry and I stop reading again, my hope rising with the realisation that luck smiled on Ludwig when he was transferred onto the armoured train. His morale would have been boosted by this. But even before I read his next entry, I know my hopes will be dashed.

19th of October, 1943

I look at my last entry and I think what a fool I was to think that I was lucky to be on the armoured train. The train got derailed and destroyed by a partisan bomb within days, when we were about seventy kilometres from the front. The ammunition car exploded and killed dozens of men. The rest of us combed the forest looking for the partisans responsible, but we didn't find any. Instead, we found something else in the depths of the forest, about a kilometre or so from a nearby village. Something too dreadful to write about. My God, the flies, and the smell in the pit. I am still sick to my stomach. Is this the handiwork of the SS or even the Wehrmacht?

We were told the Soviets did it. I'm not sure this is true. I knew things like this were happening but seeing it with my own eyes, seeing the proof, is devastating and the shame is almost too much to bear. We moved past the pit quickly, everyone saw it but no one has mentioned it. Hubert hasn't said a single word since then.

Once we reached the front, we merged with another battalion and have been securing a corridor so our supplies can get through to the front. We do our best, but not enough is getting through. They are running out of ammunition, food and fuel. And soldiers. Sometimes I see our planes flying overhead and they drop parachute containers with food and ammunition. Some planes get shot down by the enemy.

There's fewer and fewer of us every day. The enemy is overwhelming. I have no words to describe the battle which roars around us day and night. I still haven't written to Lene and my mother. But I will, I have to. Soon.

This war can only end one way. And the sooner it does, the better.

It's Ludwig's last entry. There are a few empty pages left in his journal that he didn't get to fill. Didn't get a chance to fill. And this last entry has a sketchy, disjointed feel to it. He sounds overwhelmed, weary.

I get Ludwig's letter out, the only one he wrote me. It's dated *23rd of October, 1943*. Four days after his last journal entry. But when exactly was he injured and treated in the field hospital? In her letter, Ludwig's mother said the journal was found in late spring 1944.

I read the journal again and again, but each time I read it, I am none the wiser.

CHAPTER 26

Later that night I'm in the kitchen cleaning up after dinner. Beside me on the table is Ludwig's journal which I can't bear to leave out of my sight. I dry my hands and open it again to read it for what must be the eighth time today, when the doorbell rings. I hear my aunt's footsteps echo in the hallway as she opens the front door, then hushed voices. A moment later she sticks her head in the kitchen.

'Lene?'

'Yes?' I look up.

'There's someone at the door for you.'

'Who is it?' I close the journal.

'A young man.'

My heart suddenly starts thumping like a bass drum resonating through my entire body.

Ludwig.

I rush to the door. But then stop dead. My disappointment is like an injection of poison.

'What the hell do you want? How do you even know where I live? Leave!'

I rush forward and try to slam the door, but Kurt puts his foot in the way and blocks it with his shoulder.

'Lene, wait. Let's talk.'

'There's nothing to talk about! Nothing!' Again, I try to shut the door, kick at his foot. 'Leave at once!'

'Please, Lene, hear me out.' Kurt's hand sneaks through the gap in the door and touches my arm. 'I have news. News about Schluck.'

'You don't know anything about Ludwig, not where he is or

whether he will come home or not,' I shout and push the door with all I've got, all that anger and disgust the contact with his hand evokes in me, the memory of that other time when he came to my flat during the war, attacking me, threatening me, threatening Ludwig. The door slams on Kurt's forearm.

'And what if I do? What if I was sent here with a message?' he winces, pulling back his arm.

'Who would send you?'

'Ludwig's mother.'

Could it be? I hesitate for a second. But then I look at Kurt's eyes. 'She wouldn't send you,' I say. 'Not you. You are bluffing!'

My aunt is suddenly behind me. 'Lene, what is going on here?' She comes closer, nudges me aside and opens the door wide. She grimly looks at Kurt. 'What sort of behaviour is this? My niece doesn't want to let you in, probably for good reason, so don't you block that door!'

He immediately backs away, his hands up as if in surrender, his eyes downcast. 'I just want to talk to Lene. I'll be downstairs.' He turns and hurries down the stairs.

My aunt shuts the door and looks at me for a long moment. 'Who is that man, Lene? What has he done to you?'

I realise my fists are clenched and they are shaking. 'Nothing.'

'Lene, I am responsible for you. I've already lost one of my daughters to the circumstances we are in. Your mother would never forgive me if something happened to you too.'

I don't want to talk about what happened three years ago but I come up with something. 'Kurt was a squad leader in the Hitler Youth. Later he joined the *Waffen-SS*, thought he was the elite, behaved like he was.'

'I see,' says my aunt, studying me carefully, clearly wondering if she's hearing the whole story.

'And now he's back, harassing me. But of course it's not as easy as it used to be. I think he's in hiding somewhere in the Soviet sector.'

'And he *would* be hiding with that resume! SS, ha! Your uncle was a decorated officer in the *Wehrmacht* but he despised the SS and what they stood for.' My aunt shakes her head.

I nod, grab a cardigan and cocoon myself up in it. I feel boosted by my aunt's support. Could Kurt have been sent here with a message from Ludwig's mother? He would have concocted some sort of tale for her, possibly even pretending to have been Ludwig's friend. I make a split-second decision. 'I can't let him get away without talking to him,' I say, and I run down the stairs before my aunt has a chance to reply.

Outside, the sun has set and the sky is spiked with threads of red. Kurt is sitting on the portal steps, his back to me. For a moment, I look at him through the hole in the door where the stained-glass window used to be. Despite his skinniness, his shoulders are still broad and straight. I force myself to go outside, down the portal steps and turn around to face him.

'I was starting to think that you weren't going to come downstairs after all. But here you are,' he says and stands.

I can make out my aunt in the half-open window on the second floor.

'Let's go for a walk,' Kurt says.

'I'm not going anywhere with you,' I say. 'Did Ludwig's mother send you here with a message, or not?'

'She did give me your address when I asked for it. But she didn't send me. I admit, there's no message.' He grins as though he has been caught committing a gentlemen's crime. 'I just really wanted to see you again.' He clears his throat. 'I haven't got anyone left, Lene. The house is gone, bombed, my family is gone.'

'There are a lot of people who don't have anyone left, who have lost everything that was precious to them,' I reply coldly. 'Some lost it because of what you did!'

He shrugs, indifferent. 'Don't you wish we could go back to the way things were though?'

'The way things were? You can't be serious!'

'I am very serious. I haven't forgotten what I believe in. There was order and obedience back then when we had Hitler. Girls and boys were looked after in the BDM and the Hitler Youth. Traitors and defeatists were dealt with swiftly and justly. When I was in the SS ... Anyway, look at the mess we are in now.'

Swiftly and *justly*, like hanging them without even a trial, hanging them because they dared to speak the truth! He still believes in it all after everything that has happened. How deeply it is all ingrained in him. 'That belief has brought devastation and death upon Europe,' I say, my voice shaking.

In one smooth movement he's suddenly close to me, taking me by surprise.

'Don't you dare come near me, Kurt!' I hiss into his face. 'Beat it, and don't ever bother me again!'

My words have little effect.

'We made sure justice was served. And I won't let anyone tell me otherwise. The law was on our side. Still is. Even the Americans thought so when they let me go. There's no future here for us but that doesn't mean we can't continue our work elsewhere. I've got some old like-minded friends ...'

'So do I.' My aunt has appeared in the doorway. 'I still have some old friends as well, some of whom have already been appointed into positions of trust by the Allies. My husband was a Major General in the *Wehrmacht.* Major General Feiberg, perhaps you have heard of him? He believed members of the SS were utter scum. And so did his associates.' She descends one step, towers above Kurt, her eyes as icy as I've ever seen them.

'If you ever come here or bother my niece again, we will make sure—'

She doesn't get to finish her sentence. A deeply alarmed expression flashes across Kurt's face and then he tears around and sprints away down the street. My aunt and I both watch him. His movements are now less like those of a sleek, powerful creature, but reminiscent of a terrified rabbit. He disappears behind a rubble mound.

'Is it true?' I ask when we are back upstairs. 'That you have old friends you could call upon?'

'Yes, one or two.'

I feel a sudden overwhelming desire to bring Kurt down.

'You let me know if he bothers you again,' my aunt says. 'But judging by that terrified expression on his face I'm quite sure we scared him off for good.'

CHAPTER 27

A few days later, I'm back at Frau Schluck's apartment to warn her about Kurt, although there seems little reason for him to turn up here again. I'm also returning Ludwig's journal. But when I take it out of my bag Frau Schluck shakes her head.

'I want you to keep it, Lene.'

Hesitating, I put it on the table. 'I couldn't,' I say, although in reality I don't ever want to part with it.

'Ludwig would want you to have it,' she says.

I nod. 'Thank you. I will keep it then.' The journal, which I could have sent in the mail, is not the only reason for my visit. 'The young soldier who gave you this journal, do you know him?' I ask.

'I worked with his mother in the ammunitions factory during the last year of the war. She gave it to me. I never spoke with him directly. He isn't well. He spent months in a sanatorium after he was injured and sent home. Everything I told you in the letter I found out from his mother.'

'I would really like to talk to him,' I say.

'I don't know, Lene. You can try, but his mother says he isn't talking much.' She pauses. 'He has been through a lot, of course. And he doesn't remember things very clearly. Perhaps you shouldn't bother him. He is still unwell,' embarrassed, she points to her head, 'up here.'

I insist. 'Like you said, I can try. What's his name?'

Frau Schluck sighs and gives me the address which is in our suburb. 'His name is Hubert.'

I nod. 'I will go there now.'

I'm almost at the door when something occurs to me. 'Could I borrow a photo of Ludwig?'

'Of course, Lene.' She disappears and I hear her opening a cupboard door. She returns moments later with a photo album and flicks through the pages.

'As recent as possible,' I say.

'Here,' she slides a photo out. 'This one was taken in the spring of 1943, not too long before he left for the front.' She tiredly smiles at me. 'You can keep it too.'

I'm not prepared for how young Hubert is. He's a boy; a battle-weary child. He shoos his mother, who is still explaining to him who I am, and shows me into the tiny sitting room of the two-bedroom flat where he collapses his long frame in an armchair opposite me.

'Luckily I still got these,' he says, raising his hand. He holds a cigarette between thumb and index finger. 'They had to amputate all the other fingers on this hand. The other fingers got blown off clean. The blood, you should have seen it.' He grimaces. 'Or maybe not.'

I glance at the purple stump where his right hand used to be. 'You survived,' I say.

He starts laughing, chokes on the cigarette smoke and coughs. An instant later, he starts sobbing. 'I wish the Ruskis had just finished me off. At least then I would have been a fallen war hero, right? What am I now? A war invalid! A burden! On my parents, on society. Reminding everyone of what they want to forget.' His sobbing turns into frenzied laughter again. 'My father looks at me like I am a failure. He never even fought! A paper pusher, a small-time bureaucrat, that's what he was. But couldn't wait for me to be old enough to volunteer!'

Eventually, when the crazed laughing and sobbing stops, I ask him about Ludwig.

'Ludwig? I don't know anyone by that name.' He blows smoke towards the ceiling where it hangs thick and heavy.

'Do you remember the journal you brought home?' I gently ask. 'Your mother gave it to Ludwig's mother a few weeks back.' I feel for the photo in my pocket.

'Ah, that Ludwig you mean. He was never writing any letters. Sometimes he pulled out his journal though and scribbled in it for a bit.'

Perhaps I won't need the photo. But I'm glad I have it.

'I'm told you found his journal at the field hospital. Do you remember Ludwig being treated there?'

'Ludwig and I were in the same unit. That armoured train they put us on, you should have seen it. It looked so invincible. Ha! The thing derailed and died like a damn dinosaur. Those partisans planted that bomb well.'

I nod. I know about the derailment from Ludwig's journal. There's no mention of the hospital though. Does Hubert not have any recollection of his stay at the hospital or Ludwig being there?

'Do you remember what happened after the derailment?' I ask patiently, even though I also know from the journal what happened afterwards. But I'm hoping to open a trapdoor leading to hidden memories in Hubert's mind. He's my only chance of finding out anything.

'After the derailment,' he mutters, then for a long time, he says nothing.

I wait. 'Do you remember being in the hospital?' I gently ask after a while.

'The hospital, yes, not too far from the Romanian border. I wouldn't call it a hospital, though.'

It seems Hubert is compelled to follow the random direction that his memory takes. And he doesn't seem to like giving straight answers to my questions either. I remain silent now and let him talk.

'A couple of tents and a stone hut at the rear of the frontlines. They hardly had any morphine left.' He holds up his hand. 'Got those fingers amputated without any.' He says it without self-pity.

'What little morphine we had was reserved for the leg and full arm amputations. They didn't even bother with the stomach injuries. Those poor bastards were left to die.'

I shiver. What kind of injuries had Ludwig suffered?

'There were no nurses either. They had been flown out a long time ago. Anyway, we got to stretch out on a bed and didn't have to fight. So I guess that was all right. And it was milder too, well into May by then.'

May. More than six months after the last journal entry and his letter to me, and a year after he was drafted. Why had Ludwig stopped writing? Was there simply no opportunity, was the fighting too heavy, conditions too horrendous? I nod. I'm scared to say anything because it might send Hubert's mind off in a different direction.

'Ludwig wasn't given a bed. He only had a scratch. Well, perhaps a bit more than a scratch. The shrapnel took the top of his ear off and blew a bit of a hole in his head. Looked worse than it was. Just a lot of blood. The poor bastard crawling in the mud next to him wasn't that lucky. One minute his head was there, next minute it was gone.'

Though Ludwig's injury sounds quite serious to me, I know that he was lucky. And I feel sick imagining how he was lying in the muck with a heavily bleeding head wound next to his dead comrade, probably a boy not older than him.

Hubert continues. 'So they stitched and bandaged him up and gave him a bowl of bread soup and told him he had to report back to his unit the next day. Me, they were sending home because I was useless.' He holds up his stump and his two-fingered hand. 'They were still evacuating then. It took a long time before I got out though.' He pauses. 'First, they thought my injuries were self-inflicted. Bloody morons. Why would I do this to myself? I'd rather be dead.'

Hubert is agitated now. 'And then the attack came. Earth exploding everywhere around us. Everyone in the tents gone. A bloodbath. I was in the hut, which unfortunately saved me.'

'And Ludwig?'

'Ludwig, Ludwig, Ludwig. Why is that all I'm hearing?' He stares at me, disorientated. 'Who are you anyway?'

'I'm Lene,' I remind him.

'That's right. Ludwig's sweetheart. He told me about you.'

'He did?' I forgot that I wasn't going to ask any more questions.

'Maybe he did, maybe he didn't. What does it matter in the end?' he roars. 'Nothing matters anymore!' The anger comes on from one second to the next, out of the blue. The noise alarms Hubert's mother who rushes in. She doesn't say anything, just looks at Hubert, her eighteen-year-old son, a mutilated invalid, mad and unpredictable.

'Go away!' Hubert shouts at her, jumping up like a furious jack-in-the-box. 'I can handle this myself. I don't need your help.' She leaves and Hubert curls up in the armchair.

I take the journal out of my carry bag and put it on the table.

Hubert glances at it. 'So, Ludwig,' he seamlessly and calmly continues as though his outburst never happened. 'He was there, next to my bed, dozing on the stone floor in the field hospital. And then he stepped outside: call of nature. That must have been just before the attack. And after … he was gone. Only that,' Hubert points at the journal, 'was left. He didn't take it with him when he stepped outside.' Hubert picks up the journal with his two remaining fingers. 'I didn't read it.'

'It would have been all right if you had,' I say.

'I thought it was better not to. Anyway, after the attack, outside, there were just craters, the earth turned inside out. And bits of everything. One of the tents and everything and everyone in it got pulverised. There was nothing left but a few bone fragments. Crazy that. But there had been no explosions near the latrines and there were no dead there either. Everything was completely intact.' Leaning forward, Hubert hands me the journal. There's a clarity in his eyes suddenly as they lock with mine. 'I think he got away. He fooled everyone, your Ludwig. I think destiny smiled on him.'

'How?' I whisper.

'I think he made his way westwards because he knew the commanding officer at the hospital would assume that he had died in the attack.'

That weak but stubborn hope suddenly solidifies.

The Red Cross is on the third floor of a monumental grey concrete building which also houses numerous other agencies and offices working under the Allied Control Council. In my hand, I clutch a piece of paper on which I have scribbled Ludwig's identification number, the unit and the division Hubert told me they were last in, as well as the location of the field hospital where Ludwig was treated and last seen.

There's a constant flow of people entering and leaving the building. Most have closed-off faces but are full of direction and purpose; they have probably been here countless times. It feels strange going into this building, in which, not so long ago, a Nazi ministry had their offices. Which one, I can't remember. There were so many of them.

On the steps leading up to the entrance, I slow for a moment and go over everything Hubert told me, everything I know from the journal. I re-read the information on the crumpled piece of paper in my hand. I had to have enough information to find out more about Ludwig's fate, to determine if he is or was a prisoner of war somewhere, with the Russians or the Western Allies. Nodding my head, I climb the stairs and collide with someone's shoulder. Startled, I look over to apologise.

'Herr Zoller!'

The inward and hollow expression on Herr Zoller's face lifts when he recognises me. 'Fräulein Lene, it is good to see you.' He firmly shakes my hand. 'Trying to find someone?' he solemnly nods at the building.

'Yes. Ludwig. There's hope he might have survived.'

'From the bottom of my heart, I wish you the very best of luck.'

'Thank you, Herr Zoller. You are doing the same, I assume?' I ask.

He blinks a couple of times. 'Yes, I certainly am.' He pauses as though unsure whether he should continue. 'So far without much success. But I can be very determined.'

I nod, noticing the hard resoluteness that has crystallised in his eyes.

'I'm glad we ran into each other again, Fräulein Lene.' He shakes my hand again. 'Look after yourself.'

'And you too,' I reply.

I watch him merge with the current of people and I too make my way up the stairs, where I join the end of a line on the landing between the first and second floor. The line moves forward at a steady but laboriously slow pace. Everyone has brought forms, photographs, letters and notifications. Anything that will help with the tracing.

I creep up the three flights of stairs, one step every few minutes or so, and eventually I reach the third-floor corridor. There are still countless people ahead of me in the line which has now split into half-a-dozen smaller ones; the tracing is organised in alphabetical sub-groups and I join the line for the letters S–U.

It's hot and stuffy in here, and the tall open windows make little difference. Desks with clerks behind them take up the whole length of the hall-like space. There are a couple of desks for each alphabetical subgroup. Behind the desks is a long row of doors which open and close continuously, revealing an array of corridors and offices where more clerks talk on telephones, hunch over filing cabinets or study long sheets of printed lists that are pinned on the walls. I immediately know that they are lists of names.

I suddenly feel that what I'm doing is too impulsive. I haven't filled in a form and I don't even know if I have to fill one in. Frau Schluck told me she'd been here to start the tracing process, so there would already be a file on Ludwig. But I didn't tell Ludwig's mother that I was coming here. I should have gone back and told her what I'd found out from Hubert about Ludwig. But now there's only a handful of people ahead of me. And I just spent over two hours lining up. What a senseless waste of time it would have been if I were to leave now. So I stay.

Finally it's my turn and the woman behind the desk in the S–U section points at the chair in front of her without looking up from the index card she's writing on. After a few minutes, she slides it into the bursting-full harmonica folder on her desk.

'Name?' she asks. She glances at me with small, tired eyes.

'My name?' I stammer.

'No, the person you are looking for.'

Of course. I'm an idiot. My heart is fluttering with nervousness. 'Schluck,' I say, 'Ludwig Schluck, born April 1926.'

'If this is a new inquiry you are in the wrong section.' She looks like she's about to dismiss me and call over the next person.

'No, no,' I scramble to explain. 'It's not a new inquiry, there's already a file on him. But we found out some new information which might help.'

'All right. File number?'

'I don't have it,' I whisper. 'I forgot to write it down,' I lie. 'I only have is his identification number.' I slide my scrunched piece of paper across the desk.

'So, what's your relation to Ludwig Schluck?' the clerk asks as she is reading my notes. Her face gives nothing away, her questions come automated, asked a thousand times of a thousand people who've sat in the very same chair I'm sitting in now.

For a moment I'm silent, flabbergasted.

The clerk sighs. 'His fiancée?' There's a hint of a raised eyebrow, a touch of emotion in her face now.

I nod, avoiding her gaze so she can't see that it's not quite the truth. I state my name and show her my ID card.

'Fine,' she says. 'Wait here, I'll have to find his file.' She gets up and disappears behind one of the doors. She leaves my piece of paper on her desk. It moves slightly in the weak draft wafting through the space.

I stare at the piece of paper, worried that it might get blown off the desk and vanish in the stacks of files next to it.

I become aware that someone nearby is shouting something, having an argument, a breakdown. I don't want to take my eyes off my piece of paper with those vital crumbs of information on it. But the shouting gets louder, coming from a desk a little further down the row. Finally the shouts turn into sobs.

'Now, here's Ludwig Schluck's file.'

'Yes?' Eagerly I lean forward.

My clerk sits down again behind her desk. She snatches my piece of paper, and starts copying the information onto Ludwig's index card.

'He was last seen at a field hospital at the rear of the frontlines, near the Ukraine–Romanian border. There was an attack. Another soldier from his unit I've spoken to believes he made his way west from there and possibly surrendered to the Americans,' I explain.

The clerk nods and writes. 'Good,' she says when she is finished. 'We'll try to verify all of this. If we find out anything we'll notify Ludwig's mother.'

'Is that it?' I ask.

'What were you expecting?' She pushes the index card into the harmonica folder.

'Next!' she calls out towards the impatient people hovering behind me.

'Wait! How long will it take to verify everything? To find out whether Ludwig survived?' I ask.

'I've have no idea. Could be months, could be years. He might come home in the meantime.' I can tell she doesn't believe it herself.

Dejected, I get up.

'There are always trains arriving,' she says, the next person already standing in front of her desk. 'From Italy. German soldiers released from the POW camps there. You can always try your luck. Perhaps one of them knows something.'

I slowly walk to the exit, past the endless queues standing before the letter signs, that thick line of people snaking up from the ground floor. All of them searching for someone.

CHAPTER 28

Although I didn't find out anything concrete at the Red Cross or from Hubert, the feeling that Ludwig is alive is much more than a hope now. It is something real, tangible, in my mind, more likely than unlikely. Of course I know that, even if he had deserted and made his way westwards with the aim to surrender to the Americans, he could have still been killed. By partisans, by the SS execution squads hunting down deserters. Or he could have been caught up in a battle with the enemy, or been captured by the Soviets and shot or sent off to a labour camp or the mines.

It's because of that tangible feeling that I've been coming to the train station as often as I could for the last couple of weeks. Sometimes after work, sometimes taking time off and missing out on rations cards.

And today I'm here again with Ludwig's photo in my hand. There's a lot of middle-aged women on the platform, mothers, talking with quiet excitement or waiting in silence, their eyes full of anxious and hopeful expectation. As I look around at those who most likely have been officially informed by the Red Cross of their loved ones' return, I feel foolish. The atmosphere is sombre. I suddenly feel my buoyancy seeping away. This might be a complete waste of time after all.

But then I spot others in the crowd, standing by themselves, clutching a photo, clutching at that straw of hope against the odds. There's a young woman holding a toddler by her hand, a photo in the other hand. A boy in his early teens, a couple of girls my age, an older couple.

Someone tugs at my elbow. I turn and look into a creased olive face of an old woman. She's as small as a child, shrinking away into the earth with age, but her eyes are alert and wise.

'Let me see,' she says, reaching for the photo of Ludwig in my hand.

Hesitantly I show it to her. Her arthritic fingers hover over Ludwig's image, then she touches it with her fingertips.

'There's danger,' she says.

Before I can say anything, she moves on.

'Wait,' I call, but she vanishes in the crowd. 'Wait a second, please wait,' I call again, standing on tiptoes trying to find her. What did she mean? What danger is Ludwig in? And, if he is in danger, does that mean he is alive? Oh, I shouldn't be getting worked up over words from an old woman who knows nothing about me or Ludwig!

Right then a murmur goes through the crowd, and then I hear it too: the approaching train.

It wearily steams into the station as though tired of the humanity hanging from its doors and windows, clinging to its outside like strange beetles. There are passenger cars as well as goods wagons. Even before the train stops, people jump off, climb out of windows and pour out of the open wagon doors.

I push through the crowd, trying to get to the wagons from which the returnees are spilling. As I have done for the last few weeks, I hold up my photo in front of their faces. 'Have you seen this soldier at the POW camp? Do you remember seeing him? Does he look familiar?' I repeat over and over. But they just shake their heads, barely glancing at it, looking for loved ones waiting for them.

'Please, excuse me,' I say, shoving the photo in another returnee's face in desperation, blocking his way. 'Please take a look. Do you know him? Have you see him?' I know I'm being rude. He wearily stops and studies Ludwig's image.

'Born 1926?' he asks and rubs his unshaven cheek.

I nod.

'Like me,' he says. 'Drafted in 1943?'

'Yes.'

Silently he keeps gazing at the photo; he's there but he isn't. This is hopeless. He doesn't know anything.

I scan the platform, the disembarking soldiers. More and more keep pouring out of the train. I can't be everywhere at once! My eyes catch on the back of one of the returnees, his hatless head, the unruly brown hair. He's tall and there's something familiar in the way he walks, the way he carries himself. It's like a lightning bolt of memory hitting me.

'Ludwig,' I shout, pushing my way through the syrupy mass of people, keeping my eyes trained on the man. 'LUDWIG!'

It's him, it has to be!

'LUDWIG!' I call again. My voice is drowned by the noise as soon as it leaves my mouth, reaching absolutely nowhere. I'm stuck, the throng of people is pushing me down, pulling me backwards like quicksand. As I watch the man continue to walk away, I gather all my strength and ruthlessly push past people, shoving them aside, squeezing through tiny gaps. I'm getting closer as the crowd starts to thin a little and as people are leaving the platform or getting on the train.

'Ludwig!' I finally grab the tails of a jacket, pull in desperation. 'Wait! It's me, Lene!'

The owner of the jacket turns around to face me.

My breath catches in my throat.

He looks nothing like Ludwig; it's not the man I spotted before, not the person I chased after. This man is older, shorter, with receding straw-coloured hair, his arm in a sling.

'Sorry. I'm so sorry,' I mutter. 'I thought you were someone else.'

I frantically look around at the thin returnees with strange expressions on their faces, many disabled or injured, the sobbing women, but the soldier who looked like Ludwig has vanished, lost in the crowd. Has my mind played a cruel trick on me?

Defeated, overcome with disappointment, I halt, the crowd now bumping and shoving me as they sweep away, leaving me standing alone in the same spot with my photo.

I don't know what to do. I feel so drained, so tired. I collapse on someone's suitcase, its owner sleeping next to it on the platform, and bury my head in my hands. I know nothing any longer. Is all of this useless? When I look up again the old woman from before is standing directly in front of me. She nods at me, her eyes locking into mine, then slips away again.

I shake my head. She's a deranged old woman, a ghost in the ruins of the city. But then I remember her comment about danger. And I can't get the image of the returnee I saw before out of my head.

'This is crazy,' I mutter to myself, but I leave the train station, headed for Prenzlauer Berg.

There's a Soviet truck parked amidst the rubble in front of my old apartment block. Automatically I slow as I watch two soldiers get in the vehicle. The doors slam and it drives off.

A funny, anxious feeling creeps up from the pit of my stomach. I speed up and throw open the vestibule door. Inside, an ominous silence greets me. The kind that's loaded with the negative energy of something ruthless and forceful that took place moments before; a silence that hasn't quite settled yet. I race upstairs to the third floor.

'Frau Schluck, it's me, Lene.' My loud knocks echo in the stairwell.

The door opens and I take one look at Ludwig's mother and I

know I was right. Her face is white, her neck speckled with panicky scarlet patches, her eyes red. She pulls me inside and shuts the door.

'Ludwig,' she breathes, irregular and rapid. 'Ludwig,' another gasp of air.

'Breathe in through your nose,' I tell her, 'and out through your mouth.' I put my hands on her shoulders, demonstrating slow breaths while my heart races. 'Talk to me, tell me what happened.'

'He's returned. He survived.' She's calmer now, her eyes wide and glazed. 'He's alive!'

I'm stunned. 'What do you mean?'

'He was here! With me. Minutes ago. But the Soviets came and took him, pulled him out of my arms, didn't even let him change, took his backpack too.'

'But what for?' I cry.

'He showed him his release papers from the Americans but they weren't even interested, didn't even look at them. Threw the paperwork down on the table and said that those meant nothing.'

'They took him away to interrogate him?'

'Oh God.'

I collapse on a kitchen chair, a rollercoaster wave of bittersweet emotions washing over me. Ludwig has returned safely. He's alive! And now he's gone again.

I take a deep breath. I have to calm down. 'He has nothing to hide. They'll let him go. They have to. He's not a Nazi!'

'I know, Lene. I know.'

Will this war ever end? Or will we go straight from one war into another, one between the Soviets and the Americans?

'I can't believe this,' I mutter. This, after everything. 'Do you know where they have taken him?'

Frau Schluck shakes her head. 'They wouldn't tell me. But they warned me not to investigate, that it would make things worse. Told me that if he had nothing to hide, then he would be let go.'

I know that's not always true. That they take people away on a whim, when they get the smallest whiff of suspicion or if they want more men to help rebuild their ruined cities.

We stare at each other. The thought of Ludwig having survived and returned against all odds only to be taken away again is simply intolerable, too painful to comprehend.

CHAPTER 29

I drag myself to work in the ruins the next morning. It's better than doing nothing, better than just waiting again, with my thoughts and hopes and fears. And missing out on more pay and rations cards. Heidi doesn't leave my side for most of the day; she knows something is going on, but she doesn't ask any questions.

The knowledge that Ludwig is here in Berlin, or at least was yesterday, is all I can think of. The thought that I just missed him at the train station is like torture. What is he going through right now? Was he even still in Berlin? If the Soviets decided he was a Nazi, or guilty in their eyes, or for whatever other reason, then he could be on a train to Russia already, sentenced to many years of forced labour there, sentenced to help repay for the devastation Germany has caused. Fear clenches in my stomach.

In the evening I return home, bone-tired, robotic. Gertie, Ophelia and my aunt leave me be when I lie down on my bed after work. I can hear them clattering in the kitchen and, after a while, Gertie comes in with a plate of food. She puts it down on the bedside table and I force myself to sit up.

'Do you want to talk?' she asks.

I shake my head.

She touches my arm. 'There's simply nothing you can do now. Just wait and hope for the best.'

'But that's the worst part – the not being able to do anything,' I say. 'Again.'

As usual, every bone in my body hurts but today I don't want to go home. I want to clear away the very last reminders of the ruined building that used to be here – a small pile of rubble and some leftover bricks. I want to be done. But the supervisor is calling it a day and we pack up and load our tools onto the trucks.

In place of the ruin there is now a deep, empty, rectangular plot, strangely beautiful in its austerity. It's cast in the warm light of the lowering sun, which will make way for the evening shadows soon. We've finished later than usual. The sense of despair that has been leaching through me every day these past few weeks since Ludwig was taken away is temporarily thinned by a feeling of accomplishment.

'Can you believe it, we are nearly finished here,' says Heidi, who is now standing next to me. 'Another hour tomorrow and that's it. On to the next site. It's not like there's a shortage.'

We both laugh a little at the black humour. It seems unfathomable that we will ever run out of ruins.

'You know,' Heidi solemnly says, 'I see my sister and my mother everywhere I look. Sometimes I see my father. Sometimes I see all of us together. Ten, twelve years, a lifetime ago.' She pauses. 'When Berlin is rebuilt one day, even when there's hardly any reminder left of what happened here, in fifty, sixty years, even then I know I will still see them everywhere I look.'

'Do you think you will stay in Berlin?' I ask.

'I will stay for now, though I think that I must leave eventually.' She smiles a little at me. 'I'll have to go someplace where there is more light. And perhaps then I'll be all right.' She gives me a goodbye wave. 'I'm off, Lene. See you tomorrow.'

'Yes, until tomorrow, Heidi.' I watch her walk away from the site, feeling grateful to have met her, to have her as a friend.

I shake the dust out of my hair and take off my aunt's old apron that I've been wearing for the work in the ruins. I stuff it into my canvas bag then set out on my walk home too. The setting sun touches my back and the ruins are tinged violet and pink; dust dances, slowly settling on top of the rubble.

The evening is warm and reminds me of when my father, my mother and I used to take the train out to one of the Berlin lakes for a swim. The memory makes me want to do the same thing now. The water would be warm enough and there would be daylight for at least another hour or so. Or I could wait until dark and swim in the nude like my cousins and I did when we were little! I chuckle at the thought. For a moment, I consider chasing after Heidi and asking her to go.

Despite everything, the idea brings a smile to my face but of course it's a half-hearted contemplation. A frivolity like this is out of the question. I'm too exhausted and taking the train out to the lake and going swimming after dark would be foolishly dangerous.

I'm halfway down the road, headed towards the mountain of chores waiting for me at home, when there's a hand on my shoulder.

Laughing, I turn around. 'Heidi, did you read my mind? I was just thinking how wonderful it would be if we ...'

But it's not Heidi standing behind me, touching me.

For a second I think that my eyes and mind have cunningly paired up to deceive me. I squint into the setting sun. A strange hoarse little sound escapes my mouth.

But then I hear his voice, the voice I haven't heard in years but which is as familiar to me as my own.

CHAPTER 30

Can there be a feeling of such utter happiness that hits you like a bolt of lightning out of nowhere? I feel weak with that bright and brilliant happiness. It changes everything.

I throw my arms around him, hold on to him, hold him tight. 'Ludwig,' I whisper.

'It's me. I am real, Lene. I am here.'

'Ludwig,' I whisper again, savouring the sound of his name.

'Please don't cry.'

I realise now that I am indeed crying. But tears of happiness don't feel like tears. 'You've returned,' I say. 'They let you go.'

He folds his arms around me, holding me. 'Yes, I'm here.' He sounds bewildered, as though it is only becoming real for him now, at that moment. 'I've come home.'

'I never stopped believing that you would return.' I say. 'Never stopped believing in our promise.'

Ludwig tightens his embrace around me. 'Thank you,' he whispers. 'We made it. We made it through this madness.'

I shiver, allowing myself, in the safety of Ludwig's arms, for the first time, just for a flash of a moment, to recall the last months of the war, the aftermath. The nonstop bombings, the Soviets taking Berlin, the battles in the streets, the noise, children in too-big uniforms fighting them, following orders to defend the city. People being shot by the SS for refusing. Us hiding in the cellar or the public air-raid shelter, waiting it all out. Hoping to be spared by the Soviet soldiers hunting for their rewards and their vengeance.

As quickly as the memory comes, it goes, a little weaker and a little paler.

Reluctantly we let go of one another and take a step back to look at each other, taking in each other's faces which we haven't seen in three years, thought we would perhaps never see again. Ludwig's face is narrow and tanned but still the same, slightly older, slightly more handsome, his angular features more pronounced. The little line above his left eyebrow etched in permanently. I search for any signs of the injury.

'Are you looking for this?' Ludwig asks and sweeps back strands of hair, exposing his left ear. The top of it is gone. 'I guess I'll have to wear my hair longer from now on.' He grins a little.

'The head wound?' I ask.

'That was just a nasty scratch. It's all healed.' He pauses, letting his hair flop back down. He studies me, silently. I can tell he's struggling to talk, to find the right words now for what he wants to say. Instead, we hug each other again. I don't ever want to let go.

Eventually, we sit down on a stone bench by the crumbling fountain. There are so many questions I want to ask: how he survived, what happened after the attack that destroyed the hospital, how he got away, his time at the front, the interrogation by the Soviets.

How to start? Where to start? I enclose his hands in both of mine.

'I read your journal,' I say. 'Hubert brought it back and your mother gave it to me. But we just didn't know … we could only speculate, and hope.'

'I deserted, made my way westwards and surrendered to the Americans,' Ludwig says. It sounds so muted. 'I'm so incredibly glad Hubert made it. I must go and see him as soon as I can.'

I nod. 'I was hoping that you had deserted. Hubert thought so too.'

'I didn't plan on it and I had made my choice to fight. But when I arrived at the hospital, they took one look at me and said my injury wasn't serious, that I was going to be sent back to the front the next day. And then the attack came and I just did it, just ran. I knew I wasn't going to stand a chance in battle if I wasn't allowed to recuperate from the injury. I was woozy and weak. I was cannon fodder. Next thing I knew I was hiding in the forest and started heading west. My bad conscience nearly killed me then. My only consolation at that point was that I knew Hubert would be sent home.'

His hands feel hard and tense in mine now. 'You did the right thing. What difference would it have made if you had gone back to fight? The war was already lost,' I say.

'Yes, the war was lost,' is all he says. 'All was lost a long time ago.'

I lean my head on his shoulder, control my questions. 'We can talk about it some other time.'

'Yes. It's just … I want to forget, Lene. I'm sorry. I just want to move forward and be, be here with you. I want to look forward at what's ahead, not back.'

'Me too.'

He doesn't want to talk about it all any longer. I know that he feels guilty and torn. And that, like me, he's overwhelmed by the sheer enormity, the senselessness of the war years. From beginning to end. Not just the war years, but also the years that came before, the years when all the warning signs were there and the worst could have maybe been prevented. But we simply can't allow ourselves to dwell on that feeling, to allow it to swallow us.

There are no words for it all, there might never be the right words in our lifetime. I know that's what Ludwig is thinking too. He wraps his arm around my shoulders and I lean in even closer against him.

'I'm so sorry that I didn't write to you,' he says. 'I didn't want you to hang on to a hopeless dream.'

'I understand. You did send me one letter, though, remember?'

He blushes underneath his tan and for a moment he's just like the boy I last saw three years ago. 'I meant everything I said about us in that letter. It still is true.'

'And I meant everything I said when you left too. It still is true, now more than ever.'

CHAPTER 31

On Sunday, Ludwig and his mother visit us in Charlottenburg. My aunt brought home leftovers from the American mess and we still have some potatoes; we manage to scrape together enough lunch to share between all of us. We crowd around the kitchen table, the balcony door wide open, letting in a breeze. Outside, in the courtyard, the chestnut tree sways its umbrella of leaves above the ruins.

Afterwards, Ludwig and I take an old rug and sit in the shade under the tree at the far end of the courtyard. It is bliss to be with Ludwig again, to look at him, to be reunited. It is beyond words. He grasps for my hand, kissing it. Then we just sit there, hand in hand, looking up into the green roof above us.

After a while, I tell him about my family, about my brother Gustav, my mother, and how we were reunited with my father. I tell him that my father doesn't really talk about anything. I don't tell Ludwig about the time, shortly after my father's return, when I found him madly pressing his hands on his ears, his eyes pinched shut, his face a grimace of agony. I quietly left the room without my father noticing me.

'It's a miracle that both you and my father returned,' I say.

'Yes.'

I know there is something else I have to tell him.

'Ludwig, Kurt survived too.'

'What?' Ludwig sits up straight and my hand slips out of his. 'Have you seen him?'

'Yes. When I first arrived back in Berlin, I visited your mother. Kurt followed me.' Taking deep breaths between sentences, I tell him everything about that day, about visiting Hans-Peter's father, and about my aunt scaring Kurt away when he later came to her apartment. 'And I think she scared him off for good,' I add.

Ludwig listens, his jaw working hard, silent.

'Herr Zoller was grateful I contacted him,' I say.

For a moment Ludwig buries his head in his arms. 'I'll never forget that day,' he says, his voice muffled. Then he straightens up again, now mashing the heels of his boots hard into the soft ground. 'I have to stop thinking about it, and yet, how can I? How can I be allowed to ever stop thinking about it all?'

I don't have an answer for Ludwig. Only the same questions.

Later in the afternoon we visit Hubert. His mother lets us in and shows us to his room. He is sitting at the desk, writing with a tense and concentrated expression on his face. Next to him there's a clutter of old schoolbooks and dog-eared papers. He triumphantly lifts his left hand, the one that still has two fingers on it. He's holding a pencil.

'I can actually write with this hand, even though I used to be right-handed. It's not pretty, but it's legible,' he says.

When he notices Ludwig standing behind me he goes still, his face contorts. 'You made it,' he rasps. Then he starts laughing. 'You fooled them, oh you fooled them all. You are ingenious!'

'I was just lucky,' Ludwig says.

Hubert jumps up and holds up his hand in front of Ludwig. 'I think someone up there decided that it was my lucky day when they let me keep those two fingers,' he says almost as though it was only yesterday that he last saw Ludwig.

Ludwig looks at the stumps and nods slowly.

'Are you going back to school, Hubert?' I ask, indicating his books.

'You bet I am. What else am I going to do? Become a watchmaker?' He laughs loudly and a bit too hard at his own a joke. 'You always did well, Ludwig, didn't you? You should go back to school too.'

'Maybe,' says Ludwig. 'I haven't thought about that yet.' He pauses. 'I feel a bit too old, to be honest.'

'You wouldn't be the only one. You got cheated out of an education, out of learning a trade or studying. We all did. We got trained all right, but not the kind of training anyone wants now.' Hubert pauses. 'Not that the cruel little marionette I was back then realised any of that. Thought myself superior and entitled because I'm German and all I wanted was to shoot some Soviets.' Hubert throws down his pencil and shuts the book. 'Let's get out of here. I want to go for a walk. I need a distraction.'

He marches out of his room, out of the flat, a silly, somewhat unhinged smile on his face. We are about to follow him when his mother stops us.

'Thank you for coming,' she says. 'I think he's getting better.' She puts her hand on Ludwig's shoulder for a moment. 'I would be truly grateful if you could keep visiting and stay in touch with my son.'

'Of course I will. You don't have to ask. It's the least I can do.' Ludwig looks uncomfortable and his voice sounds funny and choked again.

Hubert is waiting for us downstairs. 'Did my mother give you "the talk"?'

'Kind of,' Ludwig admits, still sounding strange. He clears his throat.

'She thinks I'm mad,' Hubert says. 'Perhaps I am, who knows? Sometimes I get so furious and my mind is, I don't know, in disarray, all messy, and I can't keep the anger in and the past bubbles up, and I want to crawl out of my own skin.'

'Just be patient,' says Ludwig. 'It takes time.'

I can tell Ludwig feels helpless. All he can offer Hubert are those platitudes.

For a while we walk in silence and soon we are in a part of Berlin that has been completely destroyed by the bombs, fires and battle. There's nothing here any longer, nothing that would even be remotely habitable. I remember that there were a lot of small businesses and offices in the tall turn-of-the-century buildings that used to line this wide street. Lawyers, doctors, accounting firms and the like. Downstairs there were cafés and restaurants which would have started to get busy now with waiters arranging chairs and setting tables for dinner service underneath striped awnings. But one wouldn't know by looking at what's left. Not a single structure remains upright. Steel girders protrude from mountains of rubble up to twenty to thirty metres high that have already partly been claimed by ivy, lichen and creepers. Everything here has been left untouched since the battle in Berlin ended. I don't even want the think about all the dud bombs that are buried beneath those ruins.

My heart hurts seeing the shreds of my city, remembering what it used to be like. Knowing that Germany started the war and the invasions and destructions does not lessen nor intensify that pain.

'We should head back soon,' Ludwig says. 'It's getting late. I'll walk you to the S-Bahn station, Lene.'

I nod. 'Yes, let's walk back to Hubert's and then we can head to the S-Bahn from there.'

'I understand.' Hubert laughs. 'You two love birds want some alone time, no problem.'

I'm embarrassed but glad to hear him laugh.

'You could be right there, Hubert,' Ludwig mutters. There's a glimpse of the old Ludwig, a slight redness creeping across his temples, a small sheepish but happy smile.

As abruptly as Hubert's lightness has come it goes and his mood darkens again. He stops, sombre, facing us. 'I envy the two of you,' he says bluntly. 'I do. I admit it. You can already see your future, I can feel that you do. In spite of all this,' he vaguely gestures at the annihilation around us, 'you are together, you're both here and that's more than enough for a future.' He lets out a long, exhausted-sounding sigh. 'You did the right thing, Ludwig, when you ran. Don't ever doubt that. If you hadn't, you'd be dead now. Mashed into the mud over there. Don't ever doubt that either.' His eyes focus on some far-away point in the distance; his words have drawn him back.

'You have a future too, Hubert,' says Ludwig.

'I can't even help with the reconstruction work,' Hubert replies. 'Everything is obliterated, not just everywhere you look but also in here,' he points at his head. 'It's wrecked.'

Ludwig pulls Hubert into a short, stiff embrace. The skin on the stumps of Hubert's hands is reddish purple, still raw looking, as they clamp around Ludwig's shoulder.

Walking together, just the two of us, we don't say much. I'm going over Hubert's words in my head. I'm thinking about the future, our future, mine and Ludwig's, in this country. The uncertainty of it. No one knows what it will be like, here in Berlin especially. There are ever increasing tensions between the Soviets and the Western Allies. Many people see no future here, and they leave Germany for America, Canada or Australia every day. But despite this, I know that I won't ever leave Berlin again, no matter what. I know this city can begin again, just like we can, here.

'I'm worried about Hubert,' I say. What I don't say is: I'm also worried about you, Ludwig.

'So am I,' says Ludwig. 'He's trying to put on a brave face but …' Ludwig stops, is struggling to find the right words. I've noticed that. His inability to articulate now, something he never used to struggle with. It's like there are no words right or strong enough to express anything any more; like everything he feels is off the charts.

Ludwig tries again. 'I guess he's putting on a brave face, but then he just cracks. And who could blame him?'

'We just have to be there for him,' I say. 'That's all we can do.'

We turn the corner and are back in our old neighbourhood.

Ludwig spins around suddenly, scanning the street behind us. 'I'll be damned,' he says.

'What's wrong?'

'I think we are being shadowed.' He puts a hand on my arm, stopping me.

I turn around too but I can't see anything but people going about their business. 'Are you sure? Who by, the Soviet police?' The back of my neck prickles.

'No.' Ludwig shakes his head. 'Kurt.'

Ha! Despite his hasty exit in Charlottenburg and my aunt's threat! I guess old habits do die hard indeed.

'I'm sure it's him. I won't ever forget that face,' Ludwig utters, his eyes narrow. 'It was just a glimpse, but it was enough. He ducked away somewhere the minute I turned around.' Ludwig assesses the ruins to the left and right. 'Come on.' He starts pulling me down the street. 'We'll turn the tables and follow him. I'm not running away from that bastard again.' Ludwig's voice is full of wrath. He slows again, squints his eyes.

'There!' He points at a figure creeping out from behind a burned-out tank.

I see the figure too now. Wearing tattered clothes that have somehow taken on the colour of the ruins, he is no more than a ghostly shadow.

'That's him,' I confirm. He scurries away, down the street, then disappears between two building shells leaning dangerously towards one another.

There is a narrow vacant block between the two buildings where the ruins of a bombed house have been cleared away. The rear building is still there, largely intact, and we catch a glimpse of Kurt disappearing in it. We dash across the cleared site and follow him into the shabby, damp and debris-littered foyer. We pause, listening for a footfall on the stairs leading up to the apartments, but it's silent. Does Kurt live here?

Ludwig moves towards the stairs but then a gate slams somewhere outside. We run down the hallway and out the back door into a rubble-strewn courtyard. Smoke is rising from a fire pit where a woman and two little children hunker down, cooking a meal. They glance at us apathetically.

On the left, next to the coal chute, we see a closed gate. It's the only way out and leads us back to the main road. We are on the south side of the intersection now, diagonally across from the building shells and the large area of rubble, opposite Café Kramer.

'Do you think we've lost him?' I ask, scanning the area.

'No, there he is!' Ludwig, his eyes narrowing, points at a figure dashing across the road a fair distance away, heading for the cover of ruins again.

We run down the road, making hurdles of rubble, dodging foot traffic and bicycles. My eyes catch on something, a shape moving in an archway. Not Kurt. The shape detaches from the charred brick wall and for a brief moment is in full view. That's when I recognise who it is. Herr Zoller.

He follows Kurt, who is a good thirty metres ahead of him. He doesn't call out to him, is in no particular rush to catch up to him. He just efficiently and silently trails him.

'Looks like we are not the only ones after him,' Ludwig says.

We dart across the road, dodging a group of displaced people with their belongings in handcarts and old prams. Ahead of us, Kurt scales a mound of rubble and disappears behind it. Herr Zoller follows, then is gone from view as well.

'Ludwig,' I grasp his arm. 'It's Hans-Peter's father.' For a second our eyes lock. Here we are, all of us, tied together by that day, by the past, by Hans-Peter, by what he stands for and what happened to him.

There's no time to talk. We clamber up the steep mound. When we reach the top, I stop and catch my breath. Below us is a wasteland of rubble, ruins and half-collapsed buildings; a man-made landscape of destruction with valleys and crevices and peaks. The scale of it hadn't been obvious from the street. Everything is abandoned and desolate. I hesitate. The ruins look largely untouched, and probably have been since the day the bombs blew everything up.

I touch Ludwig's shoulder, halting him. 'We have to be careful. There will still be bombs here, buried beneath the rubble. Maybe we should just let him go. I don't think it's worth the risk.'

Ludwig hesitates. Then he shakes his head. 'No,' he says. 'I don't want to watch my back every time I step outside. We'll put an end to this, once and for all.' Ludwig points at something resembling a track. 'Let's stick to this.'

'All right,' I say, but I'm not particularly confident. Dud bombs and shells blow up every day in the city, killing and maiming people.

Kurt has made headway. He's clambering away across the rubble as though he knows exactly where he is going. Perhaps it is here somewhere that he has been hiding out. Herr Zoller trails him, light-footed, determined and surprisingly soundless.

Kurt suddenly spins around. He must have sensed his pursuer after all. Even from this distance away I can see the array of emotions on his face: recognition, fear, doggedness. Kurt turns and accelerates his escape, though now he immediately trips and falls, scrambling to pick himself up. Herr Zoller is gaining on Kurt.

Ludwig and I start descending the steep drop, more sliding than walking, trying to disturb as little of the rubble as possible; we are no more than forty metres away from the others.

A shot rings out, fracturing the silence as it echoes in the ruins.

'Get down!' Ludwig shouts, and we flatten ourselves instinctively, sliding down on our backsides, then clamber across the rubble on all fours, diving for cover behind the segment of a brick wall, the danger of unexploded bombs beneath our feet forgotten.

Herr Zoller's voice rises above the ruins. 'Stop and turn around, you rat, or I'll shoot you in the back like you deserve!'

We peek over the top of the wall. Herr Zoller has a gun aimed at Kurt.

Kurt slowly turns around, clasping his upper right arm, his face distorted with pain. Blood is spreading across his shirt sleeve, black, drips down his hand, red. Kurt winces, then swears.

'It's just a flesh wound, you weakling!' Herr Zoller calls. He aims at Kurt's chest, his face set in determination.

'I think he really is going to kill him,' I say. 'Ludwig! What should we do?'

'He probably deserves it,' says Ludwig. He sounds unmoved.

Yes, perhaps he does. But is it right?

Herr Zoller moves a few steps closer to Kurt, sharp eyes trained on him, gun aimed. I can't watch any longer; I shift away from the wall and stand up.

'What are you doing?' Ludwig whispers.

'Don't shoot,' I call. 'Herr Zoller, it's me, Lene.' Slowly, I raise my hands above my head, just in case.

Herr Zoller glances at me. 'Don't get involved, Lene. But put your hands down, for goodness sake.'

I indicate for Ludwig to stand as well. 'Herr Zoller, Ludwig has returned. You remember what I told you about Ludwig, don't you?'

'Sure do. It's the boy who also almost hung because of this rat here. Ha, three and a half years since I took my fifteen-year-old son down from the gallows and buried him.' His index finger twitches on the trigger. 'And now, right in front of me, is the Nazi rat who denounced him, who is responsible for my son's death.'

'Shoot me then,' Kurt shouts. 'Go on! But I didn't hang him. I just followed an order!'

'Ha, that's what they all say,' Herr Zoller replies.

'I denounced him,' Kurt shouts. 'It was my duty. But I didn't know that they were going to hang him.'

'Liar!' Herr Zoller replies. 'Of course you knew.'

Kurt shrugs, which hurts his injured arm. He cries out then says: 'Perhaps I am lying. The truth is I didn't care. He meant nothing to me. Nothing, you hear? He was nobody, a traitor, a defeatist – an enemy! Back then it was right what I did, it was the law. Today it is suddenly wrong. And you,' Kurt points at Ludwig, 'I should have made sure they hanged you too that day!' Kurt's voice is high-pitched, his face a taut grimace.

'It was wrong back then too,' Ludwig says. 'The laws were wrong, the laws were designed to destroy everyone's rights! It was your decision to denounce Hans-Peter. No one forced you to do it. You could have left him alone. That would have saved his life.'

'Everyone's rights? Are you stupid? We had all the rights in the world!' Kurt shouts, mock and disbelief in his voice.

'No, we didn't have those rights. We stripped rights from others – human rights, civil rights, constitutional rights,' Ludwig replies. 'All the rights man has.'

Kurt looks at him with incomprehension. 'You just don't

understand, do you!' he yells, frenzied. 'I wanted to join the SS! It was my duty to report him and I took an oath in the Hitler Youth! There's nothing higher than an oath!

'Yes, there is,' I say.

'And he was a traitor! An enemy of the Reich,' Kurt shouts desperately. 'Don't any of you get it?'

'There is no point,' Herr Zoller says. 'He will never understand.'

'Shoot me then!' Kurt shouts at Herr Zoller. 'Go on, you Communist pig! If that's how it ends, so be it.'

'Oh no,' Herr Zoller says, keeping the gun trained at Kurt's chest. 'I'm not going to shoot you. As much as I want to. That would be the easy way out for you.'

'Coward! Come on, shoot me! Avenge your son!'

Herr Zoller's finger twitches on the trigger and the little colour that's left in his face drains.

'Herr Zoller, don't,' I call.

'Don't you worry, Lene,' Herr Zoller says, but now he aims his gun at Kurt's head. 'When I get my hands on you, I'm going to turn you in to the Soviets. They deal with the likes of you in a quick and effective way.'

I'm slowly moving in Kurt's direction, approaching him.

'I'd rather be dead!' Kurt shouts.

'You won't get that choice,' I call. In an instant, I'm next to him and twist his injured arm behind his back with all my strength. A second later Ludwig and Herr Zoller are by my side.

'That was risky, Lene,' Ludwig says. But there's a satisfied expression on his face.

I let go of Kurt's arm, and Herr Zoller and Ludwig, wedging Kurt in between them, drag him down the path. I follow a few steps behind, all of us sticking to the narrow track through the rubble. We make our way through the treacherous valleys and crevices of the ruins back to the base of the steep mound. There we tackle the arduous ascent.

When we are on the other side, Herr Zoller pauses. 'You should go. Both of you. I will take care of this now.'

Ludwig nods and lets go of Kurt's arm.

'Thank you, Lene. Ludwig.' Herr Zoller gives Kurt a shove. 'Let's go.' He tightens his grip on Kurt's injured arm. Blood keeps dripping onto the ground.

'Herr Zoller,' I say.

He turns around. 'Yes, Lene?'

'Remember what I promised you when I came to your flat?' I ask.

'I do remember.' He pauses for a moment. 'I know that I asked you for that promise. But now I also know that there will come a time when what you have been through will start to fade, and when it does, let it. Let it, so your life can begin.'

Herr Zoller nods at us.

We watch them walk away, Herr Zoller straight and tall, Kurt being dragged along, struggling, his broad shoulders collapsed. They are framed by the ruins. Dust whirls up from the rubble, and then they disappear into a crowd of displaced people.

Ludwig and I go in the opposite direction. We pass the burned-out voids where Café Kramer and our local shops once were. From the intersection we can see the rubble remains of the Sternschnuppe cinema. There's no traffic other than people on bicycles and on foot. This intersection used to be one of the bustling hubs of our suburb with a constant stream of buses, trams and cars. I remember how long I sometimes had to wait for a break in the traffic so I could safely cross the road on my way to school. People would populate the outdoor tables in the cafés as soon as the sun was out in early spring and there were always long lines outside the bakery in the morning for the freshly baked bread rolls. The bakery shop window would burst with pastries and cakes that were delicate masterpieces of icing, chocolate, candied fruit and cream. Children would crowd in front of the window, mesmerised by the magic.

I also remember some of the shops and businesses that were here before. Before the names on the shopfronts changed, before their windows were defaced with ugly slogans, before they were smashed and vandalised. I was a small child then, walking in the middle between my parents who held me by the hand so I wouldn't stumble and fall, or run off and become lost.

Now, I reach for Ludwig's hand.

EPILOGUE

I leap into the water which is cool and pleasant, just the way I imagined it, the way I remember it. The dirt and dust of the ruins and the heat and sweat of the day washes off me. I swim a few strokes, gliding through the water of the lake. I tip my head back and feel my hair fanning out behind me. Above is nothing but the pale blue late afternoon summer sky.

Ludwig plunges into the water, disappears, leaving just a ripple on the surface. I swim underwater, my eyes wide open, looking for him in the opaque green depths of the lake. I know he's there. I glide along for a few seconds, then slowly rise to the surface. A moment later Ludwig shoots up right in front of me, laughing. Rivulets of water cascade down his face and glistening drops like liquid silver fly from his hair.

We have both love and freedom; I feel weightless with the certainty of beginning and possibility.

ACKNOWLEDGEMENTS

I would like to thank my agent, Sheila Drummond, for her encouragement, support and advice. Thank you to Clare Hallifax and the team at Scholastic Australia; thank you to my editor Kristy Bushnell for her wisdom and expertise.

I am indebted to Hermann Reimer and Stephanie Reimer for answering my many questions about their lives in Nazi Germany as teenagers.

Thank you to Helen Halstead and Irina LeMaire for their support and feedback on early drafts; to Ornella Baldin, Andrea Curtis, Kerry Scholten and Janine Jasson for their friendship, long evening walks, cups of coffee and brilliant days at the beach.

Thank you to my family. Above all, I'm thankful to Thorsten, Noah and Cameron.

REFERENCES:

The following books were particularly useful to me in writing and researching this novel:

Stalingrad (1998), *Antony Beevor*; Berlin: The Downfall 1945 (2002), *Antony Beevor*; The Origins of Totalitarianism (1966), *Hannah Arendt*; To Hell And Back: Europe 1914-1949 (2015), *Ian Kershaw*; Homecomings: Returning POWs and the Legacies of Defeat in Postwar Germany (2006), *Frank Biess*; Witnesses of War: Children's Lives Under the Nazis (2005), *Nicholas Stargardt*; Blitzed: Drugs in Nazi Germany (2015), *Norman Ohler*.

Films: Die Deutsche Wochenschau, Transit Film GmbH (www.transitfilm.de).

ABOUT THE AUTHOR

Alexandra Alt was born in Germany and lived in Berlin for five years. She studied Professional Writing at Adelaide College of the Arts and has worked as a translator and tutor. Alexandra lives in Adelaide with her husband, their two sons and a mischievous little dog. *Promise* is her first novel.